D1351612

A Plea of Insanity

PRISCILLA MASTERS

First published in Great Britain in 2005 by
Allison & Busby Limited
Bon Marché Centre
241-251 Ferndale Road
London SW9 8BJ

http://www.allisonandbusby.com

1566

10 9 8 7 6 5 4 3 2 1

ISBN 0 7490 8337 9

Printed and bound in Wales by
Creative Print and Design, Ebbw Vale

B14 385 8581

PRISCILLA MASTERS was born in Halifax and is one of seven adopted children. The family moved to South Wales where she lived until she was sixteen when she went to Birmingham to work and then to train as a nurse. She is married to a GP and now lives in Shropshire. She works part-time as a nurse.

Also by this author

In the Joanna Piercy series
Winding Up the Serpent
Catch the Fallen Sparrow
A Wreath For My Sister
And None Shall Sleep
Scaring Crows
Embroidering Shrouds
Endangering Innocents

Medical Mysteries
Night Visit
A Fatal Cut
Disturbing Ground
River Deep

For Children
Mr Bateman's Garden

To Nick, congratulations on getting the MSc, good luck with the job hunting and thanks for helping me with my never ending computer problems!

Chapter One

Monday, September 1st, 9 am

She could smell the paint. Chemical, pungent, nauseating.

She stood in the doorway for a brief moment, trying to ignore the smell but it seemed to pollute her nostrils. When she tried, experimentally, to mouth-breathe it was worse. She could taste it on her tongue, in her throat, almost feel it reach her stomach and sit there, a thick oily, chemical pool which made her retch.

But still she entered the room, closing the door softly behind her.

All rooms in institutions are painted like these, in bland, neutral colours. Mushroom, cream, magnolia, beige, grey. The authorities must buy the paint in economy drums. Claire was reminded of a tongue-in-cheek lecture she had attended about colour schemes suitable for the consultation room.

Avoid red or orange; designed to inflame, the lecturer had said smugly, knowing all.

Strong blues and greens. Cold colours. Display a lack of empathy.

Don't choose black – too funereal for those already melancholic and guaranteed to tip bipolar disorders into the sludge of their depressive cycle.

Avoid sharp, strong whites. Incites hallucinations in the borderline psychotic.

Medics did this, transformed a descriptive adjective into a collective noun: Bipolars, depressives, the anxious, psychotics. The list was endless.

And so the room was predictably painted in Asylum Cream. Recently. Not the richness of Jersey milk or Welsh butter. More a contaminated white.

Already she was assessing her new office with an awareness of potential danger, seeking out sharp objects – finding a grey, metal three-drawered filing cabinet with a sharp, cutting edge. Thrown hard against that it could wound her.

Her mind rolled on to an escape route and instinctively she moved towards the window which overlooked the enclosed quadrangle where inmates could sit on benches, chat, smoke, read – if they could. Particularly on such a bright, warm day. Beyond that was the stone archway fortified by huge gates which stood shut, except for a tiny door which was left ajar.

She opened the window the regulation four inches (no wider in case of attempted suicide) to try and dispel the smell. She dragged in a lungful of untainted air and felt cleaner. One should do this – start a new job on the 1st of the month, on a Monday. It pleased Claire's need for neatness and order.

She hung her linen jacket on the hook on the back of the door and resolved to bring in a hanger tomorrow. Plastic – not wire.

After her throat had been cut her body had been hanged on the hook on the back of the door. But, she had died first. The pathologist had said so in the *Daily Telegraph*.

Claire tried to avoid fixing on the hook.

So instead she peered out through the window. Four people were squashed together on one bench. Three women, one man. All the other benches were empty. They did this odd thing, crowded each other, then got annoyed with their proximity and fell out, like children in a school playground.

A nurse was walking towards them, skirting round the half-barrel tubs filled with geraniums and petunias – a futile attempt to brighten up the concrete paving slabs. He was not in uniform but it was easy to tell he was a nurse because all four on the bench looked towards him and stiffened, like a row of paper penguins. The nurse was tall and hefty, wearing jeans and a flapping T-shirt which warned of Aids Awareness Week. She knew him from the newspaper articles too. Siôna Edwards, a Welshman, described by the Mirror as 'as kind a man as you have ever met', by the Sun as 'having a heart as big as a bear', by the Mail as 'as gentle as a lamb' and the Express as 'as strong as an ox'. One or two of the editorials had included his quote that occasionally you needed that strength when patients were 'out of order'.

Siôna Edwards had been the one to find Gulio cowering in the corridor, backed against the wall, knife on the floor, the hands blooding his face as he protested over and over and over again. 'I didn't do it, Siôna. I didn't do it. It wasn't me. I didn't touch her. I didn't do anything.' With what must have been terrible foreboding the Welshman had followed the bloody tracks back along the corridor, tried to push open the door. Found it too heavy to open, summoned help.

Afterwards he had been quoted as saying. 'It could have been his blood. They often do cut themselves. But — ' There had been a wealth of meaning even in the printed but '- *in my heart of hearts I already knew something terrible lay behind that door.'* Even though the words were clichéd Claire had sensed they had been a direct quote. An indication of his sense of terror.

So as he'd run back along the corridor his hand had flapped out and banged the red panic button.

She moved away from the window. Back into the room. She was here to work. Not to wallow in the past and her first morning had deliberately been left free to read through patients' notes. She should not waste the time. This afternoon, at two pm, her first clinic started.

She should be reading. Preparing.

The key stuck out of the filing cabinet. She turned it and slid the top drawer open. Jammed with files, A-M.

She pulled out the first one, Mavis Abiloney.

In Heidi's writing. She recognised it, from letters they had exchanged, spidery, bold writing, clear and easy to read. Making a statement. Like the letter Heidi had sent her in response to her job application apologising for being hand written but the computers were down!

She took the file over to the desk and switched the computer on.

It asked her for her ID.

It had all been fixed with the IT department the week before.

CR

It asked her for a password.

Mother, she typed.

It asked her to confirm the password.

******, she typed, then clicked the icon for clinics.

Whom would she be seeing this afternoon?

A mixture. Some inpatients, some outpatients.

Mavis Abiloney, an inpatient, was the two o'clock appointment.

Claire bent over the notes.

The last entry had been made on the 17th of March.

The day Heidi had been murdered. This was something the newspaper had not reported. Such information was both confidential and irrelevant anyway but for Claire this was the first fact about the murder which she had learned for herself.

On the day she had died Heidi Faro had interviewed Mavis Abiloney.

She read through the date again. The 17th of March. On an ordinary, dull, Monday afternoon when nobody could have expected anything dramatic to happen, Heidi Faro, consultant psychiatrist, had had her throat cut by one of her patients in the mundane environment of Greatbach Secure Psychiatric Unit in the city of Stoke on Trent famous for its china and Robbie Williams. Claire knew all the newspaper accounts had emphasised the very ordinari-ness of the day and the place. That it had been the archetypal March Monday, dull, blustery and cold. And now, from the case notes she held in front of her, Claire knew that part of Heidi's last morning on earth had been spent speaking to Mavis Abiloney, an inpatient who, according to her predecessor's notes, had made 83 suicide attempts.

If at first you don't succeed . . . Claire's thoughts flew to the iron headmistress whose voice had boomed out this particular maxim.

Would she still agree? She scanned Heidi's observations with a click of interest. On March the seventeenth she had written, '*Little Change*', and expanded underneath. '*Still expressing suicidal ideas but nothing specific. Vague threat of lying underneath a train.*' In brackets '*(No track for > 3 miles)*'.

Asked if anything in particular was bothering her.

Answer, 'No.'

Asked if she felt she was ready to return home she had again answered, 'No'.

Upon broaching the subject that she really couldn't stay here for ever she had started crying. 'Why not? You look after me. I feel safe here. I am safe here.'

Asked if she was happy here.

Answer. 'Not happy. No. But I don't think all day about dying.'

'What do you think about then?'

'I think about what's on TV. What's for dinner. Who I'm going to sit next to. The people I like. The people I don't like.'

'Who are the people you like?'

'Siôna, you. Kristyna and others.'

'Who are the people you don't like?'

'Some. I don't want to say.'

Plan: Observe, see in a week or two, prolong the Section, aim for discharge asap. When safe.

Claire noted the red star in the top right corner of the notes. Red for inpatient; blue for outpatient. Six months later Mavis was still an inpatient. Subsequent consultations had been much more cursory, little more than 'extension to Section'.

Her successors had not shown Heidi's dedication.

Claire stared abstractedly across the room at the blank walls, breathing shallowly. In spite of the window being open she could still smell the paint.

Her eyes focused sharply on the door. Usually when you had been in a room for a little while you ceased to notice background smells. But this was different. Strong. Not overpowering now, subtle but unmistakably still there.

Had they deliberately used strong-smelling paint to mask underlying odour?

She stood up, agitated again. Ran her fingertips along the wall. Not quite smooth. She could feel odd bumps, small indentations, a few raised blisters. Tiny, tiny craters where pieces of the plaster had been lifted. She put her face close to peer along the wall. Surely. . . Surely the pale paint was a little darker here and there? She could even make out the faintest of blue circles in felt-tip pen. She jerked backwards. The marks must be where forensics had ringed individual spots.

Of blood.

She stared so hard she lost her focus.

And worried.

This could so easily become an obsession.

The trouble was, knowing she was due to start at Greatbach six months later, she had read every single account of Heidi Faro's death. She could still remember them. Verbatim.

Psychiatrist murdered by patient.

Doctor's throat cut by inmate.

Madman goes on frenzied killing spree.

At home she had even cut out a piece of paper to repre-sent the room, marked out where the furniture had been, desk, chairs, filing cabinet. Hook on door, copying from the paper which had sported the most lurid detail. She had made a computer diagram of the room. Plotted out the position of the corpse then used her imagination to colour the spray of blood that would have spurted from Heidi's throat when that sharp, cruel swipe had been made. This room was home to her. Familiar. Nothing was hidden from her.

As a doctor she knew exactly how people died when they had their throats cut.

They drown in their own blood. It fills their windpipe. The trachea.

On the computer Claire had fanned the spots as they must have hit the wall had Heidi been sitting at her desk as the papers had indicated. But now she was not on a computer screen but in the very room. And it felt different than she had expected.

Computers do not fill in the senses, and underlying the paint she could smell Heidi's blood. Feel the atmosphere.

She focused on the bland room again. This would not do. She could not work in that room of her mind. She must work here, personalise the office and obliterate the past. Change it from a murder scene to her own room-of-work.

It was her name which was slotted into the metal case outside the door. Doctor Claire Roget.

Not Doctor Heidi Faro. Never Doctor Heidi Faro again. She must put up some pictures. But what would she hang?

Van Gogh, Gericault, Rousseau, Klimt, Turner, Lautrec? All odd. She grimaced. They all belonged in here. As inpatients.

Then what about Arcimboldo – the strangest of the lot? The man who specialised in the grotesque. The man who turned flowers and fruit into strange faces. Who painted so carefully trees, roots, branches and flowers only to knot them into character. Who made animals' heads, deer, sheep and something like a kangaroo into a stuffy, bloated, old man's profile. Always a profile. And wound pearls around the neck of another grotesque made of corals and fish, sea snakes and crustaceans, even hanging pearl drop earrings in the oyster shell ears. Fanning books into the face of a scholar.

Yes, she thought, Arcimboldo would do nicely here.

He was perfect for this place where the human form was recognisable but character was distorted. Invisibly.

But for now she faced blank walls with their clues so poorly hidden.

And knew there would be others.

In the centre of the room stood the desk. It was not new. Light wood – maybe ash – rather scratched and worn. Nothing on its surface except the computer, the mouse, the keyboard and now Mavis Abiloney's notes. Almost as though in a vision she knew it would not have been like this six months ago. It would have held a laptop, piles of letters, the surface smothered in papers. Heidi had been a disorganised woman. Claire had watched her at lectures, unable to find her notes, mobile phone ringing throughout, welcoming interruptions.

Put your own mark on it, Claire.

Next to the notes she put her handbag, soft leather, black.

She cleared her throat, trying to scrape out the taste of paint. The sound seemed harsh and too loud, echoing self-consciously around the room, bouncing off the bare walls back to her. She coughed again but the after-taste was still there and now the room was silent again.

She sat down on the chair behind the desk, a high-backed, deep-buttoned, black plastic covered swivel chair, the patient's a smaller one on four wooden feet, a similar one in the corner. The chairs were all new.

Not like the desk.

How thorough would the police have been?

She squatted down now underneath the desk and peered up at the drawer runners and the dusty lower surface of the wood, ran her finger along the edge.

If Heidi had slid to the floor her blood would still have

been spurting.

Claire saw: dust, dirt, dark marks. Old blood? A panic button.

So why hadn't she used it?

'Hello there.'

She bumped her head, felt foolish on her knees, scrambled awkwardly to her feet, instantly at a disadvantage. 'Hello,' she said back.

A cavalier, she thought, tall, thin, foppish, pointed tiny beard, long, thin fingers. Long skinny legs in tight black jeans.

'I'm Rolf Fairweather,' he said with a warm smile, 'and you must be -?'

'Claire. Claire Roget, the new staff psychiatrist.'

'Well,' he said, shaking her hand with long, strong fingers, 'then we shall be colleagues. I'm the clinical psychologist here. Welcome to Greatbach, home of the pathological.'

He had been mentioned but not described. Rolf Fairweather, clinical psychologist, colleague of Heidi. Quote: 'She was a wonderful person to work with, shrewd, warm, intelligent. This has been a tragedy. I shall miss her.'

His grin was attractive, asymmetrical, his teeth the faintly yellowed teeth of a smoker, the evidence born out by the scent of nicotine which clung to the air around him. One of his front incisors had a gold corner to it. In his right ear was a gold sleeper.

'Will it hold you up if I sit down for a minute?'

Her hand waved towards the chair. 'Be my guest.'

She wanted to ask him about Heidi.

Nice eyes, melty brown, but they watched her with warily sharp intelligence which penetrated right into her thoughts so she knew, with relief, that she may as well tackle the subject head on rather than skip around it, like a silly child.

'I wouldn't have taken the job,' she said flatly, 'if **Stefan** hadn't been convicted.'

That was it – said. Straight to the jugular. No messing.

He was startled. She could tell that. Mouth open, eyes flicked wider. A sudden horror sequence in a Hitchock film which was swiftly suppressed.

'Yes – well. It was a terrible time. No one knew, you see, that she was coming back here after clinic that day. We'd assumed that she'd gone home or was still in clinic dictating. But she'd come back here.'

The newspapers had asked why.

She merely fixed him with a stare.

Which he answered. 'We don't know why.'

'And Stefan?'

'He's normally in a locked ward – supervised. Somehow he must have slipped away – we think.'

'So two unhappy coincidences?'

He nodded.

She pursued the point. 'You don't think she'd planned to meet Gulio?'

He frowned. 'I don't think so. But how can any of us know?'

'Was Gulio considered a risk?'

'Yes – no – yes. They all are. He was unpredictable.'

'You have no idea then why he might have done it? Had they had words – a disagreement?'

Fairweather shook his head. 'No. Gulio was a quiet patient. He'd never been any trouble – not to us. But as I said – to some extent most of our patients are unpredictable.'

A psychiatric patient who had carried out a frenzied attack, the *Mirror* had called it.

But even scanning the newspapers she had not pictured it like that. A quick swipe with surgical precision and then the grotesque hanging of the body on the doorhook whispered to her of something else. Strange, odd, unbalanced but not frenzied. There had been no mention of multiple wounds. Only the one.

'What were the circumstances of Gulio's original conviction?'

'He set on someone outside a nightclub. It was an unprovoked attack.'

She had read the opinions of Gulio's psyche. 'A little like the original assault on him.'

The papers had been full of it.

'He fought the bouncers off too.' Fairweather blew out a long sigh. 'It was quite an assault. He's just a skinny guy. After that it was obvious he'd get a custodial sentence and with his past we expected he'd end up with us. The rest, as they say, is history.'

She nodded and moved on.

'Did Heidi usually interview patients here, in her room?'

'Oh yes. Quite often.' He rubbed the side of his nose and sniffed – a gesture which reminded her of snuff-taking. 'If she'd decided a patient needed further assessment or she wanted to take a certain line of enquiry or treatment a bit further. Heidi made her own rules.'

This, Claire knew, was the truth. Heidi had been that sort of person. An innovator – a clear mind.

'She had some amazing results.'

Claire bowed her head almost in tribute.

Fairweather crossed to the window. 'She had this way, you know, of putting people at their ease. Asking the right questions. A way . . .' He stared out at the crowded bench, 'of getting right *behind* problems.'

Claire shifted in her seat. She had encountered this before. Step into someone's shoes and their colleagues made you feel unworthy. Well, she thought acidly and with a touch of jealousy, if Heidi had been such a paragon she shouldn't have allowed herself to be in such a dangerous position. Immediately she felt guilty. Forensic psychiatrists are always in a position of potential danger. *Any* encounter with a patient was a scene of possible assault. They were, by nature, unpredictable and potentially violent. You do not always get fair warning that the pin is out of the grenade.

She rested her chin on her hands, watched Fairweather flop back into the chair, threw the puzzle back at him. 'Was there no clue – no suspicion that Gulio's condition was worsening?'

The little voice, insistent, nagging. Searching for something that might, one day, warn her.

'Surely she should have picked up on something – poor eye contact, a detachment, flight of ideas, odd behaviour – something?'

'She never said so, Claire. The police asked me to go through Gulio's notes with them. He had a history of lashing out when roused but there was usually something which had sparked him off.'

'Is it possible that Heidi said something to him that day which touched on a raw nerve? Maybe something about the original assault?'

'Possible. Anything's possible, Claire.' A swift, charming smile. 'But we'll probably never really know the full circumstances. She hadn't finished filling in her notes. Personally I would have thought Heidi was too experienced to have interviewed Gulio alone and away from his ward if she'd sensed that he was psychotic.'

'What was the purpose of her interview that day?'

'She hadn't seen him for a week or two. She'd been away for a couple of days at a conference. She liked to see everyone at least fortnightly. She was considering altering his medication.'

'Maybe he said something which made her decide against it?'

Fairweather shook his head. 'No. She'd already written that he would soon be ready for release back into the community. The entry was dated the seventeenth of March. I knew her writing well. There was no doubt about it. There was no reason for Gulio to attack.'

Again she had this feeling of out of character. Gulio's crimes were bar brawls brought on by a volatile nature.

'Maybe he misunderstood what she was saying.' She thought of Mavis Abiloney. 'Or maybe he didn't want to be released.'

But instead of slashing his wrists he cut his psychiatrist's throat.

Rolf stood up to leave. 'As I said – anything's possible. He had been a bright guy. Heidi was quite fond of him.'

Claire winced. *Fond of him? Right up until the moment when he stroked her windpipe with a knife?*

Rolf shrugged, took a step towards the door, getting bored with the conversation. 'Anything's possible, Claire,' he said gently. 'But it's time to move on now. We don't want Greatbach to be forever linked with Heidi's murder. We do some sterling work here. Our understanding of personality disorder is among the best in the country. We're responsible for drawing up the guidelines for the release of Sectioned patients back into the community. This is an innovative unit.' He took another step towards the door. 'Besides,' he said. 'We've tightened up on things since Heidi's death. A number of changes have been made. You aren't allowed to see patients alone in your office any more. Either you see them in the interview room on the ward or a member of staff is supposed to be in with you.'

'That's unethical.'

'Well – just outside the door. And as for ethics — ' There was a quick spark of anger. 'What could possibly be more unethical than being murdered by one of your patients?' He looked distressed. 'Remember. I saw the crime scene that day. It will stay in my mind for ever. The bloody scene. Changes had to be made.' He swallowed. We have CCTV along the corridors and they're recording. All the time.'

'And who's watching them?'

'The porters at the gate. They have the monitors there.'

'But Gulio's in prison,' she objected.

He'd reached the door. 'Where Gulio came from there are more. People just like Gulio – and worse – are our speciality.'

He opened the door, his foot almost through it already. 'We usually have staff meetings every morning at nine-ish – to review cases and plan the day ahead. Hope that's OK

with you. We've found it worked very well for us – saved
duplicating interviews etcetera.'

'Fine.'

'So – until tomorrow then?'

She nodded.

And was once again alone in the room.

Chapter Two

By lunchtime she was halfway through 'G' in the alphabet and felt she had a reasonable working knowledge of some of the inpatients. They were a motley assortment, many schizophrenics, depressives, severe learning disabilities, all with one thing in common – they had all committed a crime and were detained under Section 29 of the Mental Health Act because they were considered a danger either to themselves or to the wider community. As it had been months since Heidi had left quite a few were probably ready for discharge back into the community. Many were due for review. Claire heaved a big sigh. As always in the Mental Health Service she was aware of a heavy burden which never would lighten, decisions which were hers alone to make.

At one Rolf knocked on her door and stuck his head round. 'Sometimes we get sandwiches,' he announced, 'and eat them out of doors. Sometimes we eat in the canteen and at others we pop down the pub. I suggest today, as it's your first day, that we get some sandwiches from the canteen and eat them in the quadrangle. Is that OK by you?'

'Fine.' She appreciated his friendliness. 'Thanks.' Then, 'Are you in clinic this afternoon?'

'Yeah – Outpatients – alongside you.'

They queued with the inpatients, choosing sandwiches, yoghurt, a bottle of water for Claire and coffee in a lidded, cardboard mug for Rolf. Then they let themselves out into the quadrangle.

Sheltered from breezes, yet catching the sun, over the wall the tops of the brick-built bottle-kilns just visible. They found an empty bench and sat at either end, their lunch between them.

'So how long have you been here, Rolf?'

'Eight years. It was my second job out of university. I knew instantly I'd stay. Interesting cases, experimental treatments, good senior support. I used to work under a greybeard called Hartshorn. Johnny Hartshorn. He'd written lots of books on clinical psychology. Was a bit of an icon. He left after a few years and I was lucky enough to get the job as a senior clinical psychologist. He was a big influence on my life. He's well past retiring age now but I still keep in touch with him, ask his opinion on difficult cases. What about you?'

'Oh – the usual. Medical degree, interest in psychiatry, Membership and so on. Good registrar post in Birmingham. And then, like you, my big chance. Here. Only six months too late to work under Heidi.'

'Did you ever meet her?'

'I'd been to lectures of hers, corresponded a little, asking for advice on the thesis I did for my MRC Psych.' She recalled the small, plump, homely figure in black trousers and clinical white blouse with shining auburn hair which Claire had suspected was her vanity. Not commanding much attention until she opened her mouth and you listened to her words – and wanted to go on and on listening to them.

Rolf chewed his sandwich with his mouth a little open, casually, like an American, unashamed of the food inside. 'What was your thesis on?'

'Personality disorder – treatable or not?'

'Mmm. Big subject. No wonder you wanted to work with Heidi.'

With her, she thought savagely. *Not instead of her.*

'Exactly.'

'But you still came – even though . . .'

'I've always liked forensic work,' she said a little defensively.

He swivelled his head right round to look her full in the face. 'Why?'

'I think.' She took a bite out of her ham sandwich and chewed it, cud-like, to help her work this one out. 'I think it's the edge. The danger. The little clues that mean so much. I like the clinical responsibility. The thumbs up, thumbs down bit. Freedom, incarceration. I don't really know, Rolf. Only that it excites me. Interests me. It's part of civilisation, this dealing with the aberrations.'

'Mmm. Interesting.' He dug a spoon in his yoghurt and shovelled some in his mouth, licking his lips now almost daintily.

She swigged the water and knew she always found it difficult to explain why she enjoyed forensic work. All she knew was that crime – and its causes – fascinated her more than pure physical illness. It was less easy to diagnose and treat, more of a mystery. And being less exact there was more scope for personal intervention and innovation. She had always entered medicine with the explicit objective that she would one day understand the criminal mind. What made them lash out in the way they did.

The shame was that it was rarely treatable.

They swapped stories about their home life and she learned that Fairweather had lived with the same partner for seven years, ('She's a bit older than me, a professor at the university') while she confessed that she was in a relationship, knowing he would read between the lines that she was bored with it.

Before heading for the clinic she had been asked to see one patient on the ward, Mavis Abiloney, whom the staff said was agitated. Claire suspected that it was simply an excuse for the nurses to give her the once-over but she went anyway.

She ran the gauntlet of the staff's curious gaze and they directed her to the interview room. So this was the first of Heidi's patients for her to meet. Claire introduced herself to the small, wrinkled lady who stank of cigarette smoke and screwed up her eyes to peer at her. Her hands were almost mummified, as dry, wrinkled and brown as a monkey's paw. She was dressed in a black, stretch skirt with a seam wandering around the front, saggy where her seat was, a brown V necked sweater, low heeled shoes and thick brown stockings. Her hair showed half an inch of grey roots, the rest tidily hennaed and well cut into a short bob but dry as summer-straw.

'I'm your new doctor,' Claire said. 'Here instead of Heidi.'

'Better than that darky,' Mavis responded moodily.

Claire winced. Bob Karnoy had been the locum after Heidi's death. She knew him vaguely from medical meetings. An intelligent, funny and competent doctor from Nigeria. Yet to Mavis Abiloney he was simply a 'darky'.

Thankfully our generation is more enlightened, she thought, in some ways. In others we are even less tolerant. Of poverty, obesity, death, illness and poor service. And as for smokers . . .

She motioned Mavis to sit down. Little sparrow legs crossed tidily, hands dropped onto her lap, a tentative smile illuminating her face. Her eyes searched around for an ashtray. Claire did not oblige. For all her condemnation of intolerance she couldn't bear the smell of cigarette smoke – even if the habit did help patients to relax.

She opened the interview. 'The nurses told me you were feeling agitated.'

The fingers started to contort. 'I knew you were starting,' she said, dark little monkey-eyes darting around the room. 'I was worried.' Mute appeal in the eyes now, staring at her with desperate intensity. 'I was afraid. I don't want to go home,' she finally blurted out.

'Well – surely – you don't want to stay here, Mavis?'

'Why not?'

'It's for people who are sick.'

'You know something of my history, doctor. You think I'm well?'

'I think you are a woman who might consider restarting her life.'

'You think that's possible?'

'With help, Mavis, and support.'

'Huh.' She tossed her head – and the idea – aside.

Claire leaned in. 'I'm going to do nothing hasty, Mavis,' she said. 'We shall talk with you and with the others and consider the best way forward.' She had hoped this would relax her. Certainly the fingers were still again.

A stay of execution.

She smiled. 'So-o . . . How are you feeling, Mavis?'

'Not bad.' It was at best a guarded reply. She wasn't even near to trusting Claire yet as she had, no doubt, trusted Heidi.

'What are you doing with your days?'

The hands fidgeted again as though she was guilty about her inactivity. Eyes darted around, pinpointing various spots on the wall. 'Plenty,' she lied. 'We talk. We watch the TV. I help cook the dinners – sometimes.'

'Do you go out on the trips?'

'When I want to.' Evasive.

'Where do you enjoy going?'

'I didn't say I enjoyed them,' she snapped.

'Where did you go last time you did go out?'

'Ironbridge Gorge.'

'When was this?'

'Can't remember.'

'What did you think of it?'

The brown eyes stared blankly back. 'Think? I thought it was a lot of fuss about nothing. That's what I thought.'

'How are your family managing without you?'

Eyes and head jerked along the skirting board now. 'They manage.'

'How would you feel about going home?'

The two monkey paws took on a nervous life of their own, weaving fingers, wringing action. 'You know what happens when I go home,' she accused.

'But you've been so well while you've been here. You're stable on the new medication. I've been reading about you.'

'I don't think I should go home,' she said firmly.

Claire was aware that this was neither the time nor the

place. She should be seeing the patients in the locked ward at two but sometimes patients open up more to a new doctor than the physician who has treated them for years. 'Why not, Mavis?'

'I – just – don't.' Said flatly. A blind ending.

Claire drew in a deep breath. She was new here. It would take her some time to get to know the patients well, understand their circumstances. She took the easy option.

She would talk to Rolf. 'Perhaps we should meet again in a week or so. All of us together. In the meantime, Mavis, I want you to consider going home for a short, accompanied visit with one of the nurses here.'

Panic in her eyes.

'Will you think about it?'

A nod and she was gone, shuffling from the room like a woman twenty years older.

It was a short walk to the locked ward, where she was due to see four patients due for consideration of release. The first of these was Marcus Bourne. It sounded an innocuous enough name. But the story behind the ordinary name was not usual. Claire glanced through his notes. Newly on remand after stabbing his girlfriend in the lung with a penknife while they were leaving a nightclub. He'd inadvertently taken some Haloperidol which a friend had flogged him for five pounds telling him it was Temazepam and he'd been tipped into acute motor restlessness when she'd stopped to gossip to a friend. 'She just wouldn't stop talkin',' he'd told the arresting officer. 'It was the only way to get her to hurry up.'

The girlfriend had spent six weeks in hospital after contracting MRSA, the hospital superbug, in the chest wound. She had been badly scarred and would bear them for ever. The question was, how responsible for his actions had Bourne been at the time of the assault? There was no doubt that the balance of his mind had been temporarily disturbed, that he had voluntarily taken a substance but been deceived as to what it was and its likely effects. Should the charge really have been attempted murder? And the real question – How much of a danger would he be when released back into the community? After all Bourne had not gone out equipped to maim. He had been carrying a penknife – not a lethal weapon. How much was the drug responsible for subsequent events? There had been no previous convictions for violence. So while the lawyers argued the case she was left to assess the patient.

She faced the good-looking guy sitting opposite her, twenty-six years old, dark, neat hair, large eyes with ice-clear whites, a tanned, smooth complexion, an easy smile.

How appearances can lull. The temptation was to excuse this man with the honest eyes which looked straight into hers with such frankness and assurance.

But it was this very confidence which made her finger the panic button beneath the desk as she started to question him.

This was a young man used to getting his own way, accustomed to charming his route out of trouble.

The vibrations were taut enough to be an inaudible treble but she knew they were there.

Bourne had inflicted serious, unprovoked damage on his own girlfriend – not on a stranger. All because she had delayed him for a few minutes, according to witnesses. His anger had erupted like a sudden spring out of dry ground. The prosecution had made much of that plus the fact that he had spent the night clubbing armed with a penknife in his pocket. When asked why by the prosecution he had merely shrugged. Her instinct sympathised very much with the prosecution.

The defence, on the other hand, put the case forward that much attention should be paid to the fact that he had been under the influence of a rather odd drug to be peddling around a nightclub, an anti-psychotic, and argued that had he not been under the influence he would not have been a threat to his girlfriend at all. What interested Claire was the fact that he had been admitted here when he should have gone straight to prison.

Reading through the notes she almost slapped her thigh and said *Hah.* Because it was the old turkey. As the Haloperidol had worn off Bourne had claimed he had heard voices telling him his girlfriend would not bleed.

The trouble was neither the prison service nor the hospital service quite knew what to do with these people. They were tossed from one to the other like a rogue card in a game of Brag. As much of an embarrassment as a 'Q' without an accompanying 'U' in a game of Scrabble.

Instead of launching straight into the interview Claire jotted down just one of the questions she wanted to put to him. When she looked up his eyes seemed smaller – to have shrunk. She stared at him, fascinated at an impossible physical change.

She introduced herself to him and they shook hands. They could have been any couple meeting socially.

But they weren't.

'I just want to get a few facts straight,' she began. 'You took the Haloperidol thinking it was Temazepam?'

The gaze never faltered. 'That's right, doctor,' he said.

They are always polite – until. Until you rumble them. 'How often did you take recreational drugs?'

'Couple of times. Maybe twice, three times before, always when out clubbing and I needed a bit of a spark. Bit of E, the odd spliff. You know.'

She nodded.

'And the girlfriend . . .' She searched the notes for the girl's name. 'Stephanie?'

'She weren't nothin' serious. Just a bit of skirt to go out with.'

Her toes were beginning to tingle.

'And how is she now?'

A faintly arrogant smile which he tried to hide behind a fake cough. 'She's OK. Bit of a scar, my mate told me.'

'So you don't see her any more?'

'No. Like I said, she was just someone I was with a night or two.'

That was not what Stephanie had told the police. 'He – were – my – steady,' she had wheezed from her hospital bed.

Maybe she had assumed if she didn't press charges Bourne would gravitate back to her or maybe he had threatened her if she didn't stick up for him. The police might have believed her insistent story – that it had all been an accident – had not a crowd of clubbers who had witnessed the entire event said otherwise, that he had slowly drawn the knife from his pocket, deliberately opened the blade, stroked it and driven it hard into his girlfriend's chest.

It did not sound like an accident or a psychotic incident.

Claire thought quickly.

She was too intelligent a psychiatrist to ask the obvious question. It would provoke the obvious reply. Bourne was not stupid. He knew he would be released only if he displayed remorse whether fake or genuine and promised he would be a good boy in future.

She closed his file and he looked cheated – disappointed.

'Look,' he said.

'Yes?'

'Doctor,' he tried. 'It's time I was let out of here. I'm not a nut. Someone just slipped me the wrong stuff and I flipped. That's all.'

The trouble was that it wasn't.

Bourne was a sociopath. A psychopath. He had been a time bomb waiting to go off. And he would go off again.

'I don't think it's quite time,' she said, 'for a review. It's early days.'

She saw the ugly side of him then – before he buried it again deeply. 'I'm not a nut,' he said savagely. 'I don't belong here. You should recommend my release. You can keep some sort of supervision order going.'

He knew all the jargon.

Conscious that behind each set of notes lay a story she worked steadily all afternoon. By five she was through and had only one more task before she could call it a day. She had to travel to the outskirts of the city to do a domiciliary visit on another old regular of Greatbach, Harry Sowerby, fifty-seven-year-old manic depressive – or to use the current terminology, bipolar affective disorder. When on a low he was wont to cut his wrists, threaten to throw himself off a bridge, lie on railway tracks. But it was when he was in a manic phase that he crossed the line into criminal activity and attracted the real attention. Buying Porsches, throwing parties, trying to board planes without tickets, extravaganzas in expensive restaurants, movie star style – all on a pension. This time he was doing a striptease in the middle of the Potteries Shopping Centre and when hustled off by the security staff he had insisted that the Queen herself had commissioned him to do it, fumbling in his pockets for Her Majesty's letter and cheque, postmarked Buckingham Palace, so he said. He had manfully fended off the police until they had restrained him and then, not knowing what to do next, they had contacted the duty psychiatrist, her.

Nice one.

It was difficult not to like Harry – wrapped in a grey woollen blanket, humming the notes of The Stripper, arms flinging wide, little National Health glasses. Not cowering in the corner of the police cell but making a splash, hailing her with a welcoming hoot.

The custody officer gave her a broad wink. 'Hope you'll not be too shocked, doctor.'

She grinned back. 'Nothing shocks a psychiatrist,' she said. 'They train the emotion right out of us.'

Harry giggled at this and dropped his blanket, revealing a wrinkled frame.

'How do you do, Harry,' she said, holding out her hand. 'I'm Doctor Roget from Greatbach.'

'Excellent,' he said, rubbing his hands together. 'I hoped

they'd send a blonde. Real blonde, are you?'

She nodded, amused – not embarrassed at all.

'I think maybe things have got a little out of control here, Harry?'

'But if they'd only waited I know Her Majesty would have wanted to attend herself then everything would have been all right.'

'I'm sure it would, Harry, but today is a bit cold. And the shopping centre didn't seem to understand what you were doing.' She smothered a smile. 'Or really appreciate it. Let's leave it for another day, shall we. In the meantime I think you should have a nice, restful time at Greatbach for a couple of nights until things quieten down a bit. Don't you?'

Harry looked suddenly tired. 'If you say so, my dear.'

A mega dose of Lithium and in a day or two Harry Sowerby would be back to his flat, his mood stabilised into an unemotional self.

The real problem was, why had he veered out of control? Had he been defaulting on his medication or was his condition worsening?

Time to assess that in the future.

For now – home.

For him. For her.

Chapter Three

It was a long, slow drive back home. A new underpass was being built underneath the so-called D road, the A500 which links junctions 15 and 16 of the M6. She threaded miserably through the city, nose to bumper all the way, moving alongside the Trent and Mersey canal for a while before turning off towards Burslem. She was pleased to see that the warehouses on the towpath side of the canal were still being used as pottery storehouses, even though the wares were no longer being transported along the canal in horse drawn or steam driven barges. Here and there, through Stoke, as in many towns and cities in Britain, history is waiting silently for you to notice it.

It was the smell of paint which greeted her for the second time that day as she pushed open the front door. Grant was emulsioning the hall. Again. She shoved aside an aluminium ladder. He was in jogging pants and a baggy vest, a paintbrush in one hand. He planted a lager-scented kiss on her cheek. 'Hi. How's the new job? Take-away for tea?'. He stood back to admire his handiwork. 'Well – what do you think?'

Her taste was more for the simple, understated, Oriental. Bonsai trees and the palest of peppermint greens. His for vibrance, warmth, splashes of wild colour. Colours like Raspberry, Tango, Zest, Citron. She hated it and he knew it. She'd put a cross on Dove Grey. He'd bought Dining Room Red.

She smiled and said nothing. It was not worth the conflict.

But she hadn't admired his handiwork so he was offended. 'Come on, Claire. Look a bit more enthusiastic. Please. It's taken me all afternoon.'

What was the point?

Grant had been a mistake from the beginning but she was only now realising just how big a mistake at the very same moment as it was sinking in how difficult it was going to be to extricate herself from this particular error.

They had lived together for almost two years, moving in hastily after meeting at a friend's wedding. Claire had been going through an emotional time. Weddings brought out the worst in her and she had spun towards Grant, attracted by the wide smile, bright teeth and extrovert manner, the roguish, pirate look in his black eyes and thick dark curly hair. Besides – she had enjoyed seeing the look of envy her married friends had given her and the overheard comments that Claire had 'pulled something really tasty'.

But she had a habit of doing this, picking up on the wrong men, choosing the wrong types, these superficially attractive men who were stuffed full of impractical ideas, never really listened to her point of view and bowled along in their own way, doing their own thing while she tagged behind, never really comfortable with them but avoiding open confrontation.

Until she moved out, leaving always on the same note, that it 'wasn't going to work out', or they were 'incompatible'. Nothing too aggressive.

She wouldn't have minded so much had it not always been the same tired phrases, the same worn out excuses.

And then after a few months' celibacy she veered back towards the same disaster all over again.

The pattern was set and she could not seem to break the cycle.

Maybe it was part of her training – this compliance and avoidance of horn-locking. Grant was simply the latest in a succession of similar disasters and she felt cross – not with him – but with herself. She was a *psychiatrist,* for goodness sake. She should be able to weed out these unsuitable types, recognise them a mile off and take evasive action. And yet she did not. She went for the same type all over again and it exasperated her, made her irritated and angry with herself – which bordered very near to self-dislike. A feeling of being out of control of her own life, of losing this important fist-grasp of her destiny. Empowerment.

It was the buzz phrase of all young, professional women in the first few years of the twenty-first century.

So why couldn't she achieve it when she was dishing it out to her friends like orange smarties? Why couldn't she fall for some steady, professional guy who did a nine-five job in the city, wanted two-point-four kids, would mow the lawn at weekends and whose ideas did not owe all to Walt Disney? Her eyes brushed over the Dining Room Red walls while she acknowledged the answer with a small, secret smile.

Answer – because she would find him predictable and boring. And that was the biggest of sins – to be boring.

OK then. Why couldn't she fall in love with someone just a smidge less unsuitable?

This one she didn't even attempt to answer.

Grant was looking at her with a sweetly quizzical expression. He scratched his bristly chin, smearing enough of the red paint to look like a wounded pirate who hadn't even shaved today. 'Indian or Chinese?'

And just to be perverse and stake her independence she said, 'Thai' and went upstairs to run a bath.

Actually Grant wasn't as bad as her usual prototype. At least he had a job. He was trouble-shooter to the local sixth form college on computer affairs. They called him in when they had a problem with their computers and he was also involved in writing the programmes for their timetables. This made him entitled to long holidays and almost non-existent term-time work. He earned little more in a year than she did in a month.

She went upstairs and was luxuriating in the Stress Buster bubble bath when he poked his head around the door. 'Green Thai curry,' he said, 'with noodles. And it'll be here in ten minutes.' Then he flung a red dragon dressing grown at her. She caught it just before it hit the water.

Grant was one of life's charmers who get away with

doing what they want to do. And all around them people are sucked into supporting them. She might have loved him. He was easy to love. Affectionate, romantic, good looking in a hunky, roguish sort of way. But she had learned to delve beneath the surface, question his integrity – and found it wanting.

She didn't quite trust him.

Fifteen minutes later she was eying him across the dining room table – a smoked glass affair from their Habitat days.

'So,' he said warily, 'how is the new job?'

She responded enthusiastically. 'Good. Interesting. A challenge. It'll be a challenge.' She forked in some of the green curry, a few noodles sliding back to the plate on the way, like pale, small worms. 'And how was your day?'

Only a week before the college went back. She would have thought there would be plenty of preparation to do. 'You didn't have to go in?'

He gave an exaggerated yawn, arms flinging out. 'Give me a break. I felt a bit . . .'

But not too exhausted to paint the hall Pillar Box Red or Dining Room Red or whatever, she thought crossly.

But then Grant would always have the energy to do what he wanted to do.

Never mind responsibility. He and the 'R' word did not quite hit it off.

She finished her curry keeping one eye fixed on him, observing him. But oh, he was easy on the eye. His black eyes regarded her back and he raised his eyebrows. She inhaled a long, deep breath.

She fancied him.

So was it simply lust?

Maybe.

He put his fork down. 'What are you smiling at?'

'You.'

'Why?'

'Look,' she said, waving her own fork at him. 'I'm the

psychiatrist. I'm the one who asks why.'

He teased her back with his eyes for minutes before returning to the curry. His – red – to match the hall. Hers green – the traditional colour for envy.

'So tomorrow?' she ventured.

'Tomorrow – I finish the hall.'

'I see.' She resisted the temptation to ask him when he would be going in to work and finished her meal recalling their holiday in India last year when he had attracted so much attention, striding across the beach, day-glo orange Bermudas, Oakley wraparounds glinting in the sun, Reebok sandals on his feet. She had seen women follow him with their eyes and known what they were thinking. So when he had suddenly turned towards her, pulled her close, put his arms tightly around her to kiss her full on the lips, his body almost part of hers, she had known he was simply playing to the gallery.

She had been conscious of the women behind her, their emotion.

Envy.

She had revelled in it.

They spent an evening typical for them, stretched out in front of the television, making desultory conversation and finally making love in front of the fire.

Rolf was in early the next morning, a minute or two after her, well in time for the nine o'clock meeting, so she had a chance to ask him about a few of the patients she'd seen yesterday.

'Mavis?' she ventured. 'I wondered about sending her on a home visit. Surely it's time she was discharged?'

He eased his long, bony frame into the armchair and steepled his fingers, the tips brushing against the Van Dyck moustache. 'That's probably the problem. We're always being asked to consider discharge but in Mavis's case it's the discharge that sends her hurtling back here.'

'Enlighten me.'

'She has a brutal husband,' he said. 'An ex factory worker who drinks a fair bit. He's got no time for Mavis. If it was left to him we really would throw away the key. Maybe if she was one hundred per cent OK they might just about manage but as it is it's a pathological situation and without being pessimistic I'd say it is not going to improve – not ever.' He looked troubled. 'There is a daughter who lives a couple of streets away. Poor woman. She's always the one who finds Mavis after these suicide attempts. It's invariably on an afternoon when she's due round. Basically Mavis lasts a day or two outside then something snaps. Suicide attempts are her way of gaining readmission and safety. She's never tried to kill herself while she's an inpatient. There's little point discharging her, Claire,' he advised. 'She'll be back in within the week. Unless, of course, one of these days she succeeds.'

'But the guidelines.'

His eyes glistened with intense feeling. 'Bugger the guidelines, Claire. They don't allow for real life. Discharge Mavis and she'll make another attempt and another and another until she succeeds.'

'Her eighty-fourth.'

'Believe me. She's simply not capable of life on the out-side.'

She broached the subject then of Marcus Bourne, told Rolf her instincts. His smile extended as he listened but he didn't say anything until she'd exhausted her thoughts. 'He's dangerous all right but not the worst. He'd been clean right up until the Haloperidol loosened his grip. If he stays off unpredictable trips I think his chances of reoffending are pretty slim. He's just a pottery worker, you know. Just a simple guy.'

She nodded.

'If you want to meet a really nasty psychopath just wait until you've met Jerome Barclay. Now there's one who's capable of some dark deeds.'

'Tell me more.'

Rolf smiled, the gold tooth making him look a maverick. 'You'll meet him,' he promised. 'Make your own judgement. Unless I'm very much mistaken you'll meet him this afternoon in clinic. He's under a fairly close supervision order. Organised by your predecessor.' Fairweather's brown eyes were deadly serious.

She wanted to ask him more then about Heidi. But before she could question him further the door had opened and he had jumped to his feet.

'Kristyna.'

A slim blonde girl somewhere in her twenties wearing baggy cargo pants, a khaki long-sleeved T-shirt and a broad smile burst in, gave them all a wide smile and headed straight for the coffee pot. She poured herself a mug of coffee, took a deep swig and crossed the room towards Claire. 'Hi,' she said warmly, stretching out her hand. 'You must be Claire Roget. I'm so glad you . . .' She looked defiantly round the room, 'had the guts to take up the post. I'm Kristyna. One of the Community Psychiatric Nurses here. We'll be working together.'

She waved her mug. 'One of my weaknesses, I'm afraid. Can I pour you some?'

Claire took an instant liking to the nurse. 'Thanks,' she said. 'I've just had one.'

Then in burst Siôna Edwards and Claire could smell the alcohol on him as he poured himself a black coffee. He turned and stared at her completely unabashed.

'Doctor Roget, I presume.' There was a note of truculence – of challenge in his voice. She had met it before, resentment against a doctor, a female at that. Inwardly she sighed. *She could deal with this.*

She shook hands.

Two other psychiatric nurses joined them before Rolf took command. 'Right – anyone else should be here?'

'No – I think that's it. Apologies from Dawn. Dentist. Just a check-up but with appointments so tight she didn't want to put it off.'

'First of all the introductions. I think you all know Claire, Doctor Roget, taken over from Heidi.'

Claire searched the rim of faces but the returning expressions were bland. She could almost have convinced herself that Heidi had left to take up another post had it not been for a certain wariness in them all and Kristyna's words. But the bluntness of the psychiatric nurse endeared her to her. And something in the pale eyes told her a hideous truth – that Heidi never had left Greatbach – alive. Not all of her anyway. Parts of her were still here, on her consulting room walls, not quite hidden by the many coats of paint.

Edwards, Kristyna, Rolf and the others were watching her expectantly. Waiting for her to open the meeting so she outlined her clinic yesterday and her plans for the remainder of the day then invited them to continue.

Siôna Edwards told her that Harry Sowerby was settling down with the highest dose of Lithium they were allowed to give him. 'Bit of a shame, really,' he said. 'Like pricking a balloon. He gets that deflated when he realises what he's done. Don't know what's worse, really, in bipolar disorders, the ups or the downs.'

'Both as bad as each other,' Kristyna returned, pouring herself a second coffee, gold bangles jingling on the slim wrists. She winked at Claire. 'But the ups are more fun. Scandalous. I bet he said something about you being a natural blonde, Claire.'

They both giggled.

The comment sparked off a brief discussion, peppered with amusing ancedotes about manic depressives during which Claire studied Kristyna closely, taking in the smooth, olive-toned skin, the white, even teeth, her mannerisms, the throwing back of her head when laughing, the twitch of her shoulders as she talked, the animated way her hands seemed to shape words, something confident, inviting, almost provocative in her manner. There was a glimpse of midriff between her top and the trousers which were low-slung. Her hair was dragged back in a swinging sixties ponytail and she had pretty little lapis lazuli pins in her earlobes, gold studs in the curl at the top of the ear, another stud on the left side of her nose. She was sitting with her legs apart, her feet encased in leather cowboy boots, tapping in time to some secret rhythm. She gave Claire another of her wide grins which Claire returned. Then she cleared her throat.

'I've only got one concern,' she said. 'It's Nancy Gold.'

It was as though a shudder rippled through the room which Claire could not understand, as though the name touched a raw nerve.

She waited. Someone, surely, would fill her in.

That someone was, unexpectedly, Siôna.

'Nancy is a tragedy,' he said slowly. 'Twenty-three years old. She killed her baby. Held him under bath water. Then hid the body for six months in the airing cupboard. In the old days,' he said, folding his arms, 'she'd have been hanged for infanticide.'

Claire looked from one face to another.

'Thank God infanticide is dealt with differently these days. Enlightenment has shone forgiveness on women who kill their own children.'

'Steady steady,' Siôna said.

Claire met his eyes and waited. For Nancy even to be here there must be more.

'He was only ten months old, 'Siôna said. 'His name was George. The post mortem showed up bruises on his chest from where the little chap had struggled against her.' A swell of sympathy rippled around the room.

'I take it there was no doubt it *was* Nancy. It's more usual for . . .'

She had been about to say, the father – or the stepfather.

'That's why she's *here*,' Kristyna said softly, 'rather than in prison. When the police confronted her with the PM findings she confessed.'

'Oh?' Claire was no nearer understanding.

'It was her motive,' Siôna explained. 'She said she'd had it explained to her when she'd gone into the church. She was devoted to her boyfriend – a nasty, psychopathic piece of work named Hove Watson. She claimed that the statue of the Virgin Mary told her that the only way she would keep her man was to destroy her child. That he would come between them. Initially she *was* sent to prison but she attempted suicide and then kept going berserk, saying she'd only done what she was told and screaming to be with this germ of a man. Some women,' he said.

And what was that supposed to mean?

'Was this *germ of a man* the child's father?'

'Probably.'

No one spoke and yet words and thoughts were still flying around because Rolf spoke next.

'And yet,' he said. 'There is something so – untouched – almost virginal about her. It's as though . . . She's been in for four years now and we're no nearer knowing what's going on in that pretty head of hers.'

Siôna cleared his throat noisily.

'So what's your concern today, Kristyna?'

'It's hard to say. The ward staff spoke to me about her. She keeps slipping away. Disappearing off the ward, using the telephone. They think she has a secret. I don't know what it is. She isn't due for an assessment yet but there's something changed about her. Something -. Just meet her, Claire,' she pleaded. 'You'll know what I mean then.'

Already Claire knew that Kristyna's professional judgement was one she would learn to rely on. 'OK, Kristyna, I will. I may not have time today but tomorrow. I'd like to spend some time with her.'

Rolf spoke up. 'And I wonder if you'd go and see Kap.'

Everyone groaned.

'What's wrong this time?' Siôna sounded gruff.

Rolf explained to Claire. 'He's a pothead, Rastafarian guy. Very very paranoid. Like some days he won't come out of the corner. A result of years of smoking *de ganja man*.'

They all laughed.

'So what's your specific concern?'

'He lunged at one of the nurses with a knife last night. It was only an ordinary table knife but it unnerved us. It's the first time he's ever been really violent. It came out of the blue, took us by surprise.'

'Did he have an explanation?'

'The usual. Someone was out to get him. That he wasn't safe. That blood had flowed. That he would have to pay the price.'

Heidi, she thought suddenly. It was true – in fact a graphic description. Blood had flowed. Arterial blood is under huge pressure. Slice through an artery and it sprays everywhere. Like a power pressure hose.

No one else seemed to have made the connection. They were all still smiling.

Denial?

She joined them to smile too. 'I'll talk to him later,' she promised. 'He may need. . . '

'Sedation,' they all chimed in.

Her clinic this afternoon was full of routine NHS work, anxiety, agorophobia, depression, schizophrenics, manic depressives. Bread and butter stuff really until late in the afternoon she recognised the next name, Jerome Barclay. And according to her screen he had already arrived and been waiting for almost half an hour. He had arrived early. She flicked open his notes and read just one of Heidi's resumés.

Initially it was hard to see exactly why Barclay was being so closely observed. Five years ago he had apparently committed a violent offence against his mother who had subsequently refused to press charges or to submit to any medico-legal examination. But she had been admitted to hospital with injuries to her face – a depressed fracture of the zygomatic arch, a broken jaw, displaced teeth and a minor head injury which had apparently resulted from a fall backwards. It didn't exactly need a degree in forensic pathology to work out that she had been hit from the front, hard enough to cause broken bones of the face, and had subsequently fallen backwards with some force.

But her story had changed to having walked into a door and falling backwards. She said she had been drinking. And although blood alcohol levels were low – consistent with nothing more than a glass of wine – she had flatly refused to press charges against her son, had denied he was even in the house at the time and said it was lucky he had turned up later or else she might not have had hospital treatment. This in spite of a neighbour having heard mother and son rowing.

Heidi had interviewed Barclay who had backed up his mother's fable and nothing had been done. No charges had been pressed.

But a year or two later a girlfriend, Sadie Whittaker, had also accused him of serious assault. She too had been badly injured by being run over with a car which Barclay had been driving. Later, like Barclay's mother, she too had retracted her initial statement which had claimed that Barclay had driven deliberately, glassy-eyed, towards her.

She now said it had been an accident, that she had stepped in front of his car following a row and that he couldn't possibly have seen her. There had been no witnesses. The incident had happened late at night in a quiet, unlit road near where Ms Whittaker had lived so it had been her word against his.

Once again the initial charge had been withdrawn.

Claire could almost hear the police gnashing their teeth with frustration. There was such underlying brutality in both assaults and yet no conviction.

She scanned quickly through the rest of the notes. There were other misdemeanors since youth. Most of his earlier criminal charges had been minor theft from shops, garage forecourts, some casual theft of money from his work and more specifically a couple of forged cheques from his mother's bank account. She was a widow, Barclay's father having died when he was ten years old.

It was difficult to see why there was such a close supervision order on him. Heidi had spoken to Barclay every month and he was the one patient Rolf Fairweather had singled out to warn her against. Claire was very curious as she pressed the buzzer to call Barclay through.

She waited for a minute, two minutes. He should have been here by now. The waiting room was only feet away. And he would already know the way. This was hardly his first attendance. She was just wondering whether she should call him in again or if the computer was wrong and that he had not arrived when he sauntered in, without knocking.

She noted it as deliberate dominance – typical sociopathic behaviour. A kind of one-upmanship. Marking his territory and status like an animal peeing against a tree.

She stayed seated.

He was an unremarkable-looking guy – of medium height, around five nine, five ten, medium build, slightly pale skin, medium brown hair, cut neat and short. He was wearing loose-fitting grey Chinos and a cream sweater, sleeves rolled up to expose sinewy forearms, and he smelt vaguely of cinnamon as though he'd just drunk a cappuccino. He gave her a brief smile as she introduced herself. His eye contact was good. Forthright and confident. Possibly arrogant.

Which fitted.

It was time to get to know him.

He watched her warily.

'I already know a little about you, Jerome, from a brief glance through Doctor Faro's notes.'

He gave her an almost shy smile. She had meant to explain that he need not give all his past medical history but he interrupted her. 'What do you know – exactly?'

'I know that you are the subject of a supervision order in the community. I know that you have been convicted of a string of minor offences – robbery, forging cheques. I know that your mother suffered injuries a few years ago but no charges were ever pressed and I know too that your girl-friend suffered similar ill-fortune.'

She knew these types. It was better not to mince words but to set out clear parameters in the early days. Not to let them believe that they had fooled you.

Barclay blinked.

'Because of Doctor Faro's death it's been more than three months since anyone has seen you. Perhaps you could fill me in on what you've been doing.'

'Some work.' His voice was pleasant and that, combined with his shy, rather diffident smile made her wonder about him. Her hand wandered away from the panic button.

'What sort of work?'

'Office work – through an agency.'

'Full time?'

'Nah. Just when I want to go in.' Another smile. 'Don't want to overdo it, do I, doc?'

'So you go in when you feel like it.' Another black mark. 'And you're living where?'

'With my mum. I've got a sort of self-contained flat there. Over the garage. My own kitchen and bathroom but my mum does most of the cooking.'

'She's a good cook?'

It was only making conversation but something crossed his face. Anger. A flame lit the dark eyes, flickered, flared and was suppressed. She noticed he didn't answer the question.

'So . . .' She was suddenly at a loss. It was tempting to assume that everything in the garden was rosy. That Mr Barclay had finally learned the error of his ways and was going straight. Personality disorder was something you grew out of – eventually. Perhaps he had reached this point but Heidi had not recognised it. Or maybe. Just maybe he was simply being clever.

'You manage all right for money?' she floundered.

An amused smile. 'I manage. Thank you.'

'Your job pays well?'

'Enough.'

'You mother helps you out?'

'Don't you think that that's between my mother and myself?' Said almost gently, in a soft voice. She bent over the notes so he couldn't read her face.

Time to ruffle your feathers, Barclay, and see what's really going on.

She wrote something down on his notes: part time job, goes in when he feels like it.

'Have you committed any offences in the last few months? You know we will check with the police,' she added.

The nice smile was back again. 'No need for that. I'm clean.'

'Good.'

She put her pen down on the desk. 'Have there been any times when you've been tempted to commit an offence?'

He shook his head – almost ruefully.

'Why is that, Jerome, do you think?'

He blinked as though genuinely puzzled. 'I expect I've grown out of my evil ways.' Said with mockery.

'Do you regret the cheque fraud and other offences?' She deliberately left the sentence to hang, ambiguously. Let him read what he liked into it.

She only wanted him to admit to the offences. Remorse would have been an unexpected bonus. It should have been easy for him to have affected remorse.

He leaned forward. 'If you want the truth, Doctor Roget, – regret? No.' His eyes met hers, unblinking. 'If I had attacked my mother – well it might have been because she was – she could be – the most unco-operative of women. And as for Sadie – well.'

She was beginning to understand why Rolf, Siôna and Kristyna had alerted her to Barclay. Even amongst psychopaths he was King, displaying a complete disregard for the rules that existed between psychiatrist and patient – or client. And she began to realise that this consultation, like probably all the others, was nothing but a game to him, a game which he was beginning to find boring and tedious. He even smothered a yawn.

Again she tried to flush him out.

'If you needed money? If the office job came to an end? What would you do?'

'A bit hypothetical, Doctor.'

'It is hypothetical. But how else can I know what stage you've reached?'

'In my . . . cure?'

She nodded, felt exposed herself.

'If I was 'cured' you could bring the supervision order to an end?'

She changed tack. Let *him* be the one to explain. 'Why do you think Doctor Faro wanted you supervised so closely?'

Barclay shrugged. 'Who knows?'

'You enjoyed coming here?'

He shrugged again.

'Do you think it's brought about any improvement in your behaviour?'

'Is there anything wrong in my behaviour?' Said with a challenge. 'You said yourself I've only been convicted of minor offences. As for the cheque – ' With an airy wave of the hand, 'My mother would have given me money anyway.'

'So why steal it?'

Barclay made a face again. He was getting really bored now. He stood up. 'Now – it's nice to have met you but I really have to go. If that's OK. When would you like to see me again?'

Something stung her in his manner. It was for her to set out parameters. Not him. 'This isn't a game, Mr Barclay.'

Then the pale eyes regarded her. And he was still bored. 'I'm perfectly aware that this isn't a game, Doctor Roget. I'm the one who has to attend here every month or so.'

'And I would also like to remind you that if these orders aren't complied with to the letter we are perfectly entitled to admit you under the Mental Health Act. Do you understand, Mr Barclay?'

'Perfectly, Doctor Roget.'

'So sit down.'

Now he wasn't bored. He was angry.

'Have you a girlfriend at the moment?'

He yawned again. 'No one special.'

'Not Sadie?'

He looked really amused then. 'You really don't know anything, do you?'

She felt at a disadvantage but recovered herself. 'I'll learn, Mr Barclay, I'll learn. Quickly.'

His smile was supercilious now.

'Well,' she stood up now. 'Thank you for coming.'

Barclay shook her hand, smiled, asked when she wanted to see him again and made for the door. But just before he passed through it he turned, gave her another of his bland smiles. Nothing threatening. 'Might I make a suggestion, Doctor Roget?'

'Certainly.'

'Read my notes. Thoroughly. From beginning to end. Get to know me, Doctor.'

She didn't press the buzzer for another patient for a few minutes. Barclay had left her feeling drained, vulnerable, inadequate and thoughtful. She regained her equilibrium then started again, working her way steadily through the rest of the afternoon's patients. At the end she picked up Jerome Barclay's buff file with the blue star in the corner. He had thrown down the gauntlet. It was difficult not to pick it up.

But she had other patients.

At the end of her clinic Claire had promised to see both Kap Oseo and Nancy Gold. She had enough to do but still she parcelled up Jerome Barclay's files. She would take them back to her office and read through them there. They would be a useful case study.

She found Kap on the locked ward, heavily sedated, lying in his bed. He'd wet himself. She could smell the ammonia-stink of urine as soon she walked through the door.

'Kap,' she ventured. 'Kap?'

He rolled towards her, the whites of his eyes showing clearly. A skinny Jamaican with closely cropped hair. She sat down in the chair. Less threatening than bending over him.

'I'm Doctor Roget, here to help you, Kap.'

He grunted.

'How are you feeling?'

'Bad, man. I feel rough.'

'Kap – no one wants to hurt you here.'

He gave a long sigh. 'You just don't understand.'

'I do – at least I try to. No one is against you here. We're trying to help you.'

'Why they talk about me, then? You tell me. Why they do that?'

'I don't think they talk about you, Kap.'

Frank contradiction is not a good idea. Always leave a

chink of daylight for the paranoiac to creep through.

The patient is not wrong but possibly mistaken.

'Kap, they said you picked up a knife. Why did you do that?'

His eyes seemed to lose their focus. 'I got to protect myself.'

'Who from?'

He waved a hand around the room. 'I just got to. Nobody seem to do it for me.'

'You don't need protection.'

He rolled away, back to face the wall. 'Like I said, Sister, you just don't understand.'

'OK then, try and explain to me. Who do you need protecting from?'

'They come in the night,' he whispered, 'This place full of tears. I don't want to die, Sister. Not like the doctor.'

There was something shocking about the matter-of-fact way that he spoke, as though Heidi's murder was fact, well known and widely accepted. Kap Oseo didn't display horror – or shock or even distaste.

She protested. 'What do you mean – not like the doctor?'

Kap Oseo sat up then, bolt upright. He really was frightened. 'Doctor Faro. She always was good for me. Look what happen to her.' He spoke with a mature tinge of sympathy. 'Jus' look. She didn't deserve that, Sister. No one lookin' after her.'

Claire tried again. 'Kap – I don't want you to worry. The nurses are here to look after you.'

He flopped down, curved his back towards her, spoke to the wall. 'That's what you think. But maybe not all of them are to be trusted. Some of them might be listenin' to another and persuaded.'

It is easy to become involved in a paranoiac's delusions, to be sucked in to their horrid fantasy world where everyone wishes them harm. Claire could see that knowledge of Heidi Faro's death would have leaked into their brains to pollute their minds further. Maybe it explained why Kap, who had never been violent, had taken to carrying a knife.

They were both silent until Oseo started muttering to the wall. 'Anyway – who tells them to have anythin' to do with me?'

Claire answered. 'It's their job, Kap. It's what they're paid for.'

She touched his shoulder. His skin was slimy with sweat. It was starting to soak through the sheet in dark circles, making it damp and sticky, clinging to his bones. She could smell it – and mingled in was the very real scent of fear.

Drug-induced paranoia or did Oseo really have something to be frightened of?

He rolled back again, towards her. 'Who pays their money,' he asked. 'The nurses. You tell me that.'

'The government, Kap.'

He jerked upright, looked incredulous. 'And you still say no one watching me?'

It was twisted, psycho-logic. And she played along. 'Is anyone watching you now?'

Frightened eyes searched all four corners of the tiny room, finally resting on the blinds. 'Behind there,' he said, not taking his eyes off. 'All the time. Peeping through the slats with they big eyes.'

She stood up, pulled the cord, lifted the blinds completely to uncover the window, the reflection of the pair of them, he all black and bones with staring eyes, she a white, trouser-suited professional, cross-legged in the chair oozing concern. She shook her head. 'No, Kap. No one is there. No one is watching you. You're safe. You're alone. It's peaceful here. Try to rest. Sleep. Relax.'

'Listen, Sister,' the deep voice answered, 'one thing do I know for certain. It isn't safe to sleep. Not with your eyes closed. Not in here.'

She must drag him back to reality. 'Where is here, Kap?'

He laughed. 'That a trick question, doctor, by the trick-cyclist to see if I am mad or confused. I tell you now, Sister,

Doctor Roget, this is Greatbach Secure Psychiatric Unit and there are people here who are under an influence other than the one you think is in charge.'

'Whose influence? What influence?'

'The influence of evil. Of the devil. Beelzebub.' Something strange and fearful was held in his eyes. 'You are not in control here. Don't delude yourself you are. Now get out.'

She made the decision as she left the room. They would have to give him extra medication. His persecutionary delusions were increasing dangerously. This was his first really violent outburst. It was even possible that Kap's paranoia was tipping him into psychosis.

The women's ward was two floors up, again behind a keypad. She pressed the number in and the door clicked behind her. A long, windowless corridor lay ahead, parquet flooring, doors off. Halfway along, on the right hand side, was the nurses' station. She started walking. In one of the rooms a television chattered brightly. From somewhere else wafted a breeze of cheap perfume, elsewhere the sound of bath water gurgling out, muted voices. She reached the nurses' station. Siôna was playing cards with a youth and two females, the older of whom she recognised from the bench in the garden, a staring, thin woman with straggly hair framing the wrinkled face of the chronically anxious chain-smoker. Both women ignored her to concentrate on their game. Siôna eyed her. The youth simply looked her up and down, his face pale and expressionless.

'I thought I'd pop in on Nancy,' she said feeling, somehow, as though the male nurse resented her presence – misread it as an attempt to check up on him.

He stood up and ushered her out of the nurses' station. 'She's keeping to her room,' he said, 'little rebel. I agree with Kristyna. There is something funny about her.'

'What?' She felt slightly irritated. He was a male nurse. Not a member of the general public. She expected something a bit more professional that simply, *something funny about her.*

'You'll see.' The answer was deliberately mysterious. Almost dramatic. Unhelpful too. She didn't know these patients yet. They were still strangers to her. What she needed was help. Not veiled hints.

'Give me a clue,' she said to the bluff Welshman.

'You're the doctor,' he said. 'Make your own judgement.'

'I will.' She wondered whether Heidi had found him as much trouble.

'Second door on the right,' Siôna said. He put his hand on her arm with a tight grip. 'Watch her first, for a minute, through the window.'

He returned to the nurses' station and she approached Nancy's room.

She heard singing first, soft humming. 'La la la, La la la. Mm. mm mmm mm m mm m . . .'

A girl's voice. The tune immediately recognisable. Brahms' Lullaby. The tune to send thousands of babies to sleep.

We all have some memory of this melody, tucked away in the distant rooms of our childhood. Hers of her mother humming it. Not to her. To her half brother, eight years younger than herself, adored by his parents. And she, putting her hands over her ears, trying to block out the sickly song. Her mother and stepfather standing, arms entwined, staring down into the crib, as though the child was the best – the only really good – thing that had ever happened to them.

Adam.

Not half a bloody frog like Mademoiselle Roget. Adam was English to the core. She'd heard them say it.

'I'll show them,' she'd vowed. And had never stopped trying to prove herself, find their love which had somehow been displaced on to her brother.

What complicated people the human race consists of.

The sound grew no louder as she neared the room. That was the strange thing about it. It was constant. Soft. Haunting. Filling the air yet coming from nowhere.

She peered through the porthole and had a second's panicked shock.

Surely. Nancy had no baby. She had murdered it. Hidden the corpse until it mummified, like a cat or a monkey. That was why she was here.

So what was she nursing and singing to? Arms around a swaddled form dressed in baby pink wool, this crooning, traditional lullaby as treacly as honey?

Claire watched. Mesmerised, her hand raised to open the door. But afraid. Very afraid. Could you do this? Resurrect the dead? Nurse a murdered baby? Oh yes – here in Greatbach you could do anything. Strange events took place here. You could murder your own psychiatrist. She knew then whatever she might pretend Heidi's murder had affected her deeply. Oseo's veiled hints had penetrated the paper-thin armour she had donned to come and work here.

She felt stuck to the floor, her face unable to slide away from the porthole window.

Nancy was crooning to her dead baby.

What was that in her arms if not . . . *George?*

Claire watched for minutes.

Until she heard the noise of the television back in her hearing. And from somewhere she found the power to move and pushed the door open. There was a startled cry. The child rolled to the floor. Bounced too softly, the pink wool floating away, as light and insubstantial as a candy-floss cloud and Claire could see. Nancy Gold had been singing to a pillow wrapped up in a cardigan.

Siôna was suddenly behind her, breathing heavily, waiting for her reaction. 'See what I mean?' There was an edge of malice in his voice.

She said nothing to him and walked in alone, holding out her hand in friendship. 'Hello, Nancy,' she said, 'I'm Doctor Roget. I'm the new doctor here. How are you?'

Nancy recoiled as though burned. She snatched the pillow from the floor, unravelled the cardigan and twitched it around her shoulders guiltily.

Only then did she respond to Claire's introduction. 'Hello back,' she said shyly.

She was a beautiful young woman, around twenty-three years old with a tumbling mass of blonde curls and huge blue eyes. She was as tiny as a child, no more than six stone. And like a child she fixed Claire with a frank stare. 'You'd look prettier with makeup,' she said bluntly, tossing back her curls.

Claire smiled at her. Woman to woman. Not doctor to patient. 'I would. I agree. The trouble is that I can't always be bothered to put it on. And it would all be wiped off by the end of the day anyway.'

Nancy nodded and blinked her beautiful eyes self-consciously.

'You asked me how I was feeling,' she said. 'I miss my baby.'

She could have been talking about a child who was safely at school for the day, expected to return imminently. Not a little boy who had struggled against the mother who had pressed his face underneath the water until he drowned and then concealed his body for six months – just because she saw him as an impediment to her relationship.

Was this then classic denial of her crime?

Claire settled into the armchair by the window. Outside the sun had faded to antique gold. Melting into the horizon behind the silhouette of a blackened, stumpy bottle-kiln.

'You were fond of your baby?'

Nancy put her head on one side, like a little bird. 'All mothers love their children,' she said, like a catechism.

Claire knew she must broach the subject more honestly if she was to achieve anything. 'But you don't have yours any more.'

'I've learned,' Nancy said, sagely oblique, 'that you can't have everything in life.'

'So what is the solution, Nancy?' Her eyes flickering towards the last ray of sunshine as it dipped towards tomorrow.

'You have to make choices, Doctor.' The blue eyes stared innocently into hers. 'Do you think it's wrong to make choices?'

'It isn't wrong to *make* the choices,' Claire said, 'it's the choice itself which is either right or wrong and the action which follows.'

Nancy grabbed her arm with a sudden, iron grip. 'I – want – my – baby,' she said, spitting out venom as though Claire was hiding him herself.

Something cold and hard entered Claire. 'You can't have him back, Nancy,' she said. 'What's dead is dead. You can't reverse death. We cannot resurrect. We can only regret.'

That's when Nancy's face altered to a secretive, cunning expression. 'You can undo it in a way,' she said. 'All bad things.'

Claire hesitated, uncertain now how to proceed then Nancy tossed her arm away, dived into her locker, brought out a cheap fabric handbag with a broken zip, fumbling for no longer than a second to bring out crumpled photographs. A baby. The child beautifully dressed in a sailor suit, hair combed, eyes bright, gaze clear. Like a hush-a-bye doll.

Nancy eyes filled with tears. The photographs were blotched again.

'I want my baby,' she said. But this time there was defeat, an acceptance in her voice.

Siôna was watching from the doorway. 'So do you see what I mean?'

'Yes I do,' she said. 'Exactly.' She knew now why she had been summoned to see Nancy Gold. There was something worrying about Nancy's condition.

'You know, she could be a suicide risk. She should be put in a room with a monitor.'

He nodded but there was something disappointed in his face and she knew his concern had included something else. Something she had missed.

It was only when she had walked away from the ward that she put it into words.

This lust for a dead child. In such an environment it could be dangerous.

The sun had vanished completely by the time she left the ward and wandered back to her office, along dingy corridors lined with prints of bottle-kilns and famous potters whose names were still household names – Wedgwood, Minton, Midwinter. Everywhere in Stoke, you can see clues to its main industry, china. From the marl pits from where they dug the clay to the scarred landscape which yielded up its coal, the bottle-kilns where the clay was fired to the canals used to transport the goods country. No – worldwide. Stoke is justly proud of its heritage. Outsiders may joke about the ugliness of the Potteries but they have their own, utilitarian beauty.

As her footsteps tapped along the floor she contemplated the two problems she had been faced with, the woman who had killed a baby she appeared to have adored and the link between acute psychotic illness and recreational drugs, particularly marijuana, amphetamines and ecstasy. It was a subject ripe for clinical research and for her Fellowship of the Royal College she would have to produce some original, meaningful ideas backed up with case studies and statistics.

Heidi would have managed it.

For a moment she was filled with self-doubt. Perhaps she was not up to such a complicated and difficult subject as personality disorder. Maybe she should switch her specialist interest to the link between paranoia and soft drugs.

But Barclay's notes were heavy in her hands, waiting to be explored like a video-nasty, the finger ready to press play on the remote control.

You must choose a research subject which interests you – invigorates you – obsesses you, even.

It was a dull dusk. Except for that last half hour the sun had hardly shone all day. Now the greyness of the city was further dampened by a thick swathe of mist which had wrapped itself around the buildings, muffling their shapes. The hospital was on an elevated site, peering down on rows and rows of slate-roofed terraced houses and two tall tower blocks, most displaying a friendly, yellow light. But they were outside the perimeter of the hospital and seemed remote. By the time she reached her office the windows peered out on a blank, mysterious world, full of shape but with no detail. The quadrangle was deserted and black except for pools of light which spilled out from the long ward windows and the fuzzy lamps shining from the main entrance. A harsh shriek came from somewhere, maybe an urban fox, more likely a patient experiencing the horrors that sat on the shoulders of mental disturbance. The sound echoed and died. And then all was still again except for the distant sounds of a city night, traffic, the thump thump of a car stereo, intermittent claps of noise as a hundred doors opened and closed again.

It all seemed very far away and her office very near and claustrophobic, Heidi's death closer than anything out there.

She must get used to being in here.

Claire left the window, switched the small reading lamp on and began to scan through Barclay's notes.

He had first come to the attention of Greatbach as a teenage outpatient, referred to Professor Cray because of repeated petty thieving, break-ins, helping himself, basically, to anything he wanted. Initially the crimes seemed innocuous but Claire knew the words concealed something more. Her eyes were drawn to the edge of her ring of light, into the darker corners of the room.

Imagination was a strange thing. She could have sworn something moved.

Gulio?

How had Heidi first known he was intending her harm? Something in his manner? A word? Or had her first intimation been . . .

She must not think of it.

Return to Jerome Barclay.

She bent back over the notes. It was typical sociopathic behaviour which had quickly been diagnosed as such and appropriate treatment – cognitive therapy – commenced, turning the psychopath around to face himself in the clearest of mirrors.

You cannot treat personality disorder by medication but age does wither it. People grow out of their nastier behaviour. When Heidi had joined the Professor's team she had taken over Barclay's care. Quickly she had unearthed tendencies which had pointed the way to a darker conclusion. Barclay had expressed no remorse, displayed no conscience. He had scored high on all the sociopathic assessment lists and had eventually confessed to sadistic tendencies when a child, mainly towards animals. Without making any real issue of it he had told Heidi when he was six he had cut his rabbit's ears off to see what he'd look like without them. At the age of ten he'd put a sparrow in the oven to see how long it would take to die, carefully timing its death throes.

In Heidi's handwriting:

'And how long did it take to die?'

Answer 'Six and a half minutes. Much longer than I'd thought. But then I didn't preheat the oven but let it slowly come up to temperature. I thought it would be more interesting.'

By sixteen he had strung up a boy who had crossed him at school. The boy had been cut down by his friends, no harm had resulted. It had been put down to boyish high jinks.

He had admitted attending football matches armed with an eight-inch blade – just in case.

Barclay was a danger to people. Had his mother or his erstwhile girlfriend pressed charges Heidi Faro would have been asked to give an opinion on Barclay's mental state and capability of inflicting harm. Without a doubt she would have used this knowledge to recommend that he be given a custodial sentence.

But both women had retracted their statements, possibly because of Barclay's threats. So neither case had come to court.

And Heidi Faro had been denied her chance to put Barclay away. The only option she had been left with had been a close supervision order.

Claire continued reading Heidi's most recent assessment. It was not all bad news. As far as sexual matters were concerned Heidi had believed he was safe. *Promiscuous but not a rapist*, she had written.

Claire doubted it. Barclay was turned on by cruelty, inflicting pain. But Heidi's notes were detailed.

Months had gone by during which she had explored the relationship between Barclay and his parents. It had quickly become clear that his father had been the less indulgent of the two while his mother was prone to giving in to every whim.

The father had died when the son had been ten years old. Heidi had written that there were no siblings.

So she had done what she could – and should – warned the police and the courts when asked for an opinion whether he was a potential danger to society but the minor crimes had not warranted a frank psychiatric analysis or a custodial sentence; the animal cruelty had been too long ago, there was only his word for it and certainly no proof, committed when Barclay had still been a minor; and each time a cheque fraud was committed Barclay's mother refused to press charges. And the big chance of charging him with two major assaults had been thwarted.

So had begun the dance of death between them, the psychiatrist obsessed with learning more about the dark nature of the psychopath and the patient himself who craved an audience even though it had led both of them to dangerous places. They were locked together by their mutual needs.

Heidi had believed that by letting Barclay know she was aware how deep he could sink she might prevent him from committing a major offence.

But on Barclay's part the dance had merely been a mime. A year ago, six months before Heidi's murder, Barclay's mother had had 'another accident'. And this time Heidi had told Barclay quite clearly that she did not believe a word of it. She had tried to contact Mrs Barclay only to have her flatly refuse to speak to her.

Claire tried to put herself in Heidi's shoes.

As she had written these notes she must have exulted. She had foreseen this crime. Known Barclay would reoffend. And yet at the same time she would have felt guilty.

She should have prevented this, protected her patient's mother. Or else what was the point of studying these people so closely, pinning them to a board with a supervision order, if only to observe without being empowered to intervene and prevent further criminal activity?

Claire was inside her mentor's mind, reasoning alongside her. By knowing these people intimately we are party to their crimes, future, past and present, part of them, involved in them, because we know while they speak to us they are plotting and we are listening.

The assault on Mrs Barclay should have led to co-operation between the psychiatrist who has her crystal ball to predict and police who can only act *afterwards*.

But frustratingly for the police Barclay's mother, Cynthia, having got so close, backed off yet again and refused to press charges and without her statement the police case collapsed for the second time.

Reading the notes Claire could sense Heidi's frustration as she documented the change of heart. So near. And yet we cannot step across the line of conjecture and what is provable in a court of law.

She looked around the room again, decided now that she didn't like the dark corners where these moving demons lurked, pushed the chair away from the desk and impatiently flicked the central light on so she could read the notes even closer.

Heidi was here, peering over her shoulder, cheering her on, encouraging her to take up where she had left off.

She read through the full account ot the assault on Sadie Whittaker and realised it had been worse than she had initially thought. Barclay's girlfriend had actually been pregnant at the time and must have felt so strongly she did not want to spawn Barclay's child that she had subsequently had a termination even though a scan had proved that the child had not been harmed. Claire read the notes right through and agreed that this time Barclay should have been put behind bars. It bore the hallmarks of a psycho. He had confessed to Heidi that he had deliberately driven at her. But yet again Barclay had slipped through the net. To the police Sadie Whittaker had insisted she had thrown herself in front of the car and that Jerome had swerved to try and avoid her.

The police had tried their best. They had argued that the tyre tracks did not bear out this version of events but Sadie Whittaker had been adamant. She would not change her story and with their main witness denying events they could not press charges.

They had pushed Sadie as hard as they could but cleverly she had used the baby to underline her case.

'What man,' she had demanded, ' would wilfully destroy his own child?'

Barclay would.

But the news had not been all bad. From this case Heidi had been able to insist that Barclay underwent therapy and was closely watched. She had tightened her grip on him.

And waited for him to act again.

Claire could read her mind. She had been steadily working towards putting him away again under the Section of the Mental Health Act designed to protect the public from evil.

As always knowledge brings negatives in its wake. There were a few things which she would have preferred not to know. Heidi Faro had been her idol, a pioneer in the diagnosis and treatment of psychopathic behaviour, but to gather her data she must have spent a great deal of time interviewing people like Barclay. Many of the interviews had been repetitious. Yet nothing had been achieved by the hours of work. Barclay had been all too aware that he was being used as a guinea pig and had played accordingly. Heidi had lost her objectivity and Barclay was still a psycho. At loose. While Heidi was dead, having misjudged the danger potential of another patient.

Her idol had had feet of clay.

Was it the feet of clay, this loss of objectivity, which had led to her vulnerability? And subsequent death?

Claire focused on a dark spot to the right of the door. Probably where a grubby hand had fumbled for the switch and the painters had not masked it. She liked it. It helped her to concentrate. It was the inkblot of psychology.

She leaned back in her chair. So – it was now up to her to decide what to do next with Barclay.

She had the same interest in sociopaths but unlike Heidi she felt she needed to achieve results. She couldn't afford to clog up her clinics with manipulates. Maybe it was time to let Barclay go – back out into the community, unsupervised – and see what happened. She sat for a while, tapping the notes with her fingernail, hearing Heidi's arguments for close supervision but inserting her own. She re-opened the file and read the most recent letters, almost changing her mind. Objectively it wasn't strictly true that Heidi's efforts had been wasted. Barclay hadn't re-offended. He'd been clean for more than a year. He might have skipped around the periphery of re-offending but there were no documented cheque frauds, no petty thefts, no cruelty. Nothing since the attacks on his mother and girlfriend.

Had they both been so afraid?

Maybe a good way to find out the truth would be to speak to Mrs Barclay. Alone. If she would.

She picked up the phone and dialled the number in the notes.

It rang and rang and she began to wonder whether anyone was in until he picked it up.

Claire introduced herself. 'Jerome,' she said, hardly giving him a chance to wonder why she was ringing him. 'I'm considering reducing your supervision order but I thought you should keep your appointment next month. Also I could do with talking to your mother.'

Barclay laughed. 'My mother,' he drawled, 'is almost seventy years old and not in the best of health. She would find it a trial and an embarrassment to come up to the hospital.'

'Your future depends on it,' Claire said coolly. 'It's up to you, really.'

'You don't have the same . . . interests as Doctor Faro?'

'I do but you know in the Health Service these days we are measured by outcomes. I can't see what Doctor Faro really achieved by her intense interest in you.'

'I've kept out of trouble.'

He was sparring.

She couldn't voice her theory that maybe the lack of complaint from Barclay's mother was due to another reason – fear.

But Barclay was smart. And quick. 'Oh I get it,' he drawled. 'You think my old mum doesn't complain because she's frightened of me.'

How easy is it to stand over an old lady and get her to

sign the cheques?

'Well,' she said again quite coolly. 'It's up to you, really.'

'So it is. Well. I shall talk to Mummy and let you know. Is that all right, Doctor Roget?'

'Fine.'

She put the phone down with a smug feeling. She had anticipated his responses correctly.

It was up to her now. Not Heidi. For unlike the Health Service the police did not have the time to show ongoing interest in a non-case. No prosecution. No case. No witnesses (prepared to testify). No case. No certainty of conviction (according to the Crown Prosecution Service). No case.

Unlike her. *She* could work through the shadowy realms. The Land of Possibility. Not for her this black and white certainty. What Barclay *might* do was not necessarily what Barclay *would* do.

Criminal law depends on both evil mind and evil act.

Mens rea; actus reus. One without the other collapses the case.

Psychiatry is so different. So much more subtle and clever. An evil mind is recognised as potential. The question that interested her was what was Barclay capable of? Ultimately?

Claire cupped her chin in her hand and drifted off into a dream of Heidi, remembering her many encounters with her, the animated way she had talked, hands tensely to her side, voice enthuiastically high, the way she had flicked her shining hair away from her face. Clever, with an Honours degree in medicine, swiftly gaining her MRCPsych before she was thirty. Unmarried, with a succession of partners of both sexes, no children. All this had been in the newspapers both at the time of the murder and the subsequent trial of Gulio. Heidi's life had been subjected to the full glare of publicity, leaving no shadows.

She bent her head again, saddened by the sudden, vivid presence and an unexpected waft of Chanel Number 19, recognisable through the smell of paint. A stiff, strange scent for a psychiatrist to wear but over dinner one evening she had confessed to Claire that to her, Chanel was the epitomy of luxury, of Western wealth, of complete indulgent hedonism.

Claire felt a hot shaft of anger. Why did it have to be Heidi who had died in so cruel and pointless a crime? They could have worked here, together, as colleagues. Together they might have uncovered the secretive nature of a remorseless mind. Now she was left to struggle on alone. Without her.

And all because Stefan Gulio had suffered brain damage at the hand of a bunch of hooligans.

She felt angry because Heidi's death had been so futile, so pointless as to be almost banal.

She leafed through the rest of Barclay's notes.

Most of the interviews held nothing. Time after time Barclay had refused to talk, been silent in response to questions. But he did not default on his appointments. Heidi had set out quite clearly that if he did not turn up the police would be empowered to bring him in.

Once or twice Barclay had become annoyed with her but he had not threatened her – not overtly.

One interview however stood out.

J asked me whether I was ever frightened of any of my patients. I told him no, I was not. He then asked me whether I was frightened of what they could do to me. Of humiliation or pain?

I said I didn't think about it, that I had a job to do, that I must assess and protect my patients and the public and it was a job like any other.

He seemed dissatisfied by this and asked me what I was frightened of.

I answered – being wrong. Letting someone out of their sec-

*tion and them committing a crime. I said I would feel respon-
sible and that frightened me.*

*I then asked him whether he was ever afraid of what he
might do.*

He just gave me a long stare then said no.

He was trying the old trick of trying to frighten me.

*I asked him how he was getting on, living at home. He said
OK.*

I asked him whether he went out much?

He said sometimes.

I asked him who with?

He said, girls. Stupid, stupid girls.

*I said, were they stupid because they were going out with
him and he said, stupid to trust him. He named Kristyna
Gale, saying she was typical of that type. That he would enjoy
feeling her underneath him. He said she had nice ears. I did
talk to her about him and warned her to be careful. To be very
very careful.*

A week later Barclay had again lost his temper with her
probing and had threatened to cut her throat.

'*I asked him why he considered using that particular
method of murder.*'

He stared back at me. 'Lots of blood,' *he said.* 'Nice and
quick. No hanging around, waiting for someone to die.' *He
thought again.* 'Completely certain,' *he said.* 'No paramedical
intervention. The deed is done. And there is something ritualistic – almost religious about it, don't you think?'

*There is no doubt that he said this deliberately to try and
intimidate me. The attempt failed.*

Two weeks after that Heidi had died.

Claire shut the notes feeling that by reading them she had
learned as much about Heidi Faro as Jerome Barclay.

In fact, she mused, had Gulio not been around to admit
to the murder, had the confession not damned him she
would have pointed the finger at Jerome Barclay. He was a

crime waiting to happen, a time-bomb ticking away. A potential killer.

She wondered where Barclay had been when Heidi had been murdered?

Then she wondered what had made the police grab Gulio for the crime? Had it only been that he had been on the scene and only too ready to confess?

At the same time she relished and feared her next encounter with Barclay.

What would she unearth?

Chapter Five

One of the occupational hazards of being a psychiatrist is that you become neurotic about your own mental health. You start to analyse your own behaviour, spiral into introspection, find it obsessional or odd in some way. In the end you come to the conclusion that there is no such thing as normal behaviour. It simply does not exist. It is both an urban and rural myth.

As she joined the traffic queues on the A500 she hardly saw the long streets of terraced houses or the light bouncing off the slate roofs, the steep hill into Wolstanton, the pubs with their red crosses pronouncing their football allegiance or even the four-wheel-drives taking the children to school.

She crawled for a while behind a red single-decker bus almost empty of people then took her place in the queue behind even more red lights.

Such is city life.

She was glad to have the question of normal behaviour to occupy her mind.

As soon as she arrived at the staffroom she cornered Siôna and questioned him more closely about Nancy Gold. She wondered why he looked so troubled and went for the full frontal.

'What's really bothering you, Siôna?'

'She was coming up to a release order.' His manner was hesitant – stumbling. But defiant too. He was not a man who would readily admit to being wrong.

She waited.

'She'd been taking short visits out.'

Kristyna had entered the room. Behind her Claire could hear the jangling bangles. Neither of them turned to acknowledge her.

'She isn't a danger to the community.'

He was justifying something. A tension grew between

them.

'Alone,' he finished. 'We hadn't realised she was still so – ' He fished around for a word. 'Unbalanced.'

His face was suffused and red with embarrassment then pale with guilt, his eyes watery and far away. 'We haven't had a proper senior psychiatrist since Heidi . . . Just a succession of locums. And half of those can't speak English.'

Claire listened with the growing dread you experience when you sense the first vibration tingling the railway track. You know something enormous is approaching. Equally you know that nothing can stop it. Whatever it was it – was – inevitable. Already written in the shifting sands of time. Destined. She could guess the content of his next words.

'The last time she was reported as behaving like this was when she was three months pregnant a year ago.'

'And?'

'She had a termination. When it was put to her that she wouldn't be allowed to keep the baby unsupervised she agreed to it.'

'And the father?'

'She was still seeing Watson then. He raised no objection.'

She was angry. 'Don't we administer birth control on these girls, supervise their visitors?'

Siôna raised his eyebrows quizzically. 'How long does it take?'

She didn't answer.

'She's been on the contraceptive injections since.'

'So -?' She couldn't keep the anger out of her voice. But it was an emotive subject, this mother and baby, infanticide case. With women's activists so articulate, so pro-active and vociferous the mental health team and the police tiptoed across the thinnest sheet of ice. Barbaric was the word most commonly used for anyone who came between woman and her right to bear children.

Even if she subsequently drowned them.

Sometimes the tunnel through which you must pass is so dark, so damp and cold and unknown that instinctively you draw back. You do not want to touch the sides because you know it is slimy. Rats scuttle across the floor. But you know that you have no option but to move forward and keep moving. Towards the light.

'Do we keep a record of her periods?'

Siôna shook his head, his eyes never leaving her face but swinging in their sockets.

Best to face the truth – whatever that might be. 'Then we must do a pregnancy test,' she said matter-of-factly.

The worst was she hardly needed to authorise a pregnancy test. She did not doubt the nurse's instinct for the truth. Surely Siôna would not hide behind a lie just because it was more comfortable there. He knew Nancy Gold better than she did and even she had caught a whiff of motherhood at the way Nancy had sung to the soft little bundle.

This was a problem she had not anticipated.

'Uum.' She hesitated to bring the subject up – again. 'Do you mind if I ask you all something?'

They were all instantly wary. Rolf took his hand away from the arm of the chair where it had lain, brushing against Kristyna's leg. Kristyna sat bolt upright. Siôna jerked backwards. Even Bec and Dawn stilled their chatter and watched her with big eyes.

'Did any of you know that Barclay threatened Heidi?'

Kristyna answered for all of them. 'He's threatened us all at one time or another.'

'He threatened to cut her throat.'

Afterwards she realised that no one had looked shocked. 'Look.' Rolf speaking patiently. 'He's someone who loves to provoke a reaction. He does it to tease and play around. He's just trouble.'

'He's committed at least two major assaults.'

'It wasn't him,' Siôna said gruffly. 'Whatever he said it *wasn't* him.'

'You're all sure?' She scanned the room. Not one of them met her eyes.

She knew why.

They were frightened that it wasn't Gulio, that the police had got the wrong man.

She dropped the subject but she didn't forget it.

The meeting grew no easier.

She asked one of the other nurses, Bec Rowe, how Kap was this morning and was not pleased with the answer. 'Still out of it, Claire, paranoid as hell. Staring around the room like Topsy. I don't know what we're going to do with him. If he doesn't sort himself out he'll never get out of here.'

The temptation was to tack alive on to the end of the sentence.

But no one did.

Only Mavis Abiloney was causing no trouble. By temporarily extending the Section on her she was as meek as a lamb. Out of danger.

Later that week they carried out the pregnancy test which proved Siôna was right. Claire examined her and confirmed that Nancy was about fourteen weeks pregnant, which made the baby due early in March. Worryingly, no amount of questioning could extract the name of the father and to their knowledge Watson had disappeared from the scene about a year ago so that let him off the hook. When they questioned Nancy she simply gave a happy, coy smile which quashed any suggestion of a termination. Claire didn't even suggest it.

No one who watched Nancy rocking the pillow through the tiny porthole could fail to be touched by her plight. But on the other hand any child of hers would be registered at risk and almost certainly removed at birth. Nancy could only be with her child when she was supervised.

Again and again and again Claire questioned her who the father was. She turned into friend, foe, physician, spy, nursemaid. Sometimes all at the same time but Nancy would simply hug her stomach, inspect her filling breasts and sing, which made Claire bite her lip.

'Baby,' she'd say ecstatically. 'I'll have my baby.'

'Not for months,' Claire responded tightly, arranged a visit from an obstetrician and a case conference.

And although Nancy had become pregnant before she had taken up her post at Greatbach, for Claire it was the beginning of a nightmare. Reports to submit, questions to be answered. The psychiatrist's heartsink – an enquiry.

Totally preoccupied with Nancy and her problem she didn't see Barclay again for two weeks; neither did she think about him. In the meantime under pressure she had extended Mavis's Section again, seen Kap so heavily sedated he had turned into a zombie, and got to know many other patients. Her hall was Dining Room Red, the bedroom Ballroom Blue and it being term-time Grant was out of the house for an hour or two a day. And the only good thing which had happened was that the mood of Harry Sowerby had stabilised and he had been discharged.

Until the next time.

Like diabetes there is no hope of a cure for bipolar disorder – only intermittent control.

But Barclay was, of course, still part of her caseload.

A fortnight later he was again sitting opposite her, wearing a check shirt and jeans, looking deceptively anxious to please, sitting forward, eagerly in his chair, eyes wide.

Don't be deceived.

She welcomed the anonymity of the outpatients' department. Because a different doctor uses it on different days it is soulless. Neither the chairs nor the desk nor even the telephone feels as though it belongs to you any more than does a hotel room or a cinema seat.

It is yours for the duration only.

She began with the usual preamble, asking him how he had been in the last couple of weeks.

'Not bad.'

'Have you been to work?'

'No.'

'Why not?'

'I didn't want to. I felt a bit under the weather.'

'So what have you been doing?'

'Hanging around.'

'Where?'

'The city.'

'Anywhere else?'

His attitude shifted. He had been waiting for this moment. He shot her a challenging smile to warn her he was about to step up to being controversial. 'I went over to the moorlands,' he said. 'Walking.'

The intervening weather had been wet and miserable.

'Did you see many people?'

His stare was too obviously meant to be disconcerting. 'Few.'

'Did you go alone?'

'No. I went with a girl.'

It registered that he didn't say girlfriend.

She smiled blandly. 'But the weather's been horrible, Jerome.'

'It has,' he agreed. 'Simply horrible. But I think the moorlands have more atmosphere in bad weather and there's less pests around.'

'Pests?'

He blinked. A long, slow, blink as though he was waiting for her to understand. 'Other people, Doctor Roget. Other people. When you want to be alone other people can be pests.'

She was instantly alert. As he had meant her to be. He knew she would have read his notes. Everything in there. 'Who is the girl. Jerome?'

'Some slut. What's it to you?'

'You know what it is to me.'

'Ah – yes.' He put his hands behind his head, elbows

wide. 'My keeper.'

She held his eye contact with a fraction of a nod.

That is exactly who I am. The holder of the key to the cage.

He broke contact first to lean in so close she was forced to breathe the same air as he. She could almost touch the smooth, girlish skin, the fine lines around his eyes and mouth, the fringe of long, dark lashes, the strange, pale eyes which did not belong to his face, the small, indecisive chin. And for some reason it was this chin, this child-sized chin which offended her most of all. That and the reedy, petulant quality in his voice when he was not too pleased about something.

She changed the subject. 'What are you living on?'

'I get sick money.'

'But you haven't been sick.'

'You don't have to be to get the money.' A smile. 'You just have to say you are.'

'Do you think that's fair?'

'What's fair about life – and death?'

It was another challenge. She knew exactly which death he was talking about. Another piece of bloodied meat tossed in front of her for her to worry at. She wanted to ask him the one question. But would she believe his answer whether denial or assertion?

She shuffled around in her chair, refused to take the bait and turned the question around. 'What's *unfair* about life, Jerome?'

He responded with a hard, icy stare of dislike. 'I hate the way you psychi people ask leading questions that are meant to be so-o clever.'

She waited.

He crossed and uncrossed his legs, dropped his arms down, breathed quickly, showing some emotion for the first time during the interview. 'OK then. Let's go for it, Claire, Doctor Roget.' A bold stare. 'It's unfair that my mother holds the purse strings when she's past enjoying it.'

'You think the money should all be yours?

Typically he had held his trump card until the end. 'You can ask her if you like. Surprisingly she agreed to come.'

You allowed her to, you mean. Which begged the question *Why?*

He had already stood up and walked out to fetch her.

She had had expectations of what Barclay's mother would be like. She already knew she was almost seventy, that she was a widow, that she had been the victim of at least one serious assault and that she protected her son with her life. Literally. So Claire had formed a picture of a prematurely aged woman, thin and bent, in old-fashioned clothes, possibly even a little senile.

A victim.

She couldn't have been more wrong.

Cynthia Barclay was plump and short, with dyed brass-blonde hair and heavy, greasy make-up. As she entered the room she grinned at Claire's discomfort so the psychiatrist knew that Barclay had deliberately planted the picture in her mind with his phrases. 'Not in the best of health. My mother is an old woman.'

Priming her so far from the truth.

Claire stood up and shook hands with her. 'Mrs Barclay,' she said, noting that the woman's palms were sweaty with nerves. 'Thank you for coming. I'm Claire Roget, the new doctor. Doctor Faro's replacement.'

Cynthia's stare was disconcertingly like her son's with the same pale boiled-sweet eyes, eyelids rimmed with blue. 'Oh yes,' she said. 'The doctor who was murdered here in March. She used to see a lot of Jerome.' Surprisingly she blushed a little. 'He was upset at what happened.'

The reason for the blush, then, was the lie.

'Can I ask you a little about your son's early life?'

Claire could allow half an hour for this interview. It was crucial to her assessment of Barclay. If all went well and she was convinced that Heidi's interest had not been to protect the public but academic she could afford to relax Barclay's supervision order. It could be reduced if not dropped completely.

The blue eye-shadowed lids flickered. Open and shut. Open and shut. Quick, nervous blinks.

Tiny sticks of mascara'd eyelashes.

'You had Jerome a little late in life.'

'We didn't get married till late,' Cynthia said in defence.

'Jerome is an only child.'

Cynthia looked uncomfortable. 'No.'

Claire's pen had been poised. This had not even been a question. Merely an opener to a conversation. 'No?' she echoed.

'He had a brother. I'm sure I told someone.'

'Older or younger?'

When the real question was the verb. Had?

'Younger.'

'How much younger?'

Still skirting around the issue.

'Eight years younger. Peter died when he was two months old. A cot death. And then his father died. So you see Jerome is extra specially precious. He's all I've got.' Her eyes were wide with appeal – not to judge her or her son harshly.

But Claire was remembering what it felt like, to hate a baby in a cot. And coincidentally Adam had been eight years younger than she. She clenched her fists and wondered. Had Barclay hated his brother as she had hated her half-brother? Had he wished him dead – and acted when she had not?

She must ask the question. Calmly. 'How did Jerome feel about his baby brother when he'd been an only child for so long?'

'Adored him,' Cynthia said comfortably, her double chin agreeing with her words. 'Adored him.'

Claire stared deep into the woman's eyes.

Did they see nothing?

She couldn't imagine the Jerome Barclay she knew adoring anyone – particularly a baby brother who threatened to upstage him. She hardly dared delve into the circumstances surrounding the cot death for fear of what she might find out.

But why hadn't Heidi picked up on this, recorded it in the notes? This was important, significant.

Answer – Barclay must have elected not to tell her. And Heidi never had interviewed Barclay's mother.

A mistake.

She must tread carefully.

Masquerade as a friend of her son's. An ally? 'And how was Jerome in the days following his little brother's death?'

Cynthia dabbed a little of the blue eye shadow onto a flowered tissue she'd hidden up her sleeve. 'Wonderful,' she sniffed. 'Wonderful.' Her mouth trembled. 'Quiet as a mouse. No trouble at all. Even helped us choose a wreath and the coffin, helped us write the death notice and choose the hymns for the service. "Abide with me". He said what we were to put on the headstone. He followed the little white coffin into the church. Looked so sweet in his little grey suit, laid some of his own flowers. He was wonderful. A little saint. And hardly shed a tear.'

Claire's toes began to curl. Instinct. A child who would snip the ears off a pet rabbit – or watch a bird slowly cook in an oven and boast about it? Helping to choose a wreath and a coffin? She didn't think so somehow.

She felt suddenly exasperated by this woman with the blue eyelids.

'Jerome told me some rather — ' She chose her adjective carefully – 'unpleasant things he'd done when he was a young boy.'

Cynthia smiled. 'Oh yes? He did tell me you might want to know a little bit about them. Just boyhood pranks, you know, Doctor Roget.'

Torturing dumb animals?

She stared at her in amazement and knew her lips must remain sealed. She was not allowed to leak this information to Barclay's mother without his express permission.

The image of Barclay walking solemnly behind his brother's tiny white coffin slowly melted back into a question. What had Barclay gained by his brother's death?

Oh, plenty. No one to share the parental affection with. Or money.

She rolled her pen in her fingertips.

There had been another death. 'Tell me about Jerome's relationship with his father.'

Cynthia nursed her large handbag on her lap and looked away. 'Kenny didn't always understand Jerome,' she said uncomfortably.

I'll bet.

'He used to say he was using us, that I was too soft with him, that I'd swallow any story.' The eyes flicked open in a plea to be believed. 'Not true, Doctor Roget. Not true.'

'What did your husband die of?' The question was idly asked, more for further images of Barclay's responses to bereavement than any real suspicion. Jerome Barclay had been a boy of ten when his father had died.

Already cooking live birds and lopping the ears off his pet rabbit, she reminded herself.

But there were more reasons for a man of fifty plus to die of natural causes than a baby of two months old. And so much easier to destroy the vulnerable one. Much harder to kill the other. There had been almost two years between the two incidents.

But even here there was room for the sliver of suspicion.

'Well – it was odd really.' Cynthia's tone was confiding, sharing a tiny doubt that had seeded years ago and never quite been allayed. 'Kenny was a diabetic. On insulin. And for the last year or two he had had real trouble controlling it. His sugars kept going high. And then too low. They were all over the place. They kept having to change his insulin to different strengths. Different types. Pig stuff, human stuff. He found it hard to cope.'

'Had he always had trouble controlling his diabetes?'

'No. That was what I meant when I said it was odd. It was as though Peter's death had upset him more than he showed. It was only a month or two after little Peter died that the trouble first started. Before that he'd been fine. A model patient.'

There are some questions it is too painful to ask. Claire had no right to ask them, no grounds to suspect Barclay of murdering his own father except that Barclay's character was rotten to the core. What was he capable of? Already in her mind, as in Heidi's before her, Barclay's personality was attaining monstrous capabilities. She had a vision of a little boy, eight years old, understanding that to his father sugar was poisonous, playing with his father's food, tipping the forbidden substance on the special foods, even playing with the insulin, the syringes. Easy when they all lay, unguarded, around the house.

'How did Jerome respond when his father died?'

'Again he was wonderful. So protective. An absolute saint, that boy. He sat and held my hand. "Don't you worry, Mum," he said. "I'll look after you now."'

'And did he?'

Her pupils were pin-pricks. 'Of course.'

So – ask the question again. Could Barclay as an eight year old have been responsible for smothering his baby brother?

Yes. Oh yes.

Claire closed her eyes against a surge of hatred, the sugary lullaby tinkling still in her brain. Felt the familiar battle against it.

Would she?

The difference was that she was not a psychopath. Jealousy in her had not translated to murder. Adam was alive – somewhere. A student in Birmingham, she believed.

She must move on – not waste the time. 'Your son's always lived with you?'

'Oh yes. I spoil him really.' More confidences. 'Give in to him a bit. But then,' The blue eyes opened wide. 'He's all

I've got, doctor. If I didn't have Jerome I would have nobody. No one to care.'

Claire found the statement vaguely alarming. She pursued it.

'You have no brothers or sisters?'

Cynthia shook her head.

'Your husband's family?'

'He's got one sister but she's very peculiar. She lives in the north of Scotland in a remote cottage. I don't hear from her very much.'

'What about nephews and nieces?'

'One nephew but I haven't seen him in years. I could pass him in the street, doctor, and not know him.'

Her son's eyes found Claire's. 'I only have Jerome.'

It was a troubling situation. Cynthia Barclay had no one to look out for her, no one to care if she was missing or ill. Claire heartily wished it were otherwise.

Pushing it to one side she pursued a different tack.

'I want to go back to the time when . . .'

Cynthia was there before her, hooding her eyes with hostility and jumping in with her words. 'If you want to know what happened when I fell down the stairs I gave my statement to the police. I've nothing to add.'

Claire still gave her a chance. She leaned forward and spoke slowly to give her words some added weight. 'Has your son ever offered violence towards you?'

She was hotly defensive. 'You're reading him wrong, Doctor Roget. He isn't the violent type. A bit misguided sometimes.'

'Misguided? How?'

'Well – he's had a problem in the past – taking things, you know. He was a bit naughty once or twice, forging cheques. But not now, doctor. Not now. He's the model son.'

Claire sat back, thinking. One of them was wrong. They could not both be right. Barclay could not be both model son and cold psychopath who had assaulted his mother, maybe killed his father and brother. Was she the one who was chasing shadows, suspecting Barclay merely because it fitted in with her assessment of him. She had no proof.

'What about Sadie Whittaker? What can you tell me about her?'

Cynthia's lip curled. 'That – that tart,' she said. 'Nothing but trouble. When my boy made it clear she'd have to try another means of hooking him than a fake pregnancy she invented that.'

But it hadn't been a fake. Sadie Whittaker really had been pregnant. She had had a termination.

Confidentially.

'There never was a baby, was there?' Cynthia insisted.

Confidentiality.

'She was just manipulating him. Trying to lure him into marrying her. Then she threw herself in front of the car.'

Claire stared at the woman. So Cynthia believed the accepted version.

What was the truth?

Some people believe that psychiatrists have amazing powers, like stage hypnotism and mind transference. They believe psychiatrists know what a person is thinking. But psychiatrists have none of these powerrs. Their divination comes from watching people closely, observing, interpreting flickering eye movements, the movement of their hands, the muscles that bind their necks. If you think that 'shrinks' are infallible listen to two psychiatrists argue.

On opposite sides of the coin.

Then ask yourself this question. What do they really know?

Nothing.

Psychiatry is an inexact science, saturated in opinion.

'Mrs Barclay, the time has come for us to decide whether we need to continue to see your son on such a regular basis.'

She left the sentence unfinished.

Cynthia Barclay stared at her, saying nothing , simply

staring, her eyes a little wider than before as though mere words were not enough, could not encompass what she wanted to say. What words are there anyway, to express doubt, fear, imaginary threats. Yet they were all expressed in Cynthia Barclay's shrivelled pale eyes.

It struck Claire dumb. That Barclay's mother was too frightened to say anything?

Was this all learned?

She stood up too quickly. It startled Mrs Barclay. 'Sorry,' she said. 'Maybe I should have another word with Jerome.'

Cynthia scuttled out, not even asking what this new doctor's decision was. She had said her piece.

Moments later Jerome sauntered back into the room, face and manner as cocky as ever. He dropped into the chair, his face smooth and impassive. 'So,' he said, 'did you find anything out from the old dear?'

'I think so.'

She didn't want to mention the fact that she now knew Barclay had had a brother.

Which for some reason reminded her of Nancy Gold, humming Brahms' lullaby. Threads run through events as finely woven as the most intricate tapestry.

And somewhere, at some time, what seemed mere threads would be plainly seen as a whole picture.

She stared hard into the back of his eyes, struggling to read the machinations of his mind. Everything she knew about him flashed through her thoughts at the speed of light. *He had displayed classic signs of psychopathy. Tortured animals, used and abused people, treated them with disdain.* He stared innocently back, directing her own thoughts, telling her they were pure. He had never been convicted and found guilty of any crime. His slate was clean.

She made up her mind.

'It's time to let you get on with your life, Jerome,' she said steadily. 'Nothing will be achieved by your continuing to attend here, at Greatbach.' She stood up, meaning to shake his hand, to wish him well for the future, to advise him to keep on the right side of the law.

But something stopped her so she actually said nothing, simply said goodbye. And watched him turn around and walk away, knowing she would worry later whether she had made the right decision.

As he opened the door he paused to give her a friendly smile which robbed his subsequent words of malice but echoed her own thoughts with the knell of a funeral bell. 'So you're discharging me,' he said. 'Well – let's hope you don't come to regret your decision. Goodbye, Doctor Roget,' he said. 'For now.'

Chapter Six

As she had anticipated during her drive home she fretted she had not seen or heard the last of Barclay. That he would play with her – as a cat will play with a mouse. Not for food but because it amuses.

But she must continue with her work.

Grant was watching television when she let herself in. She could hear the boxed voices, chattering, gruff replies, cheap, wallpaper drama-music. A soap opera, full of fake and frothy romance and set-up dramatic situations. She could see the changing light reflected on the glass of the kitchen door, moving blues and purples, yellows and reds, bright green. He called out to her without turning around. 'Put the kettle on, Claire, will you.'

She pushed the door open, wandered into the kitchen – peppermint green with black granite surfaces, a window sporting a plain yellow blind. She took two mugs out of the cupboard and half-filled the kettle. A couple of bills were scattered across the work surface. Addressed to her and unopened. Grant did not 'do' utilities, not mortgage, heating, electricity, water or anything else for that matter. He was content to live within her means – cycle to work and live here for nothing. Claire slit open the bills and looked at them without emotion. Not even anger at the way her money was eroded by such boring mundanities as the services on which our comforts depend.

She took the coffee into the sitting room.

He wasn't even watching. Not really. He couldn't be enjoying such tripe. Stretched out on the sofa, shoes off. But his eyes didn't leave the screen as he reached out for the mug.

He practically ignored her existence except for, 'Don't suppose you noticed whether there were any choccie biccies in the tin, did you?'

Men do this, revert to the nursery when they want something.

She didn't answer and he didn't notice she hadn't answered, but smiled in empathy with the passionate snog the teenage hero was giving the crop-topped heroine.

Claire sunk into the leather chair, legs fully extended.

'Thought I'd paint the bathroom next,' Grant said, watching the TV through a wisp of steam. 'There's a whole new range of colours I saw at the DIY store near the school. What do you think of purple?'

At last he looked up and wrinkled his brow. 'Bad day at work?'

'No.'

Bad evening at home. She wished he wasn't here.

The evening passed, her in a fidget of boredom hardly relieved by an evening of reality TV. She flicked the pages of a medical journal and tried to concentrate on 'Responses to Hypnotherapy' and ignore the irritation she felt at Grant's presence. Halfway through the article she found her mind wandering towards how to tell him to go without causing an inevitable row – or even hurting him. She didn't dislike him – it was worse. Every day she felt more and more indifferent until a week, a month from now, she could sense she would not mind about hurting his feelings and she didn't want to be that cruel to him – ever.

They had had some good times together.

The evening ended with a theatrical yawn from her and a reluctant flick to off of the TV remote from him.

At the next morning's meeting she turned the subject back to Jerome and confessed that she had discharged him. The news was greeted with a sort of shocked silence – which felt like an accusation. But she was a new doctor here. She need not continue in Heidi's footsteps. She needed to carve out her own identity and way of running Greatbach. It turned out that only Kristyna Gale had had much to do with him in recent months because for a brief period after Heidi's death she had carried out the supervision order and seen Barclay herself.

'Strictly inside the hospital,' she said. 'He isn't the sort of person you'd want to meet on a dark night across the car park.'

'Did you know he had a baby brother?'

Kristyna shook her head. 'No I didn't.' A pause then, 'Do you think it's important?'

'I don't know.' Claire smiled at her. 'Or the circumstances of his father's death?'

Rolf was watching from across the room, frowning and fiddling with the gold signet ring he wore on his left little finger.

'Give me *your* opinion,' Claire prompted.

'He's . . . well . . . ' She flushed faintly, must have felt the warmth on her cheek and tried to conceal it with her hands. It only emphasised some embarrassment. 'He's cold. And when he does show an emotion . . .' Her voice petered out into nothing. But her face had changed again. Frozen into a memory that hurt somewhere privately.

Claire simply waited.

'Such a silly thing,' Kristyna confessed finally. 'You'd think I'd be immune from these punks. That I wouldn't care but he got right under my skin. He really needled me.'

It was bordering on a confession.

Claire still said nothing but waited.

'I trapped my finger in the drawer,' Kristyna admitted. 'He'd rattled me and I was slamming it shut really hard. My finger caught.' She held out her index finger, deformed by a stunted and rippled nail. 'It was painful. I'd caught the nail and it tore off taking half the finger with it.' She smiled around the room, inviting sympathy. 'I can well believe it was a Nazi torture.'

'And?' Sióna was watching her curiously. Obviously he'd never heard this story before.

Kristyna didn't even look at him, but into an unfocused distance. 'Nothing really. He just looked pleased. You know? His eyes were practically dancing with pleasure. He was really enjoying it – the fact that I was in pain.'

'What had he said to you that got you so rattled in the first place?'

'Oh – the usual. It was about rape. He was goading me. How I allowed myself to get dragged into making a comment in the first place I don't know. It was the way he was staring at me. Just waiting for me to snap, so sure I would. Confidently. And – sort of insolently . . .' Her face was pink again. She was twisting one of her gold bangles round and round.

Claire could have completed the sentence.

'Undressing me.' But Kristyna was right. Patients did this, challenged you. She shouldn't have been so upset unless there was something deeper.

'I felt so – defiled, Claire. The way he was talking. I should have ended the interview, set out some parameters, refused to be drawn, done the right thing. I wasn't very pleased with myself. That's why I was so angry. More with myself than with him.'

'What sort of things was he saying?'

'That's it. Just the usual. About girls who asked for it, the smells, the sounds, the invitation.' She looked around the room. 'We've heard it all before. A hundred times. That he saw no wrong in taking what he wanted, about women who bleated.' She stopped. 'I think it was that. The word bleated. For some reason it reminded me of Heidi and I don't know why.'

But Claire did. It was the phrase, Lamb to the slaughter. The throat cutting. Ritualistic.

Kristyna was unconsciously fiddling with her finger. 'Then the painful finger made me feel vulnerable, I suppose. I think I sort of connected the two situations – thought of Heidi's actual pain for the first time – and that made me think that he felt she'd deserved it, that he was glad and that I'd deserved it too. That he was making this mocking judgement. About both of us. I could see in his eyes he was lumping us together. So I had been determined not to let him see that he was needling me and the finger let it out. All the pain. It was throbbing and it was like he could feel each pulse. I could see it in his eyes, that he was enjoying my pain. It was horrible.'

Claire shifted uncomfortably in her chair. She felt that Kristyna was being a little over dramatic. But the nurse hadn't finished.

'I said he was wrong and finished the consultation. I just wanted him out of the room. It was the only weapon I had, the only way to assert my authority – and he didn't like it. He turned around as he reached the door and stared at me with a sort of cold hatred, then sauntered out – at his own pace. A bit like a rebellious kid from the headmaster's office. Oh no, he didn't like being dismissed.

'I grew to dread the encounters. He defaulted on one but turned up for the following one. It was just as strained.' Again she searched out the room for sympathy. 'You know how it is – once you've lost it you've really lost it with a patient. Once they know they can get to you it's hard to be professional. He'd make these sinister comments, like I had nice ears. We all knew about the rabbit incident. He'd pretend he knew where I lived by saying my house needed painting.'

'And does it?'

Kristyna nodded.

'I remember one evening the papers were full of a story about an arson attack where a woman and her three children all died. It was headlines for a whole week. The paper was on my desk and he said something about fire being a useful destroyer. I queried the word *useful*. I thought it odd and he said for the arsonist because it left no trace except the indestructible – things like bra wires and teeth and splintered bones. He was always trying to frighten me.'

'And did he succeed?'

Kristyna nodded. 'It got to me all right – and he knew it. The trouble was, Claire, he was free. Not like one of our patients – locked up at night. He was on the loose.'

She was rubbing her forearms. Agitated now.

'Then one night, about a month later, my car had acid poured over it.'

'Are you sure it was Barclay?'

'It was done late in the day,' Kristyna reasoned, sensible now. Logical even. 'I'd gone out to the car to fetch some notes in at four o clock and it wasn't done then. He was the last patient of the afternoon. The car park was almost empty when I finally left.'

Siôna made as though to speak again but shut his mouth instead.

'Even then I might not have made the connection,' Kristyna said, 'but a week later he mentioned something about cars – about them being their owners' pride and joy.' She was frowning. 'I looked at him and I knew.' Her eyes moved around the room, landing on everyone in turn defiantly, begging their support. 'I just knew.'

Claire moved her head in the slowest of nods. Having had contact with Barclay she understood exactly what Kristyna was saying. More worryingly perhaps she and Kristyna shared something with Heidi. They were all women in control of his welfare and freedom.

Rolf crossed his long, thin, stork's legs, tugged at his earlobe, the age-old gesture of disliking what you hear. 'You're very troubled by Barclay.' It was a trite observation – rather than a question.

Kristyna nodded. So did Claire.

'So was Heidi. Very bothered by him.'

He was inching towards something.

Rolf continued, unaware that Claire perceived his words as momentous.

'It's true,' he mused. 'She did really fret about that guy. She was quite convinced he was going to commit some ghastly crime one day. I argued with her a couple of times that there was nothing in his past that justified such a close supervision order but she wouldn't have it.'

Claire disagreed. 'I feel the same way,' she said quietly.

'But I'm not convinced that a supervision order will prevent him re-offending.' She wanted to say more – that according to all of them present it hadn't been Barclay who had butchered Heidi Faro. It had been Gulio.

And the more she toyed with this idea the less she liked it or believed it.

Out loud she said. 'In the end it was Gulio, wasn't it, who was the greater threat.'

That was when she realised that everyone in the room – Rolf, Kristyna, Siôna, the others – were all watching her with the same alert and wary expression.

They nodded their heads but in no one's eyes was there any hint of finality.

The case was over, she wanted to protest. Gulio was in a secure mental unit, one up from Greatbach. He had confessed.

But something clanged like a bell at the back of her head. That was just what Gulio, the brain-damaged, would do. To acquiesce was in character. Even to lash out against a perceived tormentor could be in character. But there was no indication that Heidi would have been seen as his tormentor. Claire searched the room, wanting someone to tell her why they had all been so sure Gulio was guilty. But how can a psychiatrist who inhabits a shadowy never-never land argue against the black and white evidence of the English copper? How can you say that person A is unlikely to have committed the crime and person B is therefore much more likely when the evidence points the other way?

What exactly *was* the evidence?

Probabilities are not enough to convict one man and let another go free.

They cannot point the finger away from evidence and say: *Consider this man. He could do it and feel no remorse, no guilt. Even watch another pay the price for his crime and gloat.'*

Claire stood up. It was almost ten. The meeting was at an

end but the issue was only beginning.

Not long now and she would ask all the right questions.

In the meantime it was for her to fumble – clumsily.

She was aware that Siôna's eyes were on her until she had left the room.

Greatbach was at times crowded with curios of the human race. Peer into any room and you will find them, the deluded, the psychotic, the insane, the . . . the descriptions go on and on, each one an aberration of that elusive concept a – normal – person.

And what is that? In fact the inmates of Greatbach reminded her of the bottle kilns that peppered the Potteries, stunted oddities.

Marcus Bourne was her first port of call that morning, the young potter who had murdered his girlfriend, now understanding the consequences of what he had done, depressed with the knowledge. Dispassionately Claire registered the traditional signs of remorse, the wringing of the hands, the ready tears, the eyes which dropped away from the human face, and still wondered whether it was all an act.

What could she say except that he was young and would survive when privately she knew he must live his life carrying this burden from which he could never be relieved however skilled a counsellor she referred him to. People would know – He killed someone. He's a murderer, you know.

They would always gossip about the circumstances surrounding his crime unless he changed his identity.

Murder is never forgotten.

She knew way beyond his crime. She sensed that his hands would never mould clay again, that the purity of the action would forever be beyond him because his character was tainted.

She spoke to him calmly, explained the processes, which would now be put into action, increased the medication for his depression and moved on.

To Mavis Abiloney, handing out tea, coffee and biscuits to other inpatients, no hint of wanting to end it all – until her sleeve fell back and you glimpsed the mapped territory of her forearms. Striped with razor marks.

Then on to Nancy, sitting cross-legged on her bed, not humming her theme tune now but merely looking smug, arms criss-crossed protectively over her stomach. Her very expression made Claire feel cold and shut out.

She sat in the chair by the window and waited for Nancy to speak first to her, happy to share her maternal calm.

The silence lasted less than two minutes. Nancy peeped furtively across, peering up through her lashes, a secret smile bending her mouth but not showing her teeth. It was not that warm, open type of smile but a grimace.

'I was sick this morning.'

Claire nodded. 'It's to be expected.'

'I knew I was going to be the minute I opened my eyes. I could feel my stomach rumbling around the baby.'

Claire felt tired with it all. 'Nancy, we want to tell the baby's father.'

The cunning expression took her by surprise. It was so intelligent.

'The father does know?'

Nancy leaned towards her to whisper in her ear, rocking slightly. 'I've been caught that way once before, doctor. It isn't a good idea to get too involved, you know. Men! They don't always understand as we women do. They don't know about babies.'

Claire wondered silently who was the father, what were the circumstances of Nancy's pregnancy. What she was up to. Excluding the father completely this time? Or in the very back of her mind was she planning to dispose of this infant too – if it became a nuisance?

Then she remembered the tear-blotched photographs.

No one could accuse Nancy of not feeling remorse.

She looked at the girl-child's innocent face. What complicated, intricate beings the human race consists of.

She must read through Nancy Gold's notes and try to understand better.

For now she concentrated on another issue. 'Are you feeling well?'

Nancy didn't answer straight away but carried on hugging her flat little stomach and rocking to and fro. Softly she began to hum. 'Mm mm mmm. Mm mm mmm,' until Claire's flesh began to crawl with the image the tune evoked.

She tried to stop her singing.

'Nancy, we need to know who the father was.'

Nancy stopped singing. She gave Claire a direct stare and unmistakably shook her head like a naughty child. 'Uuughugh,' she said. Finger across mouth. Zipping it closed. 'Big mistake that. Nancy keeps her secrets this time round, Doctor Roget. It's the baby I want. No accidents this time.'

There was no mistaking her determination.

She was telling her something. Claire knew it, and yet she couldn't quite decipher it. It sat in the back of her head like a shadow while Nancy's bright little eyes were morseing the information to her and yet she couldn't read it clearly. It was as indecipherable as the code to the uninitiated.

Unless. Surely Nancy could not be innocent? It could not be that she had sheltered Austin?

She was suddenly desperate. 'Nancy, you know that your baby was harmed.'

Blank eyes telling her nothing.

'We can't take the chance with this child.'

A coy smile, head on one side, like a chicken. 'I don't understand what you're saying, Doctor.' Arms even more protectively round stomach again. 'This is Nancy's baby. Not yours. Not anyone else's. Mine. To do as I please with.'

Like Barclay with his rabbit.

'We must safeguard it,' Claire insisted, blinking away rogue visions of Nancy cutting the baby's ears off.

Then the tiger jumped out. 'You can't think I'd hurt my own little child.' She almost spat at Claire. 'You can't accuse me of that. I won't let you. Nancy doesn't hurt her babies. You can't take it away. I won't give my consent.'

They learn these words without understanding their meaning. Consent must be informed consent or it is invalid. The consent clause also contains the phrase, being of sound mind.

'You may not have the choice,' Claire said flatly.

Nancy wasn't understanding any of it. 'I won't let you touch me. Or the baby.'

'At some point, Nancy, we will have to examine you – check that everything is going all right. For now . . .' She stood up and left the room. There was time enough to address these issues.

So she thought.

She met up with Kap sauntering towards the bathroom, pale-blue cotton pyjamas neatly tied around his waist, sponge bag dangling from his hand. 'Good morning,' he said, with the widest of smiles and the whitest of teeth exposed as clearly as in a skull of pure black coal.

'And how are you today, Doctor?' He spoke jauntily.

There was even the hint of healthy humour in his dark eyes.

'I'm fine, Kap,' she responded. 'How are you?'

'Better,' he said. 'Much better. I feel I am out of the woods.'

Ah – if only we can trust our patients' diagnoses. But you cannot. One minute they appear lucid. The next . . .

She touched his shoulder. 'That's good news, Kap. Very good news.'

'Exactly what I think. And now I want to go home.'

She felt weary. 'In time, Kap. In time.'

She could not release him on the streets with the chance he would have a knife in his hand.

The afternoon clinic was filled with the self-absorbed depressives, a couple of manics, a few recent discharges, a psychotic man who believed he had a parrot perched on his shoulder and kept jerking his head round to catch a sight of it. By the end of it Claire felt miserable and drained herself. But the weather was unexpectedly warm and sunny, an Indian summer on an October day, and she suddenly realised she didn't want to go home to the Disney-coloured house, to Grant, to any of it. She wanted to meet a friend, drink red wine warmed to blood-heat, spend more than an hour chomping her way through a Caesar salad and then feel white chocolate ice cream slip down her throat.

She sat in her office and toyed with her mobile phone until she reached the number who would suit.

Julia.

Julia Seddon and she had been medics together. As all Claire's friends had been – students, flatmates, colleagues and finally qualified doctors.

But Julia was special. A GP in the city with her own practice, never married, lived with another woman – an artist – no offspring and always glad of an invitation. Claire left a message on her answerphone and sat in her office for a while, waiting for the return call, watching the sun sink behind the uniform lines of grey roofs until they turned them into angular, pointed silhouettes like witches' hats, the only curve the belly of the bottle kiln on the sky-line.

Then Julia rang back.

They met at one of the new restaurants, in Hanley's cultural quarter, marked by cosmopolitan eating houses – French, Italian, Greek, Turkish, Vietnamese, Thai, a mulitplex cinema and a huge theatre. They chose the Italian where the atmosphere was as she had wanted it, garlic-scented, a background of soft, romantic arias which declined to intrude yet completed the illusion of rural Italy. Small tables, check cloths and authentic waiters completed the picture. It reminded her of New York's first generation immigrants. Claire switched the tone of her mobile off. Almost immediately the talk moved through to Grant, and Julia was accusative.

'You always do this, Claire, pick men for the uncomfortable feeling they give you.' Julia's large, slightly prominent eyes stared at her. 'You want to dump him? Throw him out?' Claire couldn't argue against what was surely the truth. 'But you haven't got the guts,' she finished.

'It isn't as easy as all that, Julia,' she protested. 'We live together.'

Julia tossed her head in a spirited fling. 'Nonsense. Just tell him to go. Bugger off. And stop painting your flat like a sixties psychedelic discotheque. Unless, of course.'

The perceptive GP peered out of her face, 'you don't really want to. Not in your heart of hearts.'

Claire had a swift vision of Grant, paintbrush in one hand, hair brightly spotted in the same colour, appealing to her to appreciate.

Julia watched her for a few moments, eventually nodded with satisfaction and changed the subject. 'Now then – tell me about the new job.'

'Interesting, absorbing, draining. Personality disorders are hard work.'

Julia groaned. 'Tell me about it.'

They spent a pleasant couple of hours, eating, drinking, talking as old friends do on one subject then another, moving from patients to new treatments, make-up, plays, books, holidays. What do friends talk about? Everything. No subject is taboo.

Finally they landed at the subject of Heidi Faro and Claire confessed.

'I'm not convinced they've got the right guy.'

Julie regarded her without speaking, certainly not jumping in with both feet to defend the police evidence.

'Too much hinged on the confession of Gulio.' She

paused. 'When there should have been others in the picture.'

Julia gave a delicate frown. 'If it was an unsound conviction an appeal would have been lodged – surely?'

'Gulio wouldn't have done. From what I've read he simply feels confused – and guilty. And from what I've heard of his mother she's been destroyed – first of all by the initial assault and then by subsequent events. It's all been terrible for her.'

Julia nodded. 'I only half remember the detail of Gulio's condition. He'd had a severe head injury, hadn't he?'

Claire nodded. 'A tragic case. He'd been a promising physics student when he was assaulted outside a nightclub in Hanley when he was seventeen years old. He'd been predicted an 'A' in Physics and Maths and had a provisional place at Cambridge to study AstroPhysics. His mother said he was a peaceful, intelligent young man. Slightly introverted. And that's what his teachers said about him too. After the assault he suffered permanent brain damage, mood swings, inability to concentrate – the lot really. And to top it all he took to assaulting anyone who crossed his path. Into which category, I suppose, you have to include Heidi.'

Julia's face was grave. 'But you're not sure?'

'Oh – I don't know.' Claire sighed. 'Maybe it's just because I'm naturally suspicious of too neat and tidy a solution. Or confessions. Or maybe I simply suspect Barclay of every single felony that happens within his circle. Or maybe – I'm just confused.'

A faint smile was spreading slowly across her friend's face. 'Then you know what you ought to do, don't you, Claire, to convince yourself?'

'Interview him. Find out the facts.'

'Exactly.'

They split the bill down the middle; Julia kissed her goodbye and held on to the hug, speaking quietly into her ear. 'And consider Grant. What is it that pushes you into pathological relationships?'

They parted at eleven, sauntering in different directions. Hanley is a hilly member of the five towns and it was downhill to a pay and display car park crowded with late-leaving theatregoers. The light was poor and she had parked in a far corner of the yard, right up against a chain link fence. But something must have registered.

One doesn't examine one's car for damage each time you return to it.

In the light of the lamp she could see there was a blistering around the bonnet, high on the right wing, over the wheel arch. An area as wide as a foot in places.

An acid splash.

She stared at it, working it out from the beginning, standing still until she had worked the first part out.

Barclay had turned his attention on to her now.

She began to panic. Vehicles were moving away. The car park was emptying fast. She must report this. She pulled out her mobile phone – then put it back. She couldn't hang around for the police. She must get out of here. Fast. As she unlocked the car door she scanned the emptying yard, peered into the back seat.

Where was he?

She dropped into her seat, locked the door behind her, glancing down only long enough to put her key in the ignition and see the splash of acid on the floor. Her window must have been left slightly open.

Her hand shook. She couldn't turn the key.

She allowed herself a swift check of the back seats, the floor, a glance in the rear view mirror.

Sometimes we are more frightened of what we can not see.

She finally started the engine, joined the irritated queue to get out and drove home eyeing the rear view mirror every few seconds. But how can you identify the anonymous headlights of a car?

She was even glad to see Grant stretched out on the sofa,

fast asleep.

She told nobody about the incident but buried it at the back of her mind where it lay, slimy and repellent, with the faint odour of something disgusting but not quite solid. Grant's lifestyle had its advantages. He asked no questions but promised to drop the car off at the garage, get a quote for the work and arrange a hire car. So she offloaded her problem on to him and he took it on while she tried not to think that Barclay must have watched her, probably at the hospital, to know which car was hers before stalking her that night while she had been feasting at the Italian restaurant, with a friend, believing herself anonymous.

Had he known that Kristyna would tell her about the acid?

Instinctively she accepted the fact that this was her punishment for summoning his mother to the clinic to check up on him and for discharging him, refusing to enter into his game of 'look how bad I can be'.

But rob an attention-seeking person of the attention and he quickly becomes frustrated.

She knew that at some point he would reappear at outpatients and she would have to face him. She could not refuse.

But the question that underlay her professional interest was: was he a danger to society?

Answer: She didn't know.

She cupped her chin in her hand and stared at the emulsioned wall. How could *anyone* know until *after* an act had been committed? She was not God to peer into the future. And Barclay was perfectly capable of teasing her, letting her *believe* he was a danger when in reality he was not.

Ah yes, argued the voice of conflict from inside. But he is also capable of doing the exact opposite – encouraging you to believe he is not a danger when the converse is the truth.

How can you know?

Answer: you cannot.

She didn't even really know whether he had revelled in the supervision order or resented it?

Later still she remembered something else Kristyna had mentioned and found another fear. *Did he know where she lived?*

Had he followed her home from the hospital?

Was her home safe?

In her worst fears she even recalled his interest in the arson case and wonderd how safe she was in her bed at night.

Because however we try to protect ourselves if someone wishes us harm we are not safe.

The phrase echoed around her skull.

We are not safe.

She was not safe. If Barclay had really decided to get to her she didn't have a chance. The acid attack proved that. And that was its purpose. To show her how vulnerable she really was.

It all came down to the question. How dangerous was Barclay? How far would he go? What was his intent?

Look for the clues, Claire.

He had all the characteristics of a psychopath. He failed to make close relationships, despised any human being within his sphere.

Except his mother who was simply a means to an end. No – *particularly* his mother because he had complete control over her. Which led her to another realisation. If he had forbidden Cynthia to attend the clinic she would not have come. Had it been *her* threat then which had forced his hand? Had she then some power over him?

So – again the continual question – how dangerous was Barclay?

She tried to be professional, to study the question from all angles, knowing that Heidi was her guide through the tortuous mind of Jerome Barclay.

And Heidi was dead.

She wished that when she even thought the name, Heidi, she did not have this vision of her mentor, a gaping wound in her throat, swinging – ever so slowly and rhythmically – against the door, as steady and regular as a metronome.

Tick – tock – tick – tock. Back and forth, her mouth still moving. Directing her. *'Questions, Claire. You must ask questions.'*

But they must be oblique, subtle enough for him not to realise she was on to him.

She didn't *know* how much the acid incident had upset her until three weeks later when she saw Barclay's name on her outpatient list and began to shake. And she knew that she had lost the professional armour that should protect her. She had discharged him, flung him back into the world, like a fish with a torn mouth. She had wanted him to swim away into oblivion. So why had he come back?

For nothing particular, it seemed.

He chatted about the usual subjects, interpersonal relationships, work ethic, the way he viewed women and more specifically how he saw his mother, while she wanted to ask only one question. Why have you come back to see me?

His chatter was less than satisfactory.

'Friends? Yeah.' Today he was well-dressed in black jeans, a white T-shirt, an expensive-looking Oakley watch, black, suede trainers that looked brand new.

Had he been on a shoplifting spree or had he wangled extra money out of his mother?

Whatever – his hair was slicked back and he looked pale and a little tired.

'I got mates,' he said.

'Tell me about them – your friends – the people you

socialise with. What do you do with them? Go clubbing, down the pub?'

The subject of the spoilt car lay fallow between them.

He looked at her as though he pitied her. 'You don't know me very well, do you, Doctor Roget? I thought you understood a little bit more about me than that. Clubbing and pubbing isn't exactly my scene.'

'So what *is* your scene?'

'I like to play records.'

'Alone?'

'Alone.'

'Anything else?'

'Surf the net.'

She wondered what websites he visited.

'What are your interests, Jerome?'

He thought about that one. 'I suppose what makes people tick.'

'Tick?'

He merely smiled. That irritating, supercilious bend of the mouth.

'So what do you do in the evenings?'

He moved his chair softly over the carpet towards her. 'I like to go to the theatre,' he said.

He was baiting her. That was why he had come. To draw her closer, burrow beneath her skin, like a scabious worm.

'Anything else?' It annoyed her that her throat was dry. Unable to manufacture saliva she wanted a glass of water. But to leave now would be interpreted as a cop-out, the doctor backing down. But if she had heard the crack in her voice, so had he.

He simply studied her before adding, 'And I like to walk.'

'In the evenings? In the winter too?'

'Best in the winter, Doctor Roget.'

'Why?'

The eyes searched hers. 'I thought you'd have worked that one out.' A pause. Just long enough for her to summon up a faint smear of spit to moisten her tongue.

'Because people leave their curtains open. They switch their lights on. And I can see in.'

'What do you see?'

'Plenty. People coming home to an empty house. Throwing their bags on the chair.'

She knew he was talking about women. Only women.

'Coming out of the shower. Dripping wet. Drying themselves. Sitting on their settees, thinking no one's watching. Talking to their friends on the phone. Watching television. Meeting in restaurants, eating, drinking, thinking no one is watching.'

That was when she understood. While Barclay was a free man no one was safe. As he had planned the acid attack over her car so he plotted other events, intimidations.

'Why do you like watching women,' she asked in a low voice.

If he said something – pathological – she could have him committed. She waited for him to fall into the trap.

She had a chance. Barclay was in a trance. Outside himself. Unconscious. His pupils were dilated, his tongue visible between his lips, a faint, pink show. There was a sheen of sweat on his forehead. He was excited.

But he was smart, in control. Too clever not to see she was setting traps. He came to. 'I like people-watching,' he said in the affected, social way folk do at parties, confessing to an odd habit which isn't odd at all. 'It's quite a common pursuit, isn't it, People Watching.'

'Every time I think I have him he slips away. But one day . . .' Heidi's words.

Claire shared the thought. But one day I shall ensnare you.

Now she was the one who stared back boldly.

And it was for Barclay to take up the challenge.

Claire gave a bland smile. Such a useful facial expression to cover up a whole host of reactions. Shock. Fear. Unease. And sneaking in on the wings of these a superiority which Barclay recognised. His eyes widened in surprise as he stared back at her.

She took advantage of the moment. 'How do you get on with your mother, Jerome?'

The mouth closed. The pupils shrunk. On the arms of the chair his hands clenched.

'We get on fine, Doctor Roget. How do you get on with yours?'

'Equally fine,' she said easily but sensed that he would have picked up on the sudden tightness of her own hand.

It was all a game.

His eyes flickered. He would save this up and use it later.

'So when do you want to see me again?'

She didn't.

'I don't think I need to,' she said.

He smiled. 'Not ever?'

'No.'

'No follow up?'

'No,' she said again.

For the second time she had thrown down the gauntlet, the challenge. How would he respond this time?

He walked deliberately to the door, turned just as deliberately and ran his index finger lightly across his throat.

She watched, mesmerised, as the door swung closed behind him.

How little of himself he gave away. How clever he was.

It was all so well-covered – just beneath the surface, hidden from view. And yet it was there, as subtle and elusive as a butterfly fluttering behind a muslin curtain.

And was her response tinged – only a very little – with admiration?

Long after he had gone she breathed in the faint scent of him. Coal tar soap. It reminded her of her childhood, the happy time before she had a brother, creeping out of bed across a cool carpet, to prop the door open with books, Treasure Island, Moby Dick, Anne of Green Gables, Pollyanna, and listen to her mother's fingers dancing over the piano keys to play Schubert and Chopin, Beethoven and

Dvorak.

But the feeling of happiness, that wonderful colourwash that all was well with the world, was gone. For ever. Destroyed.

After Adam had been born her mother had stopped playing the piano – even though she had begged her to. Something of that happiness had vanished and never ever returned. It had gone for ever.

So – back to the problem. How dangerous was Barclay?

That was when she began to understand the nature of what had spooked Heidi Faro, the reason why she had kept the supervision order up on Barclay for years, keeping it closely, and warily, like a python. Keep a tight rein on its tail, the dangerous bit, or it will wrap itself around you, crush all life from you.

Heidi had been afraid that if she relaxed the supervision order Barclay would kill.

Maybe he had.

She had been the one to uncork the bottle, let the evil genie out.

What now?

Chapter Seven

It took her less than a day to work out how she could penetrate Barclay's armour.

She looked up Sadie Whittaker's address and drew a blank. Undeterred she found that of her parents and contacted them. Naturally, once they'd found out who she was they weren't too helpful. All they would give her was a mobile phone number which gave her no clue as to where in the country Sadie Whittaker had settled.

It took four tries to finally track her down and find out she was living in the garden city of Letchworth.

Sadie had put miles between her and her one-time boyfriend.

And she didn't sound at all pleased to learn that he was still around and that Claire was the psychiatrist in charge of him. The last thing she wanted was to meet up. Claire tried to persuade her.

Eventually Sadie capitulated but she still didn't want Claire to come to her house. It was a stalemate until Claire suggested she take the train down to London and meet her at a hotel in Leicester Square in a week's time.

From newspaper articles she had a vague idea what Barclay's ex looked like but Sadie had changed. Into a pale, slim girl with a chill resolve and an odd sort of detachment from life. A woman who could fade into the background, with her neat, dull clothes, pale brown hair, eyes not quite brown, not quite grey, yet not hazel which never quite focused on you. She was a woman of negatives. Not positives. Claire realised this as soon as she saw her enter the room, scan its occupants and meander towards the bar.

It was hard to figure out just why Barclay had homed in on her.

Claire approached, ordered them both a Diet Coke and they settled into a quiet corner of the room, sinking into soft, leather armchairs.

Sadie gave a vague smile as Claire introduced herself more fully. Her gaze slid past her and roamed the room as though wondering whether Barclay was somewhere around.

'I didn't want to meet you,' she confessed quickly. 'I want to put it all behind me.'

'I do understand,' Claire said, in accepted psychiatrist's empathic talk. 'I wouldn't have asked you to come unless I'd felt it was necessary – important.'

Sadie's eyebrows rose.

'I don't understand Jerome,' she said. 'I don't know whether he is a danger to the wider community or not. I hoped you might give me some insight.'

Sadie's response was a cynical 'Humph,' and her lips tightened.

'How did you meet?' It seemed as good a starting point as any.

Sadie drew in a tired, reluctant breath. 'At a club. My boyfriend had dumped me a month or two earlier. I was out, getting pie-eyed with my mates. I lost my balance and toppled against the bar. And suddenly – there he was. Catching me before I hit the floor.' She gave a hint of a smile. 'I can't say I remember much about that first night except somehow – I don't know how so it's no use your asking me – we ended up together in the back of a taxi. I didn't feel threatened,' she added.

Claire met her eyes.

'You're right,' Sadie admitted. 'I didn't feel anything. I was too pissed.'

'So? When you sobered up?'

Sadie looked almost ashamed. 'We were back at my flat,' she said sheepishly. 'I woke up quite late the next morning and he was staring out of the window.'

Claire waited.

'He said something about it being a busy road. My flat was at Cobridge by some traffic lights but convenient for Hanley. I did have a flatmate.' Her face was a blank. 'But

she was going to Australia anyway. She had a job to go to.'
Sadie went pale then red. 'I feel such a fool,' she said suddenly. 'I should have realised.' Her voice tailed off and
Claire knew that she was going to learn something.

'You should have realised what?'

Sadie's eyes held something dark, something frightened,
something unsavoury. Her pupils contracted.

'What?' Claire prompted the girl gently.

'You won't mention the fact that you've seen me?' There
was an urgency in her voice.

'No – I promise.'

'It was all there in his lovemaking.' She moved her head
violently shaking away the memory. 'No. Who am I kidding? It wasn't lovemaking. It was – ' Her eyes almost
bounced off Claire in one, short stare. 'He enjoys inflicting
pain, Doctor Roget. He likes to be in control and he likes
you frightened. The sex act means nothing to him unless it
involves terror.' She put her hand on Claire's arm, giving
her words emphasis. 'I don't want you to underestimate
this. I don't just mean he's rough. I mean he whispers.'

Claire waited.

Sadie's face changed as she whispered, stroking the
words backwards and forwards as though with the edge of
a blade. *'I could hurt you. I could cut a slice of these thighs. I
could puncture your throat. I could kill you. I could rape you.
I can make you scream and then stop you screaming. Do you
know how much blood is contained in that pale body of yours?
Just think, Sadie, of all the things I could do without anyone
knowing.* I used to tell myself he was kidding. Then occasionally he would do something and every time we were
together I would be waiting. Usually something quite small.
A hard pinch of the nipple, a sudden movement. It wasn't
the pinch or the thump in itself. I began to realise that over
the weeks we were together. It was simply that he knew he
was able to make people frightened, that he had power over
them to manipulate their thoughts, to control the dark
rooms of the mind that normally you shut away behind

locked doors. He seemed to know what to do, what to say, to exert the most control. He is very insidious.' She lifted the Coke glass to her lips. The slices of lemon and ice cubes bumped around as her hands shook. 'Sometimes I would think I would pretend to be more frightened than I was but he knew. He knew. And then I didn't need to pretend any more. I knew something was coming. I knew I was going to get hurt one day and yet I couldn't pull away. It was like a snake holding you in its gaze. You know you should move – get out of the way – but you don't. You just stand there and wait and it bites you.'

Claire interrupted. 'Why on earth did you get into this in the first place?'

Sadie shrugged. 'I don't know. When Guy dumped me – went off with a so-called-friend – they rubbed my face in it – I felt hopeless. Useless. I lost all confidence. I felt that people were talking about me, laughing behind my back. Even strangers. I could be on a bus or walking in the Potteries Shopping Centre or even at work and I would hear them making fun. In the end I found it hard to go any-where. The night out with my friends was my first night out for ages. I was a mess. He seemed to latch on to it as though this was exactly what he wanted. I guess if I'd had more about me he wouldn't have got such a hold in the first place. I'd have moved on.'

'And then after the assault he threatened you if you gave a statement to the police.'

Sadie nodded. 'It was out of my hands at first. I was badly hurt and gave statements to the police from my hos-pital bed. I felt safe in hospital. There were people around twenty-four hours a day and I felt protected. When I realised what I'd done I was frightened.'

She drew in closer, held Claire's eyes with a stare. 'He had this little saying that went round and round my head. "Imagine a funeral pyre," he'd say. "The body burning in a car. Nothing left except splintered bones and melted jew-ellery, and those lovely teeth of yours." He'd watch me while he was speaking, seeing the effect every single syllable had on me. I'd start to shake. It was so graphic, Claire, and personal. He knew I always wore an underwired bra. He knew my jewellery. He knew the fact that my dress had caught fire when I was a child – from a firework – and that of all things I was most frightened of fire. Of being burnt. It felt so directed towards me. Tailor-made. The more he knew about me the better the hold he had. And I knew he was capable of doing it. All. So when I got out of hospital I retracted my statement. Terror, Doctor Roget, is a powerful tool and he knew how to use it to its greatest effect.'

She stood up abruptly. 'I'm sorry,' she said, politely, but there was an undercurrent of panic. 'I'm really sorry but I can't help you. I can't help you decide whether Jerome was a danger purely to me or to the public at large. I don't know. It's your decision,' she said brutally. 'You must make up your own mind. All I can say is that I never want to see him again. Not in my life. And not in Hell either.'

Claire watched her slip out of the hotel, this slim, almost invisible girl and wondered.

There was no doubt about it. Sadie Whittaker's words had unnerved her too.

A week later she applied for an interview with Stefan Gulio.

For which she had to give a valid reason.

And for that she could only tell the truth. That, filling Heidi's post, made vacant by such a violent crime, apparently caused by one of her own patients, she felt she must convince herself that the conviction was sound, that Gulio had done it and therefore no one else was under suspicion. And by extrapolation she was in no danger. Further that by understanding the assault she might, in the future, recognise some of the warning signals. She penned a careful letter to the prison governor deliberately using emotive words.

She must see Gulio, convince herself he really was guilty.

'If there is any doubt – any doubt at all in my mind that Gulio is the guilty party you realise my own misgivings could multiply and that it would make it difficult for me to function at Greatbach.' And two paragraphs later, *'I use the same office that Heidi Faro was butchered in.'*

She smiled to herself. Sometimes simple phrases were the best.

She promised not to upset or quiz Gulio unduly but to use the interview merely to put her own mind at rest, adding the titbit that it would be a useful learning curve and may, in the future, forewarn her of a patient who was likely to commit an offence. The buzz phrase was bound to tip the scales in her balance.

She signed the letter, Claire Roget, leaving out none of her qualifications. MB CHb; FRC Psych. MRCP.

You don't expect Broadmoor hospital to be in the leafy lanes of Surrey. But that is where it is, and that was where Gulio was being held. A Victorian, Gothic monstrosity which houses the most diseased brains in our country. Men and women who will tear you limb from limb and are directed to commit every perversion known to man – and some our minds are unable to imagine. She had set out in the early morning, anxious to avoid the inevitable jam on the M25, reaching a late dawn through mists and sleeting rain, flicking the radio from news analysis on Radio Four, through some beaty rhythms of Radio One, accidentally a local golden oldies' station, Classic FM and finally moving through the tracks of a Robbie Williams album. The traffic was light then heavy, then stop-start, nose to bumper, unreal through the windscreen until she turned off the motorway when the chill of who she was about to meet and the crime he had committed seemed to enter the car and made the horror vivid and the music merely a backtrack. She switched the crooner off, followed the signs to Crowthorne – and arrived.

There it lay, granite-grey, sinister as you imagine in your

nightmares, inspired by old black and white chiller films like *Great Expectations*, with Magwitch ready to spring from behind a tombstone. She hugged her briefcase to her, locked the car and reached the huge door, under the CCTV camera eye, while her own eye wandered across the grey slabs of stone and towering turrets. And she wondered: how many different shades of grey are there?

Hundreds.

The door was guarded by an intercom and swiftly opened by a round-faced man of about fifty who had obviously been briefed.

'Doctor Roget,' he said, cheerily pumping her hand. 'So you've come on a social visit to Gulio, have you? Well – he's one of our quieter inmates. Reads his books all day. No trouble at all.'

He ushered her into a small, square office, messy with the typical government noticeboard, objectives and notices pinned to cork.

From plaintive, '*And will the joker who nicked my diary please let me have it back because I don't know what I'm supposed to be doing*' to the humorous comment underneath, '*Forgetting which doll you're meant to be out with, Marty?*'

And finally artistic, two tits and a bum with an arrow. '*This one.*'

Obviously the government directives on sexual predation didn't apply here. She signed in and pinned a security badge to her jacket. 'Trouble is,' the officer offered, 'Gulio forgets everything he reads. So he could go over the same book over and over again. Shame really. Probably was quite bright, once upon a time.'

Once upon a time.

The opening words to every single fairy story and fable. And the closing words to a promising life.

So was this another fable?

The officer gave her a brief, curious look, beetling his eyebrows. 'Are you here because you think he didn't do it?'

She knew what his next sentence would be – that no one

in here had 'done it'. That prisons were, famously, full of people who were innocent.

She forestalled him. 'I don't think that,' she said briskly. 'I simply want to interview him.'

The officer was miffed at this and led her without further comment along the corridor, jangling his keys along the way, fastidiously locking, waiting, unlocking, locking again.

The visitors' room was suitably spartan, tables, chairs, more CCTV, grills over the windows, guards at the doors. Painted mushroom with grey floors there was nothing in it to lift the feeling of crushing depression.

Which hurtled Claire into wishing she had worn something other than the plainest brown Next trouser suit. Something pink – or red – or orange to introduce colour.

The door opened.

During the drive she had formed a picture of Stefan Gulio. We all do in circumstances like this. He would be tall and thin, prematurely bent up. His eyes (colour indeterminate) would slide from side to side, never quite settling, like a butterfly on a hot day. His hair would be dark and scraggy, greasy even. He might smell.

He would shuffle and manifest some of the signs of brain damage, an inability to focus either with his mind or his eye. This would be accompanied by an odd look, fidgety hands, inappropriate behaviour. A smile, a frown, a stare. All in the wrong place. There would be external clues to his turmoil.

But there was nothing.

As the door was opening she turned her head to see a slim young man of about thirty, with neat, clean, short dark hair, wearing brown trousers and a loose-fitting shirt walking slowly towards her. *Was this really Heidi's killer?*

He smiled tentatively, a hesitant, surprisingly attractive smile, and settled into the chair on the other side of the table, linking his fingers together loosely. They were long and bony and drew her gaze and she could not picture them covered in blood or committing that one terrible, slashing act.

She even felt herself warm to him.

But was this simply Gulio's trick? To appear so very different from the person he really was?

She stood, introduced herself and scrutinised his face.

It was bland, unsure, with a slightly vacant expression in hazel eyes and a quiet, studious tilt of the lips. His skin was unhealthily pale and there was a vague eight o'clock shadow on his chin and around his mouth. Was this really the man responsible for Heidi's murder?

'I've taken over Doctor Faro's job,' she said, matter of factly. 'A couple of months ago.'

He nodded very slowly, as though absorbing this one, significant fact took a great deal of comprehension. He crossed his legs at the ankles. 'Why are you here?'

'Because there's a lot I don't understand.'

His returned smile was both shallow and sad, little more than a token tilt of his mouth. 'Such as?'

'*Do* you remember Heidi?'

'I'm not sure.' It was an odd response.

'She was your doctor at Greatbach, Stefan.'

Again Gulio nodded. And there was another, tentative smile. A little rounder this time.

'Do you remember her, Stefan?'

A cloud dropped over his face. He was struggling. Finally he shook his head. 'Not really,' he said frankly. 'It's just a little . . . ' He pressed his lips together and swayed ever-so-slightly. 'I'm afraid it's beyond me. Outside my mind. Just. But they tell me. They do tell me.'

She tried another tack. 'You saw quite a lot of her in the months before.' She stopped dead. On the edge of a tumbling cliff. 'Before she died. Just describe her to me. Please.'

The bony fingers stilled. 'Perhaps . . . She was very kind. She had a nice voice. Foreign, I think.'

'She was Austrian. I heard her lecture a few times. You could hardly tell English wasn't her native tongue.'

He dipped his head, agreeing.

'Tell me what you do remember about her.'

'She wore trousers?'

'Yes. I remember that too.'

'She was a bit plump, I think.' Another smile. Mischievous. She glimpsed a boy behind the face.

'Yes,' she agreed.

'And she didn't really ask questions so much as talk about subjects.'

She was intrigued. 'Such as?'

'The Big Bang,' he said. 'The origin.'

She waited but he had lost it. 'The origin of what?'

This was a struggle for the poor, damaged brain. Bits were there but disjointed. He had understood – once. He fumbled and tried, even opened his mouth to speak – and gave up, his eyes beseeching her to go – no – further. 'Sorry, I don't know,' he apologised.

She must try another angle. 'Did you like Heidi?'

'Oh yes. I think I did.'

So – to another subject less taxing. 'Do you ever see your mother here?'

The same expression returned. That fug of confusion. 'I'm not really sure,' he said politely. 'I think we're a long way from home.'

'What do you do all day?'

'I read. I watch the television. I think I sleep quite a lot. More than before.'

'Do you work here?'

'I help,' he said, still politely, 'in the library sometimes. I classify the books.'

'Do you have any idea why you're . . . ?'

He knew exactly what she was asking.

'I'm afraid not,' he said. 'I don't think about it much. I try not to. Sometimes though I have nightmares. I hear a scream. One very long scream. I run along the corridor. I run very fast. I see blood on my hands. I try – ' He swallowed. ' – I try to help. But I don't know what to do. I tend to panic and run away. I don't like those dreams. They upset me. Then they give me an injection – something to calm me down and I feel better but still not right – something is never right but I don't know what.'

Gulio's brain had been mashed to a pulp. Only tiny windows of rational or intelligent thought still existed. The tragedy had not only been Heidi's but his too. Claire had known it but not as graphically as this. And now she was witnessing the result of the wasted intelligence.

And she had had a wasted journey.

She said her goodbyes to Gulio feeling he had been of little help. He stood as she stood, in the polite way that only well brought up men do. And the glimpse was of the intellectual he might have become. A scientist. A chemist. A physicist. A quiet man.

On the way out she spoke again to the prison warder with the rosy face. 'Does he have explosions of temper?'

'Not that I've ever seen. He's subdued is Gulio.'

'What medication is he on?'

'Couple of Stelazine a day. Keeps him tranquil.'

She nodded. It was rational prescribing.

But on the way home she tried to piece together the events of that day. Stefan had been in the room and had run along the corridor, meeting Siôna halfway down. Siôna had returned to Heidi's room, pressing the panic button on the way, but been unable to open the door. So he had pulled Rolf from his office. Together they had forced an entry and seen. But if Heidi's body had been so heavy how come Gulio had been able to get out? He was not a strong-looking guy.

Claire stopped and thought about this one. What had Siôna been doing in the building that day and why had Rolf heard nothing?

And the real question, of course, was this: had Jerome

Barclay been anywhere near?

They were all curious the next morning when she returned to Greatbach. Rolf and Siôna, Kristyna, Dawn and Bec. Their questions were endless.

'So how is he bearing up?'

'Does he remember the assault?'

'How does he look?'

'Does he still bury his head in his books all day?'

'Has he got fatter?'

' – thinner?'

'Does he look older?'

'Younger?'

'Is there any sign of his brain function returning?'

But as she had never met Gulio before Claire could make no comparison. She could only comment that he seemed quiet. So Claire reflected that they had all been fond of Gulio. The murder had not altered their affection for him. Almost as a cancer wouldn't steal our affection from a loved one.

She eyed the watching faces, soft in their benevolence, and felt a wave of fondness for them all and thoughts of Barclay and Nancy, Kap Oseo and Mavis Abiloney and Marcus Bourne faded into the background like textured wall hangings.

So the days passed peacefully.

Without drama for a while.

The cliché is that bad news travels fast.

Sometimes not fast enough. Bad news should gallop like a horse. Rip like a forest fire through tinder-dry grass. The speed of sound is too slow. It should beam at the speed of light. No – faster even than that. Everyone who has an interest in disaster should be aware within milleseconds of a terrible event happening. They should not have one fragment of a minute's peace of mind. Twin towers. Kennedy's death, Concorde crashing.

It is not so in real life.

Bad news travels slowly.

We cling to oblivion, living our ordinary lives on borrowed time.

Three – maybe four – days must have passed during which she, Claire, was happily unaware. You could also say that she was, in some measure, ultimately responsible. That she had stirred the wasps' nest. Awakened the beast.

But the next few days were spent in this illusion – this cocoon of a close, professional team working together, pooling their knowledge. Even an evening at the pub telling secret little jokes about the inmates, glances tossed over shoulders to make sure no one who was not part of their circle could possibly hear.

So it was a Tuesday morning at one of their newly chummy meetings, when she was feeling untouchable, that Siôna dropped his bombshell.

'Did you read last night's *Sentinel*?'

No one had so the enquiry provoked only a flicker of lame interest.

'It was in the Deaths column.'

They still looked at him blankly but at least he had their attention now.

'I just *happened* to see it. The funeral announcement.'

More blank faces and for Claire still not an inkling of what was to come, of the storm about to break, crashing elements around their heads.

'Barclay's mother's died.'

That was it. Three words. Enough to prick the complacency that all was right in the world and nothing was wrong. She felt the first trickle of unease which would roar into a flood of fear. 'What did she die of?'

'It didn't say. Just that she'd died last week and the funeral's on Thursday, donations to the Samaritans.'

Claire was silent, her mind clicking onto the sprightly Cynthia Barclay. No sign of a heart condition there. Funeral

Thursday so no evidence of delay, a post mortem, coroner's case, an inquest, unnatural causes. And yet it was all too convenient, just what Barclay would have wanted. To be rid of a cumbersome relative. Particularly if she was about to embark on a détente with his psychiatrist.

'It doesn't sound as though the death is suspicious.' Siôna's helpful comment.

Claire was silent. *Any death within fifty miles of Jerome Barclay should be treated as suspicious.*

All eyes were watching her, wary, this band of happy health colleagues. While she toyed with an idea. Maybe. Just maybe she should shake off the shackles of confidentiality and speak to the police herself.

Halfway through the morning, a mug of coffee on her desk, she found a window of peace to make the private phone call. Psychiatrists were asked to do this all the time, act as watchdogs for public safety. Guardian angels. To keep police informed of anyone likely to be a danger to the general public – or a specific public. Warn them. The defence union was well named. Not for doctors – for patients. But the confidentiality rules were too ambiguous. While it advised its members to consider the right to privacy it also warned them they had a responsibility to protect the public. Sometimes considering the two was a tightrope. You could so easily fall. And who is a danger to the public?

We all are capable of being.

How is a psychiatrist to know absolutely? Is he God to anticipate an evil action? There are so many possibilities: the drunk driver, the mother with an uncontrolled temper, or with post-natal depression, the wife-beater who goes that bit further. Road rage. Sudden hatred. Not only the plotter. We are all capable if you extend the circle. The unskilled builder or electrician. The careless, the mad, the psychopathic. Ah. The psychopathic. This is the one the law of disclosure is specifically aimed at. The psycho of noir fiction. The person diagnosed as having Severe

Psychopathic Personality Disorder.

Barclay.

But even here there are pitfalls. How can we know who was a potential killer until after they have killed? Psychiatrists do not have foresight or crystal balls, the power of peering into the future although they are supposed to be psychic. All they have are pointers – personality characteristics – to flag up the dangerous psychopath.

They are: Aggressive.

Often drunk.

Full of threats.

They break the law.

They accuse others of letting them down. Nothing is ever their fault. They delegate responsibility.

They lack closeness with another human being, fail to make relationships, keep jobs.

There is an aura of unprovoked violence that clings to them.

They are unpredictable, manipulative.

Claire rolled a biro between her fingers back and forth, back and forth. Barclay fitted the bill perfectly.

She had the number on the keypad of her mobile phone, the Medical Defence Union. But she was not about to leak information, only to fact-find.

So instead she dialled directory enquiries and asked the number of the local police station. Then asked to be put through to the officer investigating the death of Mrs Barclay, reading the address from Barclay's notes.

'There isn't really one.'

'Then the officer who attended the scene?'

'It was Young. Sergeant Young.'

She explained who she was and asked again to be put through.

She was not reassured. A slow, Stoke voice came down the line minutes later, 'How can I help you, Ma'am?'

She needed someone of sharper intelligence than this. Someone with subtlety.

But she tried. 'I'm a psychiatrist who works at Greatbach Psychiatric Centre.'

'Oh yes.'

'I simply wondered how you viewed Mrs Barclay's death?'

'May I ask what is your interest in this?'

'I'm not at liberty to say except that I do have a legitimate interest.'

'I don't quite see the connection.'

She backed down. 'There probably isn't one. I simply wondered whether Mrs Barclay's death was being treated as suspicious?'

A pause. 'Who did you say your name was?'

'Claire Roget. Doctor Claire Roget. I'm a psychiatrist.' She had a feeling he was scratching it down on some dog-eared ledger or tapping it – one-fingered – on a computer. 'Look – I simply wanted to know whether Cynthia Barclay's death was considered suspicious.'

'Is that R-o-g-e-t?'

'Sergeant Young,' she said firmly. 'If there is nothing unusual about Mrs Barclay's death then that's fine. I simply wanted to reassure myself. And – ' she hesitated. 'I'd really rather you didn't mention the fact that I'd been in touch to anyone.'

'You want me to keep this phone call a secret?'

Claire was tapping her foot on the floor in frustration. 'Please. Can you just answer the question.'

'Mrs Barclay was in her late sixties. Her doctor tells us she was not in good health. She was very nervy and needed pills to help her sleep. According to the pathologist she took too many, was a bit sick and breathed it in. She'd had a drink or two. She died. There isn't anything odd about it.'

Aspiration? Of course there was.

'Her death is not being investigated as suspicious. It was simply an accident.'

She put the phone down and went home.

No sign of Grant. There was a football match on at the college. He would be getting muddy, in his strip, and in an hour or so downing his beer like a man. Claire fidgeted and channel-hopped through the entire TV network but sometimes it is not the programmes but our state of mind which makes us bored with the whole spectrum of entertainment. We cannot be entertained.

Her mind was busy, frantically exploring possibilities.

Barclay walking. Walking. Peering into basement flats. Peeping Tom into kitchens and living rooms, hallways and bathrooms. Watching.

And then what?

Who knows?

Walking. Stalking.

She could do the same. She took her coat from the chair, shoved her key in the pocket and slammed the door behind her.

This was the time of year when the leaves make a noise as they die and fall, dry and crackle. The sky was a luminous navy, bright and speckled with stars, a crescent moon beaming down from the apex. Branches like bony fingers grasped at empty air and the sounds carried clearly through the stillness. TV, car radios, pub doors opening to chatter then closing again, the mournful, enquiring bark of a lone hound. A few walkers, like herself. Some traffic.

She crossed the road.

A Mercedes garage boasted its wares, each car on the forecourt carefully clamped. She walked on. A dark road led down to Festival Park, neon lights throwing up to the sky. The light changed subtly, the hues taking on the brittle depth of an October night. She walked on.

A couple, holding hands, chattering, the girl eager, the boy indulgent, passed by.

Behind her a car door slammed and she started, aware that whatever her eyes had seen, her thoughts had been of Barclay.

Out of town shopping precincts are hell to walk through if you stray from the painted footprints. They deliberately make it hard for the pedestrian with cobbled slopes, walls in the centre of the road, no walkway but a wide sweep for the traffic.

She left Festival Park.

In a trance she stepped along a street of terraced houses and did as Jerome Barclay did, peered in, at families, old and young people, girls, boys, men, women.

All unconscious to the fact that she was watching them.

It could become a habit.

She turned to go home feeling detached from the entire human race.

Except one.

Barclay was getting under her skin.

Grant was singing as she put her key in the front door.

They must have won.

Chapter Eight

Though she didn't want to she knew she must summon Barclay again.

But, oh, how neat. It was not she who summoned Barclay but Barclay who presented to her, the very next morning. As though he had guessed at the timing. His mother had been dead for a week but he had gauged precisely the length of time between the event and her knowledge.

The call was put straight through, during the morning meeting, at which she had found herself tongue-tied, unable to voice her suspicion and so isolated from this new warm family circle because she was excluding them from her private thoughts. She had a secret.

Jerome's thin, reedy voice followed the formal enquiry as to whether she would speak to a patient.

She knew it would be Barclay. He would do this, thrust and parry, parry and thrust.

'Doctor Roget.'

She confirmed.

Unnecessarily Barclay introduced himself. Then, 'I don't know whether you know but my poor mother passed away last week.'

The euphemism sounded an affectation.

'One of the nurses here saw the funeral announcement in the paper.' She didn't offer her sympathy. She would not play that game.

'It's next week. Next Thursday.'

He was waiting for her to suggest an appointment.

She fell in. 'Did you want to come in and discuss this?'

'Yes.' Said almost humbly. Was it possible she had been wrong about him – that he was experiencing grief over his mother's death?

'I have a clinic tomorrow, Jerome. Come at three.'

'Thank you, Doctor Roget.'

Again – said humbly.

Rolf looked across, a finger stroking the point of his beard. 'That wasn't who I think it was, was it?'

She nodded.

'What does he *want*?'

'An appointment.'

Kristyna was perched on the arm of Rolf's chair, almost leaning into him. 'Why?'

'I don't know.'

Maybe the looming appointment excused the fact that her ward round that morning was cursory. Perhaps she should have listened harder to what Nancy was saying, hesitated before discharging Kap Oseo, fought Marcus's transfer to an open prison. He was no longer deemed a danger to the community at large or to himself. Her excuse was that her mind was fixed on Barclay, firmly focused on the appointment that stuck out in her mind, like a granite headstone. A psychiatrist who deals habitually with such oddities should not allow his or her mind to be distracted. The results are potentially too dangerous.

Let a tiger out of his cage and see what happens before you recapture him.

She spent a restless night dreaming up all sorts of scenarios. That he would confess to something. Having killed his mother?

Unlikely.

People grow out of personality disorders. We normalise with age. Maybe he was, for the first time, experiencing real grief. But then he was equally likely to try and shock her by telling her he was glad she was dead. Anything really. And this was the trouble. With Barclay, she knew nothing for certain.

And as he sat down opposite her, in neat dark suit and mourning tie, she still didn't know what was going on so she let him take the cue.

'Why did you feel you wanted to see me, Jerome?'

He crossed his legs, treated her to a cold stare. 'I imagined you'd want to know how I'd react to my mother's death.'

'Well?' She returned the coldness. She wasn't going to help him. No clues.

'I was the one who found her, you know.' He spoke excitedly, truculently. Eyes bright, mouth shining wet.

She merely looked enquiringly, with a little lift of the eyebrows. The only way to expose the entrails of Barclay's mind was to affect indifference. Psychopaths hate indifference, boredom. They hate it so much they will do anything to provoke some emotion – anger, fury, anxiety, fear.

'I found her in the morning,' he added, agitated now at her refusal to engage. 'She'd been dead for hours. She was quite cold, you know. My own mother.' He took a sly glance at her from underneath thick, dark lashes.

She put her head to one side in an attitude of concern.

'I tried to wake her but I knew really.' He let the sentence fade away into nothing.

'Jerome, how do you feel about her death?'

'Sad.'

She tried to search into his eyes, to read off what his involvement had been. Had he fed her the pills? Added alcohol to her drink? Contributed, somehow, to her demise and then exulted? Or was she wrong? Had he entered the bedroom to wake her, only to be horrified at her death and then grieve?

She looked long and hard into his eyes and read – nothing.

Did you kill you mother?

His eyes mocked the silent question.

She waited. They both waited but there was nothing more.

She tried to prompt him. 'What will it mean to you?'

He thought about this one, tried to work it out. It took a long time. Minutes ticked past before he spoke. 'Well – I shan't have her at home, to look after me.' He sensed this wasn't good enough. 'I'll miss her company.' He was struggling to find an appropriate response.

'And what will you do now?'

He couldn't resist a smirk.

'Well – she's left everything to me, of course, so I thought I'd sell up.'

'Do you mean the house – everything.'

'Yes.'

'Then what will you do?'

'Maybe travel a bit. That was one of the reasons why I thought I'd better come in and see you.' Accompanied by an innocent stare. 'You don't have any objection to my being out of the country for a while, do you?'

His eyes were frank and open, wide, bland, staring. He was calling her bluff – and she had no other way open to her but to let him go.

He stood up then, taller than she, but not a physically threatening presence – until you read his eyes and the sheer, brittle mockery they held.

She watched the door swing behind him.

Let a tiger out of his cage and see what happens before you recapture him. Only then can you truly know whether he is a man-eater.

Chapter Nine

Afterwards she could recognise that this had been the turning point, the time when Barclay had 'gone underground', stopped playing the part of an errant patient humbly presenting for treatment to a concerned psychiatrist, and started to expose his true colours. The game had changed. The rules had changed. Later she would understand more and even excuse the tangled mess which she misinterpreted, bleating that her attention had been deflected. Events became more complicated – a double helix of characters, a twist of malevolence and intent.

Cynthia Barclay was buried. No more was said.

It was almost a month later, during the pre-Christmas frenzy of shopping, eating, parties and hangovers, this chaos that our lives become to celebrate a Christian feast in the most un-Christian ways. Hangovers and lateness had became the norm so when Kristyna Gale failed to turn up for a Wednesday meeting not one of them turned a hair. In fact later they would remember cringingly that they had smirked at each other as they had waited. Rolf smothered a giggle as he tried her mobile.

'Switched off,' he said when he'd dumped a joky message about 'indulging at the pub last night'.

Only the shorter psychiatric nurse, Dawn, looked concerned. 'Funny she didn't ring in. Not like her.'

'Probably too hung-over.'

Something – not complete enough to be an instinct or an advance warning – made Claire ask an idle question.

'Does she live with a boyfriend?'

'*Girlfriend*,' Rolf said meaningfully. 'Didn't you know she's gay?'

'No.'

'She lives with an older woman called Roxy who works for local government. Roxy was in an unhappy marriage when she and Kristyna kind of hooked up through a gay website and that was it. Roxy left her husband, she and Kristyna moved in together and that, as they say,' said with an expansive wave, 'was that. They've been an item for a couple of years and seem happy.'

Everybody has somebody.

Right on cue the telephone rang.

Rolf reached for it. 'I bet that'll be Kristyna now, mobile battery flat and she's got a puncture.'

There was an inevitable wait while the switchboard put an outside call through then they all heard the voice of panic, of desperation that Rolf was getting a blast of. They watched his face change from concern through deep frown to worried puzzlement and finally settle into lined anxiety. They listened to his suggestion to the person on the phone that maybe she'd crashed out somewhere then a forceful rejoinder – almost a scream – that they all heard perfectly clearly. 'No. Absolutely not.'

'Then – staying with a friend?'

Another vehement denial.

They froze with apprehension. Something bad was happening.

Finally Rolf covered the mouthpiece with his hand. 'Looks like Kristyna's gone missing. I don't suppose -?'

One by one they shook their heads. But there was a variety of possible explanations. Christmas is a time of heightened awareness about personal relationships. An uncertainty can magnify under the contrast of consumer celebration and private evaluation and thought. This is the time when we ponder whether our lives really are as neat and right as they appear for the rest of the year. These were veins of thoughts that ran through Claire's mind.

Nothing sinister. Not then.

But it was the beginning of the nightmare. Wednesday, December the 10th. A date which would grow in significance. A date they would prefer to erase.

Coincidentally or not the following morning's post deliv-
ered a handwritten card from Barclay, addressed 'To all at
Greatbach', postmarked Dijon, with a picture of the mairie
on the front and a jaunty message inside.

'Hi, everyone. Back for Christmas. Having a great time,
Jerome.' And in brackets, '(Barclay – patient)' as though it
was all part of the joke and a P.S. 'Hope you're not worrying about me.'

Claire read it through and realised he had begun to fade
from her mind.

During the last month she had, at last, started to concentrate properly on her job without the distraction of Heidi's
murder. She no longer looked around her office with an
apprehensive stare, obsessively searching for some residue
of the assault. Heidi had been murdered. Gulio, strange
man as he was, was in prison, serving a life sentence for the
crime. Admittedly her personal life was not quite so neat
and tidy. Grant was still at home but she had grown used to
him being there. She would not oust him. Privately she
admitted he suited her. He, the homemaker, she the career
woman. He was happy, humming and decorating the terraced house, planning various projects.

She had bought him a book on decorating for Christmas
and a year's subscription for a magazine about interior
design. She had enrolled him on a day's course with Jocasta
Innes learning about different paint effects.

Secretly she had even begun to scan estate agents' windows and look at more ambitious properties in need of renovation. Maybe after Christmas they would move. It would
make Grant happy. They should make a healthy profit on
this house. They could buy another property, do it up and
sell it. It was the one area Grant found fulfilling. Well then
– let him do it. The night before she had tousled his hair and
dropped a kiss onto the top of his head, stroking his neck
until he had turned and kissed her with a gentle, 'Hey.'

Her tolerance had turned to affection.

Yes – things had changed for the better.

Two days later the police called at Greatbach.

They had heard nothing from Kristyna despite numerous phone calls to both her mobile and her landline. They had connected with a distraught Roxy twice and, dreading this, none of them had rung her. They had their excuses. They had been busy with seasonal admissions. Christmas may be portrayed as a time of family, harmony and happiness but it is a bad time for depressives and the lonely. And there is a group of people who, happy throughout the entire year, have a terrible tether to the Festive season. They are those who have lost a child, a husband, a mother or son during Christmas and the time of year fills them with remembered dread. Every year when the tinsel is hung and the battery Santas start gyrating and singing their tinny carols these people are tipped into depression, suicide and self-harm and the most isolating type of loneliness. After all – the world merrily closes down and shuts its doors on unhappiness so these people congregate wherever a door is propped open: churches, pubs, hospitals.

The police arrived at four o'clock on a dull afternoon. It was Friday, the 12th of December, another date to stand out like March the 17th, the date Heidi had died.

They arrived at an inconvenient time, halfway through Claire's inpatient ward round. She had called in an obstetrician to examine Nancy Gold and he was with her just as a pair of burly shoulders blocked out the light in the little porthole window in the door.

You sense when something looms to darken a room – or a day – or an innocent moment you are not entitled to.

Claire left the obstetrician to attend to the door in an attitude of impatience.

'Yes?'

'Are you Doctor Roget?'

'Yes.'

'I'm a police officer.' He flashed a card. 'Do you mind if

I ask you a few questions about a colleague of yours, Kristyna Gale?'

A pointed glance behind her to emphasise that this was not a good moment.

The policeman was, however, implacable.

'OK,' she said, 'if you can wait – just a few minutes.'

Doctor Crane, the obstetrician, had finished his examination of a very smug Nancy. 'Everything seems to be fine,' he said, putting away the Sonic Aid with which he had broadcast the baby's heartbeat, to the squealing delight of Nancy. 'Is it a boy or a girl?'

Claire's head jerked round. *For you to murder, child-woman?*

The obstetrician was calm. 'I don't know without doing a scan – and there's no indication for that.' He flicked the clasps of his case. 'We don't want to harm the infant.' His blue eyes searched across, found Claire's with a tired acceptance of the world as it is.

Only when they were safely outside the door did he voice his concern, speaking for both of them. 'The baby will have to be made a ward of court,' he said quietly. 'Either Nancy is supervised all the time she is in attendance or the baby is taken away from her at birth.'

Claire felt a flash of sympathy. 'That's a cruel . . .'

'I *heard* that baby's heartbeat,' Doctor Crane said curtly. 'It is a living thing. It has the right to remain so.'

'When is it due?'

'Middle of March, I should say.' He glanced around. 'Best you keep her here until she goes into labour.'

Claire sensed a movement behind her and knew too late that Nancy's curious little face was filling the porthole window.

Doctor Crane walked briskly away up the corridor and Claire turned reluctantly to her side. The policeman was hovering. He flashed the card again at her and this time she read it. Detective Constable Peter Martin. An ordinary looking guy, tall, brown hair, brown eyes, smart jeans, sweat shirt. Nothing remarkable about him except an inherent honesty about his face.

'So – what can I do for you?'

'We're looking into the disappearance of Kristyna Gale.'

'Disappearance?' It seemed too strong a word. 'Has she disappeared?'

'Well, we don't know where she is. I understand she hasn't been seen at work for more than a week and her partner reports her as missing, which is out of character. How would you put it?'

Claire felt her face tighten into a frown. 'Surely there's some other explanation.'

D.C. Martin looked around anxiously. 'Is there somewhere we can talk, a bit more private than a corridor?'

She felt an odd reluctance to admit this policeman to her private office. The taint had only recently been cleansed, the ghost laid to rest. She didn't want him there to resurrect spectres.

There were plenty of visitors' interview rooms spare. She led him to one, small, square, soulless. He didn't seem to notice.

'There are a few pointers,' he said when he had settled into a saggy, vinyl covered armchair, 'which give us cause for concern.

Claire raised her eyebrows politely. 'Such as?'

'Kristyna's mother has M.E.,' D.C.Martin said. 'Kristyna was in the habit of ringing her every day to check how she was. For her not to ring for two nights is most unusual.'

Claire waited.

'Her sister is going through a divorce. She has two small children who are a bit of a handful. Kristyna usually babysits once or twice a week to let her have a night out with friends. Only up the pub. Nothing special. She was due to babysit last night and didn't turn up.'

How little we know about people.

'Roxy, her partner, says she's never ever done this before, gone AWOL. They hadn't had a row or anything. All her clothes except the ones she was wearing – her work clothes – are hanging in the wardrobe. No money has been taken out of her account and her passport's in the drawer. There's been no word from her since Tuesday evening when she left here. You see my point, Doctor Roget. I take it there's been no trouble at work?'

'No – no trouble at all.'

'When did you last see her?'

'I can't remember. Sometime on the Tuesday, I suppose. The first I knew she was missing was when she failed to turn up for the Wednesday morning meeting.'

'And how did she seem on the Tuesday?'

'Normal.'

The policeman looked bored, as though he'd expected something better from her.

She tried. 'She was talking about her Christmas presents, sending off for something for her mum, I think. I can't remember. Have you no clues?'

'Not really. There is one thing that strikes me,' D.C. Martin said. 'I don't know if you remember but Tuesday started off very cold but dry. Later in the day clouds came over and it poured with rain.'

Claire was puzzled. 'So what's that got to do with it?'

'She worked here all day, last seen in the afternoon. Her car was in for service so she'd walked to work, a distance of over two miles. That morning she'd worn a heavy winter coat – not a mac. If she had walked all the way home her coat would have been soaked.'

'So why didn't she ask someone for a lift – or call a taxi?'

'Maybe she did,' D.C. Martin said meaningfully.

Claire worked it out. The police would have contacted local taxi firms. So – a lift.

'Thousands of people go missing every year, don't they,' she said anxiously, searching for some explanation. 'Most of those have not come to a bad end, have they?'

The policeman shook his head. 'Quite the contrary. Most of those people want to disappear, are anxious, in fact, not to be found.'

'Well maybe she found the job, her partner, her mother, her sister . . . maybe she found it all a bit much.'

'Maybe,' said the policeman.

But she knew what she was doing, struggling to convince herself that Kristyna Gale was somewhere, safe and sound and perfectly well. The obstacle was that she wasn't even sure she believed it herself.

D.C. Martin cleared his throat, a sure sign he was about to say something unpalatable. 'You get a feel for these disappearances, Doctor Roget, and I have a bad feeling about this one.' Another scraping of the throat. 'Some very odd people are inpatients here. Outpatients too.'

She believed he was about to mention Barclay and his mother. 'Are you suggesting a patient?'

But he skated away.

'We're exploring all avenues, Doctor,' the policeman said flatly. 'There was a murder here earlier this year and that did turn out to be a patient. Patients and their families frequent this area.'

She felt bound to defend. 'You can't extend the illness of our patients to their families.'

The policeman blinked. 'I can only suggest that you all take extreme care.'

It was on her tongue to mention Barclay. But implicating him in his mother's death was one thing – dragging him forward when a member of staff had gone missing was another. Besides – he was out of the country.

A few hours away.

She said nothing.

D.C. Martin gave her a cue of silence then stood up. 'Well,' he said, 'I'd better be off. Plenty to do. If you do think of anything I'd be grateful if you'd get in touch.' He handed her a card.

'I suppose I ought to warn you. If she doesn't turn up we may decide to stage a reconstruction.'

She bowed her head.

'*One of the outstanding features of patients manifesting severe personality disorder is a pathological degree of attention-seeking behaviour. They will do anything to draw attention to themselves or their deeds – sometimes – whatever the consequences. In fact the conviction itself can be part of the necessary gratification bringing with it public recognition and revulsion.*' One of Heidi's lectures.

That evening Claire searched her car and found it, Barclay's little mark. A small splash of acid on the front of her car. Dead centre of the bonnet. It had not been there when she had driven into work.

The nightmare had returned from his holiday.

Chapter Ten

The temptation was to involve D.C. Martin in her suspicions but Barclay was clever enough to cover his tracks. Besides – what if she was wrong? About everything? What if Kristyna was still alive? And Gulio, Heidi's killer? What if Barclay had nothing to do with Kristyna's disappearance and that she really had tired of her commitments and deliberately vanished? What if her own instincts, that Barclay was hovering in the background, were misleading her?

What if this was obsession?

But she couldn't silence the quiet voice that warned her insistently that Jerome's danger was that he was both elusive and clever. He was capable of outsmarting her, leaving her with nothing concrete, only these vague shadows which disappeared when you turned on the light. She was annoyed with herself. She – of all people – should know how dangerous were these formless suspicions. She only had to talk to Kap Oseo to know that they could chain you into a corner and leave you there without the power ever to come out. They could form a barrier between you and the rest of the world. The mind is all powerful. There is only one way out – to turn around and face these suspicions. Say Boo to the bogeyman. Otherwise like Mavis Abiloney her fears not faced and dealt with firmly would grow bigger and bigger until they swallowed her up.

If anything did lie behind her suspicions it was up to her alone to turn them into hard evidence if *Jerome was guilty* in the first place.

And if he was not – if all in the happy valley of Greatbach was as it should be – she should preserve her sanity and disengage from his game.

So she bided her time.

But Kristyna did not turn up so the week before Christmas, on one of the busiest shopping Fridays of the year, when damp snow sat in the clouds and threatened to tumble right into the bright warmth of the festive shops, the police staged their reconstruction.

They all hung out of the window and watched the girl who was pretending to be Kristyna, their friend and colleague, stride across the quadrangle, in a long camel coat, chased by cameramen pushing cameras on wheels, technicians dangling huge, fluffy microphones and a cluster of local press.

It was unnerving, Claire thought, how convincing these reconstructions were. By squeezing her eyes almost shut she could convince herself it really was Kristyna crossing the quad. The missing nurse had come back. Flanked by Siôna and Rolf she pressed against the glass and watched the Kristyna lookalike in the long coat, hands thrust deep into pockets, bag slung across her shoulder, walking briskly, with the measured wide steps and firm conviction of someone who knew exactly where she was going as she had passed through the hospital gates.

Had she? Claire leaned forward eagerly, wanting to find the answer.

Kristyna Gale had stepped out of Greatbach into oblivion. The question was: had she known where she was going or was this scene being played out in front of her eyes merely illusion, a blind guess by her doppelgänger?

Was the truth something else? Had there been another, secret, Kristyna, a life behind her life, a clandestine lover, friend or admirer waiting for her to step into some new existence, one without all the encumbrances, lover, mother, sister all with their demands?

Claire watched and guessed again. Had she stepped outside the gates and entered a completely different scenario – a dangerous one – kidnapper, malicious patient, sadistic killer or rapist waiting to snatch her?

Jerome?

Was she dead or alive? Claire found that her fists were

clenched, her head hard against the window frame.

Was Kristyna free or a prisoner?

Happy or sad?

Reflective or relieved or beyond feelings altogether?

Claire turned from the window restlessly.

Why did she continue to sense Jerome Barclay behind this? Why did she feel the same cold fright that she had felt when she had first entered the room where Heidi Faro had been butchered months before?

Obsession, whispered the voice.

What was going on here with Greatbach at its epicentre? Faces rolled past her eyes, staff and patients alike. All strange.

Rolf was watching the Kristyna-girl too, his hand poised beneath his chin, almost touching his pointed little beard, his eyes heavy and unreadable. Sad. The word slid into her mind as she looked at him then slid straight out again as though it should not have been there in the first place.

She continued to watch him. Did he know something? Any more than she did? Or did he *think* he understood? He had known Kristyna for years longer than she had.

A vignette formed in her mind: Kristyna, legs astride, cargo-pants, bangles jangling, tiny gold stud in her nose catching the light with a cool, yellow glow, the skin as smooth as the surface of a pebble, polished by the sea. Her gaze moved around the room.

They all knew Kristyna better than she did as they had known Heidi Faro too. Not as an adoring pupil in the front row of the lecture theatre but as a colleague – a friend – an intimate. In this new light she studied everyone in the room in turn and sensed that they all had something they were happy to conceal.

Siôna spoke for them all. Angrily. 'Where the bloody hell is she? Where's she got to?'

He spoke as though it was all Kristyna's fault.

No one responded to his outburst. Each person merely looked embarrassed, as though it was something they might all have thought but no one would have spoken aloud.

The reconstruction with its unsatisfactory ending of the camel coat whisking through the gates cast a dampener over the entire day even more acute than usual. It seemed to put a formality, a finality on Kristyna's vanishment.

But now there was work to do. They must address the issue of Mavis Abiloney spending Christmas at home. Her worried daughter had made an appointment to speak to her. She was an interesting woman, in her early forties with a hefty frame, well-applied strong makeup and a confident manner. One would have thought the diametric opposite of her mother. And yet . . .

'I'm a teacher at the Special School in the Meir,' she said. 'I work full-time. My husband and I split up eight years ago. I have a daughter of sixteen.'

She met Claire's eyes with a searing boldness. 'My mother can't stay in here for the rest of her life,' she said formally. 'And I don't really want her to come and live with me. Much as I'm fond of her I have my own life to lead.'

Claire supplied the alternative. 'Which leaves her home.'

Beatrice Harvey gave a long sigh. 'And we all know what happens if my mother goes home. Within hours – or at least days – she's back in here.'

'Well —'

Beatrice Harvey gave a sigh. 'I hope you don't believe her fables about my father being violent.'

Claire gaped.

Beatrice Harvey continued. 'She simply says it to excuse her behaviour. The truth of the matter is that she's institutionalised. But I don't know how to cure her.'

'What does your father think?'

Another sigh. 'Poor Dad,' Beatrice said. 'He always starts off really wanting it to work but within hours he gets frustrated. She can be difficult, you know. Dad's always had a short fuse. He can't stand it. He does shout. And then.' Part of her confidence began to crumble. 'I do want Mum home for Christmas but I don't see . . .'

'You live close by,' Claire stated. 'Is there any chance you could stay with your parents – and your daughter of course – for the two days – just to try and keep things on an even keel? It might even be the starting point of rehabilitating your mother. Otherwise she'll have to be discharged eventually to some sort of halfway house which won't really help her. It really isn't in Government Directives for us to keep patients like your mother as an inpatient. She doesn't fulfil any of the criteria.'

'It's keeping her alive, 'Beatrice argued sharply. 'Surely that fulfils a Government Directive?'

Claire knew better than to argue.

Kap Oseo was also fit for discharge. His family were coming to collect him. Wife, son, daughter, son-in-law. Eight people had crammed the tiny interview room as Claire, Rolf and Siôna talked to them about emergency numbers, duty psychiatrists and restraint. As one they nodded their heads solemnly, accepted responsibility and signed the discharge forms. Kap looked dubious as she shook his hand, wished him well and handed him the outpatients' card for early in the New Year.

Claire did her final Christmas shopping on December the 20th, Suicide Saturday, with her festive spirit replaced by irritability, and returned from the shops to an empty house. Grant had gone to visit his parents. She went to bed early, tired yet anxious she would not sleep. She woke at 3 am, in a sweat, from a dream which had been so vivid she sat up, convinced it was the truth.

Christmas morning, waking up with an instinct to destroy. Tiptoeing to Adam's room and watching him sleep. A sour Christmas Day, she sitting alone in the corner, opening her presents unobserved while they fussed over Adam. An over-whelming feeling of jealousy and hatred that poisoned her.

She sat up in bed, hugging her knees and remembering.

She slept again only to find other monsters in her dreams.

An insubstantial woman who melted through the closed doors of Greatbach. Kristyna in her camel coat, hands thrust into pockets, her shoulderbag swinging, like a pendulum. Tick tock. Making the noise of a metronome set by a strict piano teacher. Claire tried to catch up with the girl in the camel coat, to walk with her and ask her where she had been but Kristyna, as people often are in dreams, was always one or two steps ahead, not even turning around to acknowledge Claire's calls, as though she was stone deaf.

Head down, hands deep in pockets, striding like a man, Claire could only see her back view and – occasionally when she turned – her profile and the bag swinging. Tick tock. Tied by invisible rope they walked in tandem through the city, as Claire had on that strange night, a few months ago, passing windows and derelict factories, bottle-kilns, lighted shops, health clubs, the noise punctuated by car doors slamming around them.

Claire hurried but she never caught up. Was never close enough to touch Kristyna. So finally they were in a car park, the one near the theatre, both walking towards her car, which was parked crookedly, she a few paces behind when she noticed acid bubbling on the bonnet, like a witches' brew. She drew close enough to feel the bubbled paintwork beneath her fingertips, Kristyna, somehow, now behind her. Then the car door was flung open and Jerome Barclay peered up at the pair of them from the driver's seat, arms casually wrapped around the steering wheel. 'Well, hello,' he said. 'Hello. You've been ages. I've been waiting.'

As she had known he had. She sat up with certain knowledge. Words were needling her mind, puncturing holes into her consciousness.

Need for stimulation. One of the ten commandments of

personality disorder. She knew how Barclay achieved it.

He had a need to frighten people. So what was he planning next?

All day Sunday she was distracted, unable to concentrate on the Sunday papers. Feeling she should do something but not knowing what. When Grant returned in the early evening she was hugely glad to see him and stood, in the kitchen, drinking white wine, leaning against the units and for the first time ever she began to confide in him. He listened quietly, cooking a meal of pasta and chicken, fresh basil and a plate of tomatoes and onions drowning in balsamic vinegar. As she spoke she was aware what an irrevocable step this was. She never had shared confidences with Grant before but she had a need to talk to someone she could trust. Someone away from Greatbach.

Eventually he put the food on the plate, carried it through to the dining room and they ate.

'I think,' he said, chewing his dinner slowly, 'that you should speak to the police.'

'But — ' she started to object.

He put his fork down. 'If you're so sure, Claire,' he said, unsmiling. She was grateful he had recognised the seriousness of what she was saying. 'After all – you're the psychiatrist, trained to recognise psychopathic personalities. 'If you think he's a danger.'

'It's just that he mentioned *her*, in particular.'

She put her knife and fork down too. 'It's no good, Grant. There isn't anything specific to go on. I've no evidence. The police can't *do* anything.'

'But I thought . . .'

'It's a grey area, Grant.' She hesitated. 'If I *knew* one solid fact I'd act. I really would. But . . .'

He carried on eating his meal.

Chapter Eleven

But she did nothing.

Christmas was an anticlimax, the presents not enough of a distraction from the fact that Kristyna had not turned up. And as time went on not one of them believed she ever would – alive. Each one tucked away their conviction and said nothing to each other, which made them isolated and stilted. Their morning meetings had become increasingly strained and the camaraderie had melted away, leaving them uncomfortable colleagues. It was as though a hard lump of ice sat in the middle of the room, chilling them all.

There was a tangible edge to add to the disappearance. Roxy had been haunting the outside of Greatbach, like the heroine of a tragic Russian novel, a headscarf wrapping her face against the sharp Easterly winds and flurries of snow which rained in on the exposed site. She would catch each of them in turn, by the sleeve, begging them to tell her if they knew anything. Anything . . .

At first Claire had not recognised her but Roxy had introduced herself and over the weeks she had become a tragic figure they all avoided, even leaving the hospital through the kitchen exit so they didn't have to run the gauntlet of that ravaged face with its raw hurt.

Which reminded them they had no answers to offer her.

Besides – none of them knew that Kristyna hadn't simply tired of her commitments.

All the staff except the ward nurses had had two days off to celebrate the festive period and many of the inpatients had been allowed home but even on Christmas Day Claire could not help wondering where Kristyna was, what had happened to her, and riding on the back of that where Barclay was and what he was doing. Because like locating a shark by its fin in the water he was at his most unnerving when he was invisible.

So for them all there was a terrible unfinished feeling to the entire festive season. Not helped by the fact that privately Claire wondered whether they would ever know what had happened.

They returned to work on Monday the 29th of December.

Nature, we are told, abhors a vacuum.

Therefore one imagines that a void must always be filled.

Not true.

Emotional voids spread to form uncrossable chasms, growing deeper, wider, darker, by the day.

After the Christmas break a new trend developed. Starting with Dawn, staff began to avoid the morning meetings. The numbers dwindled from eight to seven – to six – to five and finally to Claire, Siôna and Rolf. People made excuses but the real reason was the awkwardness that stifled conversation. You cannot constantly skirt round the main topic occupying your mind. It is not possible. By Freudian slips, accidental words and unconscious gestures everyone knows what everyone else is thinking. You are united but you cannot mention what unites you.

No one sat on Kristyna's chair. So it was left, empty as a grave plot, silently protesting while each time Claire even glanced at it she was distracted with the last sighting she had had of the psychiatric nurse, perched on the arm of the chair, leaning across and grooming Rolf's hair.

So she waited.

Although he had no follow-up appointment she knew Barclay would be in touch. He had to keep the attention on himself. If her assumptions about him were correct he must have some contact to keep her under his influence.

She was right.

But in the meantime there were endless visits from the police and during one of those she caught the name Young,

Sergeant Young, the police officer she had spoken to briefly after Cynthia Barclay's death.

Two days later she met him.

He turned out to be a stolid, slightly plump, Stoke man of around thirty. His questions were routine, predictable, unimaginative, almost irrelevant, dealing with Kristyna's last few days at work, lists of patients she had seen. The name Jerome Barclay didn't crop up. Sergeant Young had no original ideas, no answers. She eyed the policeman across the staff room and decided not to mention Barclay – yet. The time would come. But it confirmed her suspicions that Cynthia Barclay's death *could* have been suspicious, the police naively unsuspecting. Barclay could still be getting away with murder.

She sat and puzzled over this. She had always assumed the police were naturally suspicious beings, questioning seemingly innocent statements and delving into people's past. Instead the opposite seemed the case. They accepted alibis and statements, failed to investigate properly. She was disappointed.

Barclay loved to do the unexpected, to appear like Houdini. He caught her unawares by not making an appointment. He simply turned up at one of her outpatient clinics and demanded from the receptionist that he see her. She heard his voice outside, unusually raised. (*Was he losing control?*). She moved towards the door, pulled it open a fraction and caught part of the conversation.

'It'll be on your head . . .'

'I shall make a complaint . . .'

The high-pitched voice of the receptionist protested weakly and Barclay pressed home his point.

'Look. I have a mental condition. You go in there and ask Doctor Roget if she wants to risk not seeing me. Go on. You go in there and ask her.'

Claire opened the door wide. 'It's OK, Sophie,' she said.

'I'll see him.'

And to Barclay, 'You have ten minutes, Jerome, to explain just what is so urgent. Then I shall have to get on with my clinic.'

Firm control. That was the key. That and to be unemotional. Don't waver or let them manipulate you, rattle you, or get you on the hop.

Stay in control.

Heidi's words.

She closed the door behind him, waited for him to sit down, settled into her chair, dated a fresh sheet of paper for his notes, gripped a pen – and waited, her gaze square on him.

'I read in the paper,' he began carelessly, 'about Kristyna Gale.'

She offered him nothing.

He licked his lips, smiled just a little. 'You don't like me much, do you, Doctor Roget?'

She leaned forward then, across the desk, her elbow on his folder, her hand lightly on her cheek. 'Get this straight, Barclay,' she said. 'I'm a doctor. A psychiatrist. I have a job to do – to treat the problems you have merging with society. It isn't part of my remit to either like you or dislike you. In actual fact I feel neither emotion.'

He chewed his lip at that. 'Liar,' he muttered.

She let it pass.

'What if I told you I think something's happened to Kristyna? Something awful.'

'I would ask you what evidence you had.'

She tried to forget that in her estimation he was responsible.

She tried to forget what had happened to Heidi.

It would not help her.

He met her eyes boldly, his mouth open, his tongue dry and rasping over his lips. She caught his scent, a cigarette, Lynx deodorant, toothpaste and chewing gum mixed with something chemical. Maybe the acid he marked her car with. There was a stain on his thumb.

'If I said a feeling – a strong feeling.'

'I would suggest you stop playing games with me, Jerome, and tell me what you know. If anything. Tell me if you do know something why you've come to me and not to the police. We have limited time so don't waste it.'

Now wait for it. He would want to puncture her adult control, impress her, catch and keep her attention. But how far would he go?

'You were a bit suspicious about my mum's death, weren't you?'

So this was how he would play it, prick her with a tiny lance, the picador of the bullring and she the bull, meant to become fierce and careless. To the death.

Well she wasn't playing.

'I did speak to the police,' she admitted. 'They told me your mother's death was not being treated as suspicious.'

'Oooh,' he sneered, mocking her admission.

She retained her role as doctor/patient. 'So stop playing around with me and tell me whether you know anything about Kristyna's disappearance or not.'

He leaned back, folded his arms, crossed his ankles, stared at his shoes. 'Do you know why I keep coming here?'

I think I do.

'You – and Heidi – and Kristyna. You are all a challenge. Difficult to break.' His voice was quiet, but she was not scared. All of this could have been anticipated.

Barclay observed her for a moment, his face perfectly impassive.

What lay beneath that bland exterior, that smooth skin, those pale, odd eyes, that pink mouth?

Suddenly her overwhelming emotion was that she was glad that she was in the outpatient department and not in her own office. She knew her eyes would have betrayed her by wandering around the room, that she would have searched out and stuck to the spots where they both knew Heidi's blood had spilt. And she knew her fingers would have grazed the underside of her desk, felt the tiny patches of dried blood.

And he would have known.

Instead she was here.

Chloe was on the outside with a row of waiting patients, the psychiatric nurses, a couple of porters. All within shouting distance.

He knew that too.

As he studied his fingernails. 'A shame about poor old Heidi.'

He looked up at her.

'What are you saying, Jerome?'

'And as for Kristyna . . .' He left the sentence dangling dangerously like a live cable which has been severed, sparking and jerking.

'Have you ever thought,' he said next, 'how much destruction a body can take.' He stood up, splayed his hands across the desk. 'What fire can do?'

For her to stand up too would be to acknowledge she found this disparity uncomfortable.

He whispered his next sentence. 'Bones splinter. Jewellery melts. Nothing left but the underwires of her bra.' His eyes dropped deliberately to her bust-line. As though he had X-ray sight the underwires of her bra seemed to grow hot.

He sauntered out then and she knew he had won this first round while she had learned nothing except that *she* was in his sights now.

Should she tell the police?

Yes. This was the point at which she was justified.

She did ring the defence union, explain the facts surrounding Heidi's death and that Barclay's mother too had died, also that one of the nurses had vanished just before Christmas and now one of the most disturbing patients was dropping hints.

'They may help the police,' she pointed out and the lawyer employed by the defence union could not help but agree.

Rolf was in clinic in the next room. She waited until his patient had left the room, knocked and walked in. He gave her a warm smile. One of the warmest she had seen on his face for days.

'You look worried,' he said. 'What's up?'

She flopped into the 'patient's' chair. 'Only Barclay gate-crashing my outpatient clinic to make the same sort of threats he used to make to his ex-girlfriend.'

'How do you know his ex-girlfriend?'

'I chased her up,' she admitted. 'He worried me – right from the first – so I thought I'd find out a bit more about him.'

'And did you?'

'Oh yes,' she sighed, 'but I almost wish I hadn't. He's an unsavoury character, a danger. And yet I have so little to go on to get him Sectioned. It's all in my mind, Rolf.'

He touched her arm then and she was reminded of one of the last meetings when they had all been together and him stroking Kristyna's arm. It seemed a friendly gesture – as though he was singling her out for friendship – rather than sexual.

'What sort of threats?' he asked.

'Oh – Barclay, you mean? He has this thing about fire destroying bodies, bones splintering, underwires – nothing left but teeth etcetera etcetera.'

'He does? Now that's interesting-'

She grinned across at him. 'Well, I'm glad you find it so,' she said. 'Because I find it alternatively intimidating and downright frightening.' She stood up. 'But I feel better for having chatted about it. Thanks, Rolf.'

'Any time,' he said.

As she reached the door she paused. 'I spoke to the Defence Union,' she said. 'I think I will have a word with the police. As a sort of insurance policy.'

'Good idea,' he said.

* * *

So Claire spoke to D.C. Martin and this time held nothing back. The acid attacks, Heidi's death, the death of Cynthia Barclay and finally Barclay's hints on Kristyna's disappearance.

Martin listened for a while then asked some questions about Jerome Barclay's condition without comprehension.

'Just what are you saying?'

'I'm saying he is a psychopath,' she said. 'I'm saying he is capable of committing crime and feeling no remorse – no pity. I'm saying he is clever and should be watched, that his idea of fun is to unnerve people, make them frightened, control them. I'm saying that it is possible he abducted Kristyna Gale. I'm telling you he is capable of it.'

'And you really think?'

She knew what he was building up to saying. 'I did believe he killed Heidi Faro. Now I'm not so sure. I met Gulio. Maybe I didn't see him as a killer but it's possible. I don't know how thorough your original investigation was – whether there's room for doubt. Whether my patient, Jerome Barclay, was even on the premises at the time of Doctor Faro's murder.'

'As far as I remember,' D C Martin said slowly, 'there isn't any record of someone called Barclay being questioned or in the vicinity of the assault.'

'We don't like re-opening cases,' he added. 'Makes a lot of extra work. Causes no end of trouble. But I can look into things if you like.'

She left the sentence dangling.

She needed someone of higher rank than a Detective Constable.

Chapter Twelve

There were other events to absorb her mind. Mavis Abiloney had spent a successful Christmas with her husband, daughter and granddaughter and Claire felt it was time for her to be discharged. She spent time preparing Mavis and watched the woman gradually come to terms with the fact that she could not stay at Greatbach for ever. She must pick up the strands of her life. But as she talked to the middle-aged woman she watched a spasm of fear tighten her face. She called in Karl Abiloney.

He was a small man, no more than 5 feet 4 inches tall, with dyed black hair slicked back from his face, a swarthy complexion and over-large hands with stumpy, out-of-proportion fingers. He was slim and wiry-looking with an accent she found hard to trace. From Mavis's records she knew he was an electrician.

He seemed genuinely concerned about his wife's condition. 'I can't understand it, doctor,' he said worriedly. 'I never have raised a finger towards my wife. I am fond of her but when she comes home from here she seems always to accuse me of all sorts of things. I am upset. I defend myself. We argue. I shout. I don't deny that. But almost the next thing I know is that she is back in the hospital threatening death again.'

It was hard not to feel some sympathy for the man. Looking at the situation from his point of view he hadn't had much of a married life and yet Claire knew he was not strictly speaking the whole truth. A few times on re-admission Mavis had displayed bruises on her chest, her upper legs, back and bottom. They had got there somehow. There had been no explanation from either daughter or husband and the bruises had been puzzled over but no explanation found. Yet she did not believe Karl Abiloney was violent towards his wife. It was more probable that she had inflicted self-harm. Heidi had concentrated on the repeated suicide attempts and glossed over the cause, a fatal omission, Claire thought smugly. More evidence that her idol had had feet of clay.

She decided to try herself. 'Mr Abiloney,' she began. 'When Mavis has returned to us she has, at times, displayed some bruising.' He was watching her very warily, keeping as still as a cat.

'She's not able to explain how she came by them. Have you any idea?'

'She is – clumsy.' He waved his big hands. 'She has a drink. She falls. She does not always remember things.'

'Are you saying that when at home Mavis drinks excessive amounts of alcohol? That she falls because she is drunk?'

He defended her. 'Not drunk,' he said.

She waited for further explanation.

He answered obliquely. 'My wife,' he said sedately, 'has had a very strange life.'

There had been little focus of Mavis's history in her notes. 'Tell me more, Mr Abiloney.'

He folded the big hands away. 'She comes from a country background. Somewhere in West Wales. Far away. Her father was a farm labourer. They had not much money. Mavis told me she was isolated as a child, that she was frequently in trouble with her father and punished for her misdemeanours. When she misbehaved she was made to sleep in the cowshed with the cows and the rats and mice. She was told she was not fit to come in the house. Naturally she then got dirty, even more of an animal, and even less was able to live in the family house. When she was fifteen she became pregnant. She never told me who was the father. I have my suspicions but,' he shrugged, 'who can tell? Who can be sure what has happened in someone's life before you knew them and were a part of that life yourself. It is not right to point the finger.'

'Quite. And Mavis's mother?'

'She does not mention her. I think she did not know her – ever.'

'And you, Mr Abiloney, what about you?'

'I am from a small island in the Pacific,' he said. 'I too have had an isolated life away from twentieth century living but thankfully, unlike my wife, not a cruel upbringing. I came to England when I was seventeen and learned my trade.' His face was sweating.

'We were married when I was twenty-one years old. Unfortunately, Doctor Roget, when we leave a country we do not leave the past behind. We take it with us. Mavis was fine for a small while before the wedding but once we were married she seemed to fear I would change, in a bad way. And she has not stopped expecting that. Into what I do not know. Maybe into her father. Maybe we should separate but where would she go? It is not me who is the problem, Doctor. It is Mavis herself. Something inside herself. I think she will not be cured. Not ever.'

'How much is she drinking?'

'Some,' he said warily. 'I do not know the exact amount.'

'Than maybe you should have no alcohol in the house,' Claire suggested. 'Or pills. After discharge I'll see her every week for a period of time then every fortnight and so on. We'll arrange therapy for her and hopefully bring around a change or at least some stability.'

Karl Abiloney stood up. 'I don't mind to have her home,' he said wearily. 'I do understand about cuts in the Health Service. All this is okay but . . .' He stopped mid sentence. 'I'll be honest with you, Doctor. I don't even mind if she were to die because . . .' Again he stopped. 'Because really we have had no life. I have a fine daughter. I have a job I understand. I have a home. When I left my island at sixteen I was full of all sorts of dreams but now I am not. Love, money, success, status. One by one each little dream has disappeared. I have no dream left now except to find warmth, food, peace. And to be frank I could have had that back on my island home. I'm happy to have Mavis back,' he said again, 'but I would not want her to die in this miserable way of suicide, trying to escape imaginary threats. It has not been a good life. Not for her; not for me.'

'Two weeks,' Claire said, extending her hand. 'We must prepare her. Then she'll be home with you.'

Karl Abiloney walked to the door then turned around. 'You will not win,' he said – almost pityingly.

January passed slowly as January invariably does. Six weeks between pay-days and the hype of Christmas gone like a pricked balloon with almost no difference except huge credit card bills. Claire opened hers and winced. Surely she couldn't have spent that much? It seemed part of the post-Christmas gloom that there was still no sign of Kristyna.

All through the entire month Claire had a feeling of impending doom, as though something terrible was about to happen and how ever much she analysed the sensation she was unable to decide on the cause. Adding to the panic this engendered was that she wondered whether the root of the feeling was caused by waiting for Barclay to make the next move, like a very tense game of chess. Or it might simply be waiting for inevitable bad news of Kristyna. Then there was the responsibility of the new job and difficult decisions to be made and stood by. She was not short of areas which could make her stressed and nervous and she knew from experience it was worse not to know from where the threat came.

Some of the time she acknowledged to herself that they may never know what had happened to Kristyna.

It didn't help that Nancy Gold was wandering the corridors patting her stomach and looking increasingly secretive and self-satisfied. Claire sat in the room with her one day and asked her questions.

'I expect you're very excited about the baby,' she began. Nancy hummed her signature tune, her face turned towards the floor but her eyes were watchful and her shoulders tensed, a kitten ready to spring.

'It won't be long now,' Claire commented.

Nancy seemed to shrink back into the chair, trying to make herself invisible. Her arms folded tighter around her stomach. The humming stopped.

'Nancy, you know that your last baby died?'

One last sobbing cry. 'I'll look after this baby,' she whispered. 'I promise I will. Keep its life.'

Claire wanted to believe her.

'Nancy we can't take the risk. Someone will have to stay with you. You can't be alone with the baby.'

Nancy started humming again. 'I don't need anyone.' This time she spoke fiercely. 'I don't need *anyone*. I don't *want* anyone.'

'She'll help you.'

'Aagh agh.' A vigorous refusal.

It was something else to worry about.

To add to all these worries Kap Oseo had missed his outpatient appointment and telephone calls to his home number had provoked no response. He could be away, staying with relatives, but Claire had tried numerous times, day and night, and it was something else to rock her equilibrium.

Marcus Bourne had been transferred to another unit and from reports she knew he was becoming increasingly withdrawn and depressed.

Only Harry Sowerby appeared to be toeing the line, turning up early for each appointment, a fixed smile on his face. And his blood levels proved he was complying with the medication.

Sometimes the job can be too heavy a burden. One cannot solve the problems of the world. Increasingly she turned to Grant as solace for the job. Bravely they put the house on the market and cast around for somewhere else to renovate. Grant was ecstatic. He kept hugging her and talking about ideas, colour schemes and plumbing. She gave him Karl Abiloney's card to keep. They may well need a good electrician and he had struck her as just that.

January is such a glum month.

Gradually the waters closed over Kristyna and by the end of the month even Roxy had stopped haunting the front gates of Greatbach. It was beginning to seem as though the nurse had never really existed. Rolf had moved the chairs around and now sat in the soft, squashy affair that Kristyna had used while Siôna had changed to Rolf's old chair. The entire room had been rearranged with the coffee table now against the wall. All was different. And from the police she heard nothing.

Then on the very last day of January two things happened.

The first was that someone – they never did find out who – pinned up a photograph of Kristyna Gale. Resplendent in leather mini skirt, leaning across a bar towards the photographer – wearing spiky black mascara and odd plum-coloured lipstick, her hair in asymmetrical bunches which stuck out like a St. Trinians' schoolgirl.

The second incident was that she found herself talking for a long time to Rolf Fairweather.

The photograph sparked it off. She walked into the staff room one lunchtime and found him peering at it. She approached it too and then she saw that his face was haggard and would have sworn his eyes were bright with unshed tears. Instinctively she put a comforting hand on his shoulder. He started then passed a hand across his eyes.

'Sorry,' he said. 'I was miles away.'

She thought he would say he had pinned the photo up but he didn't. Instead he wondered when and where the picture had been taken. 'She looks super-tarted up,' he commented. 'On the pull. It must have been before her lesbian days. She'd have sparked off too much hetero-attention like this.'

'What do you think's happened to her?' It was the question they'd all asked themselves countless times.

He sat down, his eyes focused far away, 'It could be, Claire, that she was abducted and murdered on her way home that night and it could just as easily be that she'd had enough of her life and wanted out or even that she had a secret lover and simply wanted to be with him or her.' A tinge of humour softened his face. 'See how little we know.'

'We *need* to know,' she said, suddenly realising it herself. 'We need to be able to draw a line under this experience and move on. Otherwise —'

'Yes, Dawn and Bec will crack. And what with Heidi's murder last year I wouldn't take bets on the rest of us either. Greatbach depends on us all, the team, our functioning properly. It'll fall apart if something doesn't happen.'

The worst was she knew he was right.

This then was the waiting period. The calm before what they all knew would be a catastrophic storm.

Ominously Barclay stayed silent and invisible. And there was nothing they could all do except wait.

There is much discussion of how sensitive humans still are after centuries of urban living. It is an uneasy thought that our instincts have been bred out of our inherent character. Yet maybe they have not vanished but changed into something else. Another warning system which utilises other factors.

Certainly when Claire woke on Monday the 2nd of February with a wrong feeling she lay without moving and wondered what it was. Like Scrooge, she toyed with the idea that it was possibly the result of a bad meal last night. Still sleepy she smiled. Cottage pie and mushy peas were not responsible for this. It was something else. Not a dream this time. She must look elsewhere. Afterwards she would search her mind before attributing it to a sharp, icy stillness. But that was wrong too. So maybe it was this evolved instinct.

Even before she opened her eyes she knew that something was amiss.

She turned her head to the side.

Grant was asleep, an arm flung across her. He grunted and smiled in his sleep. She lay and studied the ceiling. It was still dark with the first glimmer of a light outside the curtains, visible where they failed to meet. She sat upright, pushed Grant's arm away, showered quickly and while pulling her clothes on drew the curtains back and looked out of the window. That was when she noticed that her car door was not quite shut. The interior light was on. Dimmed but shining.

Her first thought was prosaic – she would have a flat battery.

Her second thought was that she'd locked her car door last night.

Running downstairs, buttoning her blouse, she rationalised.

Perhaps Grant had wanted something out of her car and pushed the door to without properly locking it and it had wafted open.

By the time she reached the bottom stair she had already worked out that the thing Grant would have wanted would have been their current favourite CD, a moody work by The Beautiful South.

So she shouted up to him. 'What did you want from my car last night? You left the door open, you . . .'

He appeared at the top of the stairs. 'No I didn't. I never went near your car.'

By this time she was running towards it, *knowing* she had locked it firmly. If not Grant, who?

She pulled the door wide open.

On the seat, neatly folded, was a camel hair coat.

Chapter Thirteen

Time stretched.

She seemed to stand there for hours, staring at the coat, noting over and over again the fact that it had been so very neatly folded and placed on her seat so carefully.

She sensed Grant beside her. Heard him speak, puzzled, looking to her for explanation. 'Claire?'

Slowly she turned around. 'It's Kristyna's coat.'

Then he too entered that elongated timezone to stand by her side, stare at the coat, note, like her, that it was displayed neatly enough for a ladies' dress shop. Neither of them stretched out a hand to touch it. They simply stared, both knowing that this was evidence. Grant spoke softly, in dream words. 'We – should – tell – someone.'

She still didn't move and after a further pause he turned around, walked slowly towards the house, disappeared inside and returned, carrying the phone. He pressed the dial and spoke one word into it. 'Police.'

Only when a squad car came screaming around the corner did time re-enter the normal zone.

The police were wonderful.

It is a cliché, but they were. Around in minutes, cordoning off the area. Taking charge competently, speaking into walkie talkies, looking business-like while a dazed Claire fed them the facts.

'My colleague. She vanished a few weeks ago. I think this is her coat.'

Knowing, all the time, that HE was playing games with her, spinning her around like a wooden top until she was so dizzy she would soon topple.

The police took it all perfectly seriously.

One of them detached from the rest to introduce himself as Detective Inspector Paul Frank. He was a no-nonsense forty-year-old, deadly serious, with grey-streaked hair.

'Doctor Roget,' he said, his eyes not on her but on the cordoning off of the vehicle behind her. 'Pleased to meet you.' A firm, reassuring handshake. 'I've heard about you from both Sergeant Young and Constable Martin. ' His eyes searched out the coat. 'This is an unlikely turn of events.'

She nodded. Shock had made her cold and clammy. Somehow instead of the suit jacket she was wearing one of Grant's thick, huge sweaters. She didn't remember putting it on.

Inspector Frank must have noticed her shivering. 'Would you prefer to go indoors?'

She nodded and they trooped inside.

The warmth of the kitchen was welcome after the damp chill of the bleak, February morning, dank, grey and now threatening.

'I must ring work, tell them I'll be late.'

Grant's hand was on her arm, restraining. 'I've already done it', he said. 'I told them there was a problem with your car.'

She concentrated back on the policeman. 'What will you do now?'

'We'll be examining the car and sending the coat for forensics.'

'What will you look for?'

He knew she knew.

'Trace evidence, hair, skin cells, blood. Evidence as to whether the coat really was Kristyna's, how it got there, who put it there. When. How.' His eyes regarded her steadily. Blue-grey with dark rims around the irises. It gave him the look of a man of mystery. 'And if it is Kristyna's whether there are any marks on it that indicate what has happened to her.'

She concentrated hard on the simple. 'How did they get into the car? I know I locked it. I remember.'

He dismissed the action with an abrupt jerk of his head. 'It's not that difficult. They just get a skeleton key, a piece of wire. A scanner.' He stopped talking for a moment then changed tack completely. 'Tell me, Doctor Roget, do you think this has any wider connection with Greatbach?'

She nodded.

She thought he would pursue the subject immediately but he didn't. She would learn he was not an impatient man. Instead he contented himself with a comment.

'I was the senior investigating officer over your colleague's death,' he said, 'Doctor Faro. And Sergeant Young tells me you were asking questions about the death of the mother of one of your patients?'

Again she nodded.

'Then we had the disappearance of Kristyna Gale. And now this.'

He waited before making the comment. 'A sequence of occurrences, don't you agree?'

The kettle was boiling. She didn't remember filling it and switching it on but made coffee anyway.

The Inspector accepted it. 'I take it you believe these occurrences are connected.'

He was watching her. 'And I suspect you have an idea that just one person could be responsible.' He sipped his coffee, licked a drop from his lips. His eyes found her again. 'And as Gulio is currently incarcerated I also imagine you have your doubts we got the right man in the first place.'

'He can have had nothing to do with Kristyna's disappearance.'

'True.' He waited for her to volunteer more information and when she didn't he prompted her. 'So – would you like to tell me more?'

'I don't know whether I should,' she said slowly. 'It's a patient of mine who has a personality disorder.'

Paul Frank made a face. 'It doesn't sound a hugely *dangerous* disease,' he said dubiously.

'Most serial killers share the same diagnosis, Inspector.'

He raised his eyebrows. 'Then tell me a little about the condition.'

'They start off as juvenile offenders,' she said, 'manifesting delinquency. They are glib, intelligent and plausible, with a superficial charm which makes them dangerous – and credible confidence tricksters. They are pathological liars, have shallow characters, a lack of remorse. Constant need for stimulation, a sense of grandiose self-worth. They lack empathy and are callous, cunning, manipulative, impulsive and irresponsible. How far do you want me to go?'

'I think I'm getting the picture,' he said. 'It sounds all too familiar. I guess virtually any young offender would fit into that picture.' He gave a wry smile. 'Apart from the intelligent bit. Most of the kids in custodial care haven't got two brain cells to rub together.'

'These are more dangerous,' she said, 'in that they are cruel as well as criminal. There is no moral argument you can successfully use against them. They make their own rules.'

He rubbed his chin. 'And I take it that the innocent enquiry about Cynthia Barclay's death to Sergeant Young is connected.' He waited for a comment and when she still said nothing he added, 'I also believe she has a son.'

It was enough. Between herself and the policeman there was a tacit understanding.

He cleared his throat. 'So,' he said. 'Tell me a bit about Kristyna. What sort of a person was – is – she?'

What could she say? 'Stable, normal. Average. Friendly. Good at her job. Sweet-natured.'

'Not given to histrionics? Abnormal behaviour? Attention-seeking?'

'No.'

'So you don't think she put the coat in your car to alarm you, reassure you, warn you?'

It hadn't even entered her head. 'No. It wouldn't be her style at all.'

'So I take it you think her abductor . . .' He carefully avoided using the word *killer* but it lay between them, awkward and obvious, ' . . . is responsible.'

'Yes.'

He stood up.

'My car?' she ventured feebly.

'We'll have to impound it,' he said. 'There may be evidence on it or in it. We'll get another car for you. In the meantime can we give you a lift somewhere? To the hospital, maybe?'

'Yes, fine. Thanks.'

'We'll obviously let you know how our investigations are progressing and we'll want to speak to you again.'

She bowed her head.

She was over two hours late for work but meeting Siôna in the corridor he said nothing. Which made her paranoid. He *should* have asked her why she was late. He should have grilled her. Not slunk past. He must know something.

She quickly visited each of her four wards and found little to delay her so an hour later she was ready to eat her lunch, on the bench outside her office window, sitting in the yard. It was cold but she wrapped her down jacket around her and welcomed the chill, clean, damp air, as she watched the watery grey sun make an effort to brighten the scene. Gradually she stopped asking the same four questions: Was it really Kristyna's coat? Who had put it in her car? When? And most chillingly, why? Acknowledging that she already knew the answers because it was like a real-life Cluedo game. Barclay had killed Kristyna Gale, somewhere, put her coat in the car in the middle of the night, with a dual motive, both to gloat that he alone knew what happened and to frighten her, his psychiatrist. She knew all this but she didn't know what had ultimately happened to Kristyna. Except that she must surely be dead. And although she believed Barclay was capable of murder and that he could have killed his mother by switching her pills she couldn't see how he could have abducted Kristyna – the nurse had known Barclay was potentially dangerous. She wouldn't have got into his car. Even on a wet night. What about when she had worn her best coat to work and had no car? But surely Kristyna would have fought for her life?

So would Heidi.

She took a bite out of an underipe pear and chewed it thoughtfully, the flesh gritty and hard between her teeth. She was becoming ashamed of her inactivity. She should be doing something more positive. It was no use sitting here and trying to work out what had happened. She should be doing something. Not only for Kristyna. For herself. To protect herself. What? How? Be more observant. Watch out for him. She knew he was around. She should be more vigilant.

In contrast to the tranquil wards her outpatient clinic was muddled, chaotic and busy with patients complaining they'd been kept waiting. No member of staff made any comment and when she glanced in the mirror while washing her hands at the end of the afternoon she knew why.

She looked wild. Odd and strained, pale with a background of fear. It was then that she realised that throughout the entire clinic she'd half-expected Jerome Barclay to appear.

It was dark and late. She was tired and desperately wanted to go home, to a hot bath and dinner, but she needed to dictate the letters. She had a brief tussle with her conscience. The clinic was deserted. It had over run and the ancillary staff had gone home. Only a few cleaners were left. Finally she decided to drop the notes off at her office and come in early in the morning to dictate the letters.

But returning to her office was a mistake. She realised she had begun fearing the room. Now she hated it. It was the scene of a crime, a manifestation of Heidi's weakness, a place where her own weaknesses would be exposed. She sat down in the chair and stared at the wall.

Waiting.

Psychiatrists deal with fear. Real or imagined. You must turn around and face your fear or it grows monstrously, into something too big to live with. Sanely.

She drew her mobile from her bag, located phonebook, scrolled to A, found Adam's number and pressed the dial button. He answered at once, recognising her caller ID.

'Hi, Sis. How're you doing? New job OK?'

'Reasonable,' she said. 'Grant's knee-deep in decorating. How's your course, Adam.'

'More work than it should be, Sis.'

'Adam,' she said and stopped. 'Come up and see us soon.'

'Sure.'

'No – I mean it. I'm not just being polite. Keep in touch and come and visit us. Soon.'

'Yeah. OK. I'll give you a ring in a week or two. Got to go, Sis. Football calls.'

She felt cleansed when she had replaced the phone back in her handbag. Dealing with phobias, brushing out the dark corners of our mind, makes us feel cleansed. Strong. Pure and powerful.

Empowered.

She sat, still and quiet, sensitive to every noise in the building but hearing no creeping footsteps. Tonight she was alone in this wing. She ran her mind's eyes along the corridor. Dark, still, empty. Beautifully empty. No crouching figure.

She switched the light off and left.

Chapter Fourteen

It was at that precise point that events took a turn for the sinister. She stopped being the stalker, the watching eye, and began to realise that the interest was turning on to her. Barclay was stalking her.

She had ended the evening sweetly, Grant and she, entwined on the sofa, still revelling in this newfound intimacy. She'd had a bath, full of aromatic oils, wrapped herself in a huge white bath towel and they'd eaten a simple meal of chicken with pasta, followed by fruit. They were almost celebrating. They'd had a good offer on the house, the would-be purchasers gushing over the bright, 'happy' colours and 'contemporary ambience', the 'sense of air', whatever that might mean. Even Grant had looked bemused at that. Life seemed good. But she should have remembered that optimism is a temporary state – like its twin brother, pessimism.

Neither lasts for long but of the two it is optimism who has the shorter lifespan.

The police had loaned her a Renault Clio and she liked the nippy little car, arriving in her office a full half hour early, prepared to dictate the letters from yesterday's clinic. She was still perfused with yesterday's happiness, not yet knowing it would not belong to today. She sat down at the desk. She picked up the top set of notes and immediately re-entered that strange time zone last experienced when she had looked at Kristyna's carefully folded coat.

The top set of notes was Jerome Barclay's.

A thousand thoughts crowded her mind.

He hadn't been in yesterday's clinic. His notes shouldn't even have been out. They should still have been in the gun-metal filing cabinet in the corner which was always kept locked. How had he got in here in the first place? Unseen – because if he'd been spotted he would surely have been stopped?

Agitated she stood up, crossed the room, tugged at the top drawer.

The filing cabinet was still locked.

He must have got in here, unlocked the cabinet, taken the notes out and put them where she would find them.

Her brain was filled with such stupid, illogical thoughts. Only Houdini took notes from a locked cabinet. And she had the only key on her own keyring.

Her mind was still working slowly, cranking in low gears. She picked up her bag and fumbled for her own bunch of keys then dropped them onto the desk before checking them. They were all there.

So how had Barclay's notes been magicked from a locked cabinet to the top of her pile of notes?

Panic burst through.

It gave him supernatural powers. He could open locked drawers without a key, move, unseen, through the hospital, know where she was when he was nowhere near, anticipate her next move. Get away with murder.

What did he plan next?

Shakily she replaced the notes in the drawer and tried to concentrate on her dictation.

But her eyes seemed fixed on the door handle. If it moved, she felt she would go quite mad.

But now events began to cascade into tragedy, fast and furiously tipping her into a downward spiral of terrible confusion. Had she been a disciple of Bio-rhythms she would have had no need to check the calendar.

All the signs must be bad. As bad as they could possibly be.

Sometimes psychiatrists get things wrong. Badly wrong. They misjudge intent, misinterpret symptoms, underestimate real misery and they are held, ultimately, to blame. Or perhaps it is the victim mentality, this feeling of ultimate responsibility, that makes doctors blame themselves for their patients' tragedies.

The news filtered through, in dribs and drabs, Chinese Whispers in the staff room that a suicide attempt had been successful. Then a name was pinned to the anonymous story. Mavis Abiloney. No details yet except this, identity. Their worst fears had come true. Her final suicide bid had succeeded. And Claire felt terribly responsible. She had misjudged the situation, discharged her patient, believing it was better to turn and face the opponent. She had been wrong wrong wrong.

The police came to take a statement, two young constables; the coroner's officer interviewed her. Kindly he did not ask the vital question, *Why, given such a history, Doctor, why in heaven's name, why did you discharge her?*

Then Detective Inspector Paul Frank came to see her.

He arrived unannounced, during her lunch break. She suspected he had asked her secretary when would be a good time to catch her and her secretary, like a conspirator, must have told him without informing her. Between one and two she invariably was in her office, working, reading, doing something. She was surprised to see him, had been startled by the knock on her door. She did not usually have visitors at lunchtime. Since Kristyna had disappeared it was almost as though the staff had ceased to trust each other and these days they rarely shared their lunch break, perhaps respecting each other's need to be alone.

She had an idea the detective had picked up on both the surprise and the apprehension in her face as well as, maybe, an ounce or two of resentment when she opened the door. 'Can I come in?' he asked, his hand still poised in knocking position.

'Sure.'

He entered cautiously, peering around him. 'It's a while since I was here,' he said finally.

She knew exactly what he meant.

His eyes flickered passed her, around the walls. She knew he was looking, as she had done, for blood stains, for some residual sign. He had, after all, been the Senior Investigating Officer for Heidi's murder.

With an effort he switched crimes.

'We've got some news,' he said cautiously, 'from the forensic lab.'

She lifted her head.

'Is everything all right?'

'No,' she said, 'not really. Nothing is all right.' And somehow this encompassed everything, from Heidi to Kristyna, from ill-fated Gulio to malevolent Barclay and everything else between, connected or unconnected. 'One of my patients has committed suicide.'

'You've just got to mean Mrs Abiloney.'

She nodded.

'Well – excuse me for stating the obvious,' he said, 'but she was a copper's nightmare. You were never going to be able to stop her topping herself ultimately. It wasn't exactly the first attempt, was it? One of these times she was going to manage it. No doctor in the world was going to keep her alive for ever. Not even you.' Said with a grin. 'She had a death wish, Claire.'

'We never thought so,' Claire said stiffly.

'And I thought *you* were the psychiatrist,' the detective said, laughing. 'I thought the new thinking was that there is no such thing as these "cries for help". I thought they were all serious attempts to die.'

She dipped her head. He was right. It *was* the current thinking. But she simply didn't agree with it. She thought the other way round, that the deaths were more often attempts gone wrong. But that didn't stop her being impressed that this 'copper' was up-to-date with contemporary and fashionable medical thinking.

He put a friendly arm on her shoulder. 'You can't blame yourself for everything that goes wrong,' he said. 'It's like my job. The bottom line is your clients are nuts, ours are criminals. We do our best to keep law and order, you to keep some semblance of mental health. The lines where we cross are the most difficult. There are limitations but we all do our best. That's it, Doctor.'

She managed a smile. 'So what did you come about?'

'The coat,' he said.

She had a hundred thousand questions to ask about the coat and he seemed to sense it.

'First things first,' he said. 'We've confirmed it was Kristyna Gale's coat. We found some hairs on it which have been positively identified as hers. She'd used a quite distinctive mix of hair dyes,' he added with a mischievous smile that crinkled his eyes.

'We know that they got into your car with a key. It isn't difficult. A twelve-year-old with the right intentions would have managed it.'

'But it wasn't a twelve-year-old, was it,' she said wearily.

Frank shook his head. 'No.'

The unspoken words were the most fearsome. It was Kristyna's killer.

'Did you find anything else?'

'Plenty. Probably too much to go into now but there were rain spots on it which implies she'd walked at least some part of the way in the rain the night she was abducted.'

'And?'

That was when the detective's face changed. It became graver, older, sadder. She thought it must mirror her own face when she had to break bad news.

Sometimes we can only despair at the human race.

Claire gripped the sides of her chair as though she was on a terrifying death-defying fairground ride, the anticipation making her queasy.

'I'm afraid we did,' he admitted. 'There was some blood-staining.'

She let out a little gasp of air. 'How extensive?'

'Quite a bit on the collar,' he said. 'A lot.'

Throat cut?

'What does the pathologist say?'

Detective Inspector Paul Frank looked haggard. 'I don't have to point out that this is not to be in the public domain,' he said, his voice hoarse with anguish.

'How much blood?' she asked again. 'Does it mean she's dead?'

'Hard to say.' He counter-attacked. 'You're a doctor. You know you can lose a great deal of blood without necessarily dying.'

She waited.

'This is only an opinion,' he said wearily. 'The pathologist thought the amount of blood and the distribution indicated she – ' His eyes were almost hooded. *He didn't want to say it.* He cleared his throat noisily, wiped the skin underneath his eyes. 'He thought that it was compatible with a major wound, something like having her ears cut off.'

'While she was still alive?'

The room receded and swam back into focus. Frank was nodding.

That was when the room span. She just made it to the sink to vomit up her lunch while the Detective Inspector stood by, helplessly watching.

She emptied her entire stomach contents before she stopped retching, made a futile attempt to clean the sink out. Frank was quiet, not embarrassed, watching her without emotion. It must have drained from him when he had learned the facts from the pathologist.

'I'm sorry,' she said. 'I have this tendency to . . .' She didn't really need to elaborate.

And now Barclay's opportunity for confidentiality had passed.

She had to tell him.

Without speaking she fumbled beneath the desk for her handbag, took her keys from it and opened the filing cabinet, found the letter 'B' and removed Barclay's folder. She opened it to the right place and turned it round so the policeman could read the relevant paragraph. Then she sat back opposite.

He took a minute or two to read through, re-read then looked across at her.

'You were the senior investigating officer for Heidi Faro's death,' Claire said. 'Are you still sure you got the right guy?'

His face was set, old-stone. 'If I hadn't been sure, Doctor, I wouldn't have brought the case to court.' The suspicion of a smile softened his face. 'I do have my morals, you know. Jerome Barclay wasn't even in the picture.'

'And now?'

His eyes dropped to the file again. It was an answer.

'All I want is for you to contemplate,' she urged. 'If there is any doubt. Just look again at them all, Cynthia Barclay's death and Heidi's murder, in the new light. Then consider the fact that not only is Kristyna dead but she almost certainly suffered terribly before she died. Please. Just consider the entire scenario as a whole with Greatbach as your background.'

They had trouble enough at Greatbach without anything more happening. But trouble is a fickle entity. It seeks out those who already have an overload and dumps more misfortune on them.

And so . . .

Only Nancy Gold seemed impervious to the atmosphere which had stretched as taut as the 'E' string on a violin. She alone seemed detached, floating in clouds of baby pink and blue, humming lullabies softly to herself as she sat cross-legged on her bed, smiling dreamily and waiting for her baby. Claire spent time observing her through the porthole window, wondering what was going on in that pretty little head as she sat and hugged her swelling abdomen. But there was something guileless about Nancy, something small, child-like and innocent that misled you so no matter how frequently you recalled her history you were inclined to disbelieve it, to tell yourself that someone, in the past, must have made a mistake.

Afterwards Claire wondered how she could have been so wrong and made the excuse that the minute she stopped watching Nancy she forgot about her because at the time her mind was too saturated with another worry – Barclay.

She sensed him always behind her but however fast she turned her head she never quite caught him, only his shadow, marked by the swiftest of movements, little more than an alteration in the arrangement of light and shade. Still a threat.

She dared not confide in Rolf or Siôna or any of the others that D.I. Frank was questioning Stefan's guilt and, encouraged by her, focusing his attention on Barclay. But typically Rolf picked up that something had changed. He just wasn't sure what.

The following day he too knocked on her office door and invited himself in.

People react differently to worry. Rolf had lost weight, making his face appear longer and thinner, and with his small, pointed beard he reminded her of the man in an El Greco painting, The Burial of Count Orgaz.

'Umm, hi, Claire.' He began with a friendly note. 'I know we're all upset about Kristyna.' He sat down, uninvited. 'I wondered if you wanted to talk about it?' Said with a bright, encouraging smile that belied the sadness in his eyes.

It made Claire remember. He had been fond of Kristyna.

She longed to tell him that the investigation had taken a turn but none of this was her secret to confide. 'I can't,' she said, a smile softening the refusal. 'I'm sworn to secrecy, Rolf.'

'It is something about Kristyna, isn't it?' he prompted.

She nodded.

'Just tell me,' he pleaded. 'I'm a friend too. I've known her longer than you. Have they found her? Is she dead?'

'They don't *know* she's dead, Rolf,' she said softly, 'but I think she must be.'

'What have they found?'

'Her coat's turned up,' she said. No need to tell him where. 'It was heavily bloodstained. I'm sorry, Rolf. If I was allowed to say more I would. I really would but there's more to this than meets the eye and . . . I just can't say more.'

A certain steeliness set his face. His pupils were pinpoints, the eyes hard and unforgiving, the face still El Greco's but hostile now instead of sad. She watched him with a detached fascination. This was not the Rolf Fairweather she knew, not the gentle, counselling psychologist, but an angry man. Who had lost a friend. It was an intriguing transformation. He stared around the room, his Adam's apple very prominent as he gulped and swallowed, finally regaining his composure before leaning forward from the waist. *'There's a lot you're not telling me, Claire.'*

It was almost hypnotic.

She could only nod.

'And some of it . . .' Again his glance was rolling around the room. ' . . . Some of it,' he repeated slowly, intuition surfacing with an air of satisfaction, 'is not only to do with Kristyna. It's Heidi too, isn't it?'

She nodded again, realising fully, perhaps for the first time, what a very good psychologist Rolf Fairweather was.

He spoke slowly and very deliberately. 'You never did seem very convinced it was Gulio. That's why you went down to see him, isn't it?'

He was getting there patiently, inch by inch, scrabbling with his fingernails over loose rocks.

'You've got your sights set on Barclay, haven't you?'

A penetrating perception.

Another nod from her as she watched him unravel events with the precision of a heart surgeon.

Rolf was so clever she feared he would work it all out before her. And yet until she had come he had not travelled along this path.

His eyes narrowed and he looked down his nose at her. 'Have you got any real evidence, Claire, or is this pure guesswork?'

She did not want him to explore any further. 'I can't go into it, Rolf.'

'That means you *have* got something.' Intuitively he snatched at it, terrier-like, and worried at it. 'And either you've persuaded the police round to your point of view or they've got there on their own.' He scrutinised her. 'My guess is a bit of both. But,' he mused, 'it must be something concrete. Not just an idea, a feeling or intuition. They wouldn't listen to that.'

When she still said nothing he stood up, tall and thin, reminding her now more of Charles I, King of the Cavaliers, sartorially elegant, dressed today in a wine-coloured cravat over a dark shirt and black narrow-legged jeans. 'OK, Claire,' he said. 'But be careful. Be aware. If it is Barclay you've got in your sights he is frighteningly dangerous. Be very very careful. Please.' A hand brushed her shoulder.

And then he was gone, closing the door softly behind him.

It is difficult to worry about more than one thing at a time. The brain reaches saturation level. Enough is enough. Barclay held the central position while Nancy Gold was relegated. As with Mavis Abiloney, Claire was too preoccupied and her management was not square. Maybe if she had not been so taken up with Kristyna's disappearance she might have spent more time worrying about Nancy and her unborn child. As it was she gave her fleeting, cursory thoughts and then continued with the work which swamped her. Sometimes it seemed that the five towns had more than their fair share of people with mental problems. She found herself working late simply to see her quota of patients and dictating long into the evenings, taking work home.

She could not keep this up for ever.

The house was sold and they were doing their best to keep the purchasers at bay, spending all their spare time hunting for their new house. But Grant was fussy. He wanted to try his hand at some building work. He wanted somewhere with potential. Suddenly, fearsomely, he wanted to make money. Sometimes in the evenings, Claire would look up from the sheaves of house details and muse. They had both changed – altered in their preoccupations and perceptions over the last few months. Why? And why this search for the perfect house when Claire wondered whether it even existed outside her partner's brain.

The shame was that while Grant's waking and sleeping moments were filled with Shangri La hers were always spent with the same person and the eternal question.

What more could she do?
    Echoed a week or so later with another, worse question.
    What more could she have done?
    And later still,
    What more should she have done to prevent . . .?
    But there was no answer.

A week after the coat had been found in her car Paul Frank rang her.
    And asked her to put an hour aside to speak to him.
    Apprehensive and intrigued, she used her office again.

There is a belief that inanimate objects or a location hold atmosphere in their air or their very fabric. This is why the price of haunted houses or houses where there has been disaster or violent crime is sometimes low. Paradoxically it is also the reason why major auction houses sell for huge prices the shoe of someone who drowned on the Titanic or the notebook of the well known poisoner from Rugeley, the waistcoat of a Victorian felon, the bridle of Dick Turpin's Bess. People are intrigued by tragedy. They fear it. They respect it. They are endlessly fascinated by it.
    Claire was not immune from this superstition. That was why she chose to use the room where Heidi had died to begin to learn the truth.

D.I. Frank arrived promptly at two o'clock on the first afternoon of the year that could possibly be thought to herald spring. The air was light and clean outside, the central heating stuffy and cloying inside, the scent of paint still tainting the air, but less noticeably than before. It would soon be a year since Heidi's death. In an attempt to blow away the ghost Claire had thrown open the window the inches it was allowed and was enjoying the purity of the air that streamed in. Spring air is so much cleaner than summer air full of pollen and flies.
    The detective was carrying a couple of brown manila

files which he placed on the desk. He scanned the room curiously before sitting down without making comment.

'This is a private conversation, Doctor,' he warned. 'None of this is official. It isn't on the record and it won't be used in court. There are no witnesses.' He settled into his spiel. 'Think of this as being two friends chatting informally, pooling our resources. You're a psychiatrist with a depth of knowledge about criminal behaviour and I'm a policeman with years of experience. I suggest we at least start by communicating all that we know.'

'If we're going to communicate,' she said – almost archly, 'I think I should call you Paul and it'll save a lot of time if you simply call me Claire. Excuse me for being cynical but if this is off the record is there any point to it?'

'Oh there's point,' he said, unoffended by her bluntnesss – rather his pale face softened into humour.

'Have you located Jerome Barclay?'

'No. There haven't been any definite sightings – except that we do know he's in the area somewhere. Mobile phone and cashpoint,' he explained. 'Just remember, Claire, we've no reason to arrest him. We'd like to locate him, watch him even, I agree. But we have nothing admissible on him.'

'Nothing admissible?'

'We can't charge him with anything. If we bring him in for questioning we'll have to release him. Likewise if we go after him too hard he'll go underground and we'll lose him.'

'True.'

'When we do drag him in we're possibly going to have to reopen your colleague's murder, look at the death of his mother and try and get something on Kristyna. As it is there is a chance.' He held his hand up to fend off her comment. 'Just a chance that she could still be alive. I don't want to find out we'd scuppered her chance of survival by being too heavy-handed. I don't want that on my conscience.'

Claire was silent. She was recalling the details she had learned about Heidi Faro's murder. It had been brutal, cruel, without compunction. In spite of herself her head was shaking. 'Kristyna won't be alive, Paul,' she said.

He stared at her for seconds, must have followed her thought processes and nodded. 'I know,' he said. 'I agree. But . . .'

She chipped in, frowning. 'There isn't a but, is there? So let's get on with it. Have you any leads?'

A swift vision of Kristyna, small and blonde, in khaki, golden bangles shaking on the slim wrist, the stud glinting in the pointed nose, the dark tattoo on the smooth skin, tiny, golden hairs, almost animal. The vision hurt her more than she expected. She winced in real pain.

Perhaps he didn't notice, too busy shaking his head. 'Not a thing except the coat. We'll have more when he chooses to give it.'

'Defeatist,' she said, bordering on angrily. 'We must pursue. What did you find on the coat? Apart from blood?'

'Trace elements. Potash, bone, chinaclay. Cobwebs. Dirt, dust, some glaze. Lead.'

She sat, mesmerised. A vision rising in front of her eyes. Period Stoke, the land of the bottle kiln, place of the manufacture of the country's china and porcelain, fired in the stumpy little bottle kilns, each one now with a preservation order. Almost too late. Thought to be ugly hundreds had been knocked down. Few remained. They were a sign of the past. Kilns were electric now. Not coal-fired bottle kilns. But the Potteries had originally been built on clay and coal. You cannot eradicate the past. Slash a potter's wrist and clay pours out. The women may have contracted breast cancer from feckling and filing cup rims smooth enough for a lady's lips. The men may have got coal dust and clay dust in their lungs. But they had loved their heritage, felt real pride in it. Then progress had roared in. The electric kilns had been installed and the Potteries had almost completely lost their emblem. And yet bottle kilns were still their heritage.

There are still potters in Stoke but not many. Manufacture of fine china has largely returned whence it came – the Far East. China.

More importantly for Claire there were still a few pot-banks in Stoke on Trent. Places where you would find traces of cobweb mixed in with china clay, pulverised bone, dirt and lead glaze. 'So she was held in a potbank,' she said.

Paul Frank nodded. 'There are still quite a few dotted around. Derelict sites. We're checking them all.'

'This must be a neglected one to have lead glaze.'

'We've searched and found nothing yet.'

'It could be a red herring,' she said suddenly. 'If I am right and it was Barclay who took her he isn't above playing a little game of false trail with you.'

Frank gaped.

'I told you he was clever,' she said earnestly. 'I did warn you. He will toy with you like a cat with a mouse. Even the blood may be part of the game. Do you *know* it's Kristyna's?'

A shake of the detective's head answered her question.

'What I'm saying is, don't limit your search. Remember he will always be one step ahead. Sometimes two. Sometimes more.'

Frank regarded her steadily then nodded. He pushed the one buff file to the side and brought out a second.

'Cynthia Barclay,' he said. 'Police photographs.'

Claire opened the file.

The photographs were on the top.

She had met Cynthia Barclay once only. She would not have recognised her again. Not from these.

People who have ingested tablets and alcohol are inclined to vomit. Unconscious and lying on their back their vomit stays in their mouth and they breathe it in. Into their lungs instead of the fresh clean air that blows across our country so their lungs fill with acid. Hydrochloric acid to be precise. If they do not die from suffocation they will die from pneumonia caused by this alien substance in an organ which depends on oxygen. Inhalation pneumonia is a not uncommon cause of death for drunks and people who overdose on drugs. The noxious substances bubble from the mouth and nose as the dying person breathes their last.

Sometimes the bubbles are pink, blood-stained and frothy.

Other signs are less constant. The eyes may be open. They may be shut. The body may be convulsed.

The first photograph was clear and well-coloured enough to discern everything. Cynthia Barclay lay on her back, her eyes, devoid of makeup, slightly open, as though she was peeping slyly from underneath the lids. *An illusion only.*

She was wearing a pale blue nightdress, demurely tied around her neck, with a narrow, darker blue ribbon. She wore a gold crucifix which lay, like a religious statement, halfway down her cleavage.

Pink vomit trickled from the side of her mouth.

Claire studied the picture for a minute before flipping it down on the desk, a discarded playing card.

The next photograph was of the side of her bed, a small table, with a drawer, a cupboard beneath. On the top was a bottle of tablets with its top unscrewed, a bottle of Gordon's gin, its label clearly visible, a half-full glass and a travel alarm.

'The tablets were barbiturates,' Frank said. 'The glass was full of neat gin. No fingerprints were found except hers on either the bottle of tablets, the drinking glass or the bottle. The tablets found in her stomach were pink Soneryl, the same as the ones in the bottle.' He met her eyes. 'We went right through the house looking for something suspicious. We've got Barclay's record. We knew his mother's death was convenient. We found nothing, Claire. Her G.P. informed us that she was addicted to Soneryl. She'd been prescribed them by his senior partner at the time of her husband's death and no one had been successful at getting her to stop.

In fact she would have to have been treated aggressively by the substance abuse department to stop her habit. The lesser of two evils seemed to be to keep her on a maintenance dose, not increase, and stop her picking up more than a month's supply at a time.'

Claire nodded. It all made perfect, logical sense.

But her original instinct had been to suspect Jerome Barclay of his mother's murder. And that instinct was not melting away even with the police evidence.

'Did she leave a note?'

The detective's eyes were firmly connected to hers as he shook his head very slowly.

He wasn't happy either.

'There is something else that more or less tipped the balance,' he said. 'She had called the Samaritans earlier in the evening.'

Claire opened her eyes very wide, questioning.

'It was a bit of a longshot on our part.' Paul Frank couldn't help preening a little. 'We got a computer printout of her telephone calls. It's more or less routine in a case like this. Added to that in the newspaper deaths column there was a request that any donations be made to the Samaritans. We contacted them, explained what had happened and they were quite helpful. She'd been in the habit of ringing them once or twice a week when she was particularly worried about things. Two things in particular. Her son, behaviour bordering on criminal, and her own addiction, concerned about what would happen if one day her doctor simply refused to continue prescribing for her. That night, they said, she was quite tearful and on the phone for almost twenty minutes. They log all their calls,' he explained.

But it would have been Barclay who would have inserted the death notice. And this alone made her smell a fat rat. But she tucked this little fact away, said nothing and reluctantly closed the file on Cynthia Barclay.

Now her eyes were on the second file.

Without opening it she knew that this file would contain graphic crime scene photographs of Heidi's murder-scene, the pictures that never would have been released to the general public. But they would have been shown to the jury in Stefan Gulio's trial. She focused on the cover, knowing that Paul Frank would wait for her to open them.

'In your own time,' he said.

She reached out.

The photographs were clear and in colour, Heidi recognisable before she was cut down.

She gasped. 'I hadn't realised.'

Heidi was hanging upside down.

She had been strung up by the ankles, her trousers flapping around her calves, arms and hair hanging downwards, her neck wound gaping, blood – seemingly gallons of it – pooling on the floor.

Claire felt faint. It looked so – animal. One word pushed into her mind.

Halal.

'Upside down?'

He nodded. 'As you can imagine the blood loss was . . .'

'But *this*.' She jabbed her finger angrily on the colour plate. '*This* wasn't made public. Why not?'

Paul Frank was unruffled by her anger. 'Partly the indignity,' he said. 'It was unnecessary for the public to know. It would have achieved nothing except further revulsion for a sufficiently horrible crime.'

Her eyes narrowed. 'And partly?'

'It was thought sensitive in the current political climate.'

'*Halal*,' she breathed again.

The detective looked uncomfortable. 'We had a Muslim officer,' he said. 'A Pakistani guy. He explained that this was how halal meat is prepared. Upside down, the throat cut. The blood drains out. Quick, clean.' He smiled. 'The animal dies quickly. It wasn't as though it had any bearing on the case anyway,' he said defensively, 'and we thought it was potentially inflammatory. It could have done more harm than good.'

'And if Gulio had been a Muslim?'

'The same,' he said. 'We would still have kept the detail of Doctor Faro's murder secret.'

'How did he manage it? Physically, I mean?'

'Stunned with a blow to the back of the head, strung up and . . .'

'How sure were you that you had the right man?'

'We were sure. At the time.'

'Did you seek a psychiatric opinion?'

'Of course.'

But they both knew that Heidi was the one who could have given the most valid psychiatric opinion on Gulio. No one else would have known the secret passages of Gulio's mind. And Heidi had been unable to speak either in his defence or to damn him.

'Put your cards on the table,' Inspector Frank said, 'if you have any.'

She told him then about Barclay, holding nothing back from his history, telling him Sadie's story, about the acid on her car, the story of the 'dead bird and the rabbit's ears – even confiding to the detective the eerie feeling he gave her. 'I have no firm evidence', she said. 'No real proof. Nothing except for the fact that I know he is capable. If I were an offender profiler I would describe Jerome Barclay and you would be picking him up on my evidence alone. He is a danger.'

She closed her mind to the image of Kristyna's terror, shut her ears to her colleague's screams. Drew in a deep breath. 'And now he's turned his attention on me.'

Frank looked rattled.

It was hard not to look again at the picture.

Heidi had been wearing navy blue trousers with black, kneelength popsox. The trousers flapped up around her knees, which were pale and swollen. She wore no shoes and her right big toe stuck through the popsock. The cord was looped tightly around her ankles, biting in to the flesh.

In crime scene photographs it is often the detail rather than the whole which you remember afterwards.

Paul Frank waited while she studied the pictures. 'I've looked back over Gulio's conviction,' he said, tossing statements towards her. 'If you removed his confession we would have had a weak case. Between you and me it might have served us well to have kept more of an open mind. If you look at it from another angle most of the evidence was circumstantial. The blood stains *could* have come from him stumbling across the murder scene. He had no good reason for being there. But just remember he never retracted his confession. We gave him plenty of chances.'

She looked up. 'Knowing Gulio's history I could explain that. He has a sense of guilt. He's likely to blame himself even when he is innocent.'

'Maybe.' The detective looked dubious.

'And as for the second case, Barclay's mother. You know how difficult these poisonings are, how little evidence there often is.'

'She'd had quite a lot to drink that night – the equivalent of a bottle and a half of wine plus the gin. Her fingerprints were quite clearly on the pill jar. There was just nothing to make us believe otherwise.' He chewed his lip, frowning and thinking. 'And as for Kristyna – we've nothing. Absolutely nothing. Completely nothing. We can only convict when we've evidence – hard evidence. What I'm saying is, Claire, our hands are tied. We can do nothing.'

'You can do one small thing', Claire interrupted, 'apart from finding him, that is. You can at least check the dates he was in the country. See if they tally with the date Kristyna disappeared.'

'I take it the hospital doesn't have any way of finding Barclay?'

'We've tried his mobile,' Claire said. 'It isn't even ringing and we don't have a current address for him. The one we have is his mother's house which, of course, has been sold. So we have to wait for him to contact us.'

The policeman scratched the side of his mouth now. He was unhappy. 'That,' he said, 'is a bit of a bummer. We'll have to put out a find and apprehend which I didn't want to do. You see, Claire, we've nothing really against him apart from your suspicions.'

She blinked. It felt a heavy responsibility on her shoulders. 'He'll be in touch,' she said confidently. And in answer to his quizzical expression. 'Barclay doesn't function without an audience.'

She laid her outstretched hands flat on the desk, palms down and stared across the room at the miniscule bumps in the paintwork, splattered around the lightswitch. 'Paul,' she appealed. 'Get to him before he gets to me.'

Almost without being noticed Nancy Gold slipped away. No one registered her absence as the sun began to rise, early on a Wednesday morning.

She had gone to meet her lover.

The night shift was shattered. Six am and they'd spent half the night with a thirty year-old who'd tried to kill himself while suffering delirium tremens, the hallucinations caused by chronic alcohol poisoning. He'd screamed for hours about ants and spiders crawling up the wall. Eyes distended, pointing with a shaking hand at insects and arachnids which were as real to him as the nurses who tried to convince him otherwise. He was strong too – and terrified. They'd pumped him full of Chlorpromazine and waited while he sunk back into oblivion. He was a thin man, an ex-sailor, with numerous tattoos and hands that shook so badly it was anybody's guess where he was pointing. It was hard to imagine him ever otherwise.

Nancy Gold was cradling her pillow when the summons came. Who knows how. It came and that was enough. She hugged her pillow one last time before laying it down gently on the bed. Then she fished some loose cotton trousers out of her locker and a dark blue sweatshirt. All the time she dressed she kept her eye trained on the porthole window. No one must see her. She must remain invisible.

Seconds later she slipped out of the room, opening the door only as wide as was necessary to ease herself through. Her blue eyes darted up and down the corridor, making sure no one was around to see her. Then she tiptoed towards the door at the top end. She heard the alcoholic man ranting and raving, both nurses trying to restrain him. He could almost have been in his employ. He was so provident.

'Get outside and to a phone.' It had been her instruction

and mouthing it to herself she followed it blindly.

Like a wraith she passed through the front gate while the porter was attending his burning toast and then, exhilaratingly, she was outside, in the city. The fast, thumping city, sleepily coming to life after another ice-cold night. She stood and breathed in the scents and sounds of freedom, her hands stroking her bump. Almost in response the child moved inside her, alerted by the unfamiliar noises.

Nancy shivered. It was a frosty morning and her sweatshirt was thin. Added to that she was accustomed to hospital central heating which made it summer all the year around. But she would be all right. She knew that. So far she had done well, saying nothing to anyone. No one had prised the name out of her, the magic name which would grant her what she wanted most in the whole world – her own baby again. She whispered it to herself to conjure it up.

'*My baby.*'

Back on the ward the nurses were just pouring their early morning tea, rubbing their eyes, discussing what a night they'd had. Their hallucinating alcoholic had responded to the sedation and there was no need yet to check on their other patients. It was a window of peace, a haven of rest when they believed that nothing was happening.

At home Claire was under the shower. Grant had finally found a suitable property. A late Victorian house, detached in a rundown area in Burslem. Waterloo Road, connected for years with the red light district. But eighteen months ago a property developer had finally realised that these houses were truly wonderful, Victorian 'greats', full of style and original features, ten minutes away from the city centre. So he had bought up two and converted them into luxury flats, landscaping the back gardens and adding private parking and secure, electric gates to the front.

The tone of the place had started to alter slowly and subtly.

Grant had discovered a third property. Only slightly smaller than the others, missing out on a few original features. The fireplaces had gone from the ground floor when it had been turned into offices and the rooms had been divided with sheets of plaster board and batons. But upstairs little had been touched. They had viewed it the night before and Claire had listened as Grant had muttered in her ear about reclamation and authenticity, stone mullions and perfect plasterwork and she had realised with piercing clarity. It was in his blood, this renovation.

He had come to life, found a purpose and changed.

As for her, she had been convinced the moment she had stepped through the french windows into the garden. A high brick wall trailing with honeysuckle surrounded it. No one had touched it yet so it had retained an ancient cricket pavilion in the corner, damp, green wood, a gnarled apple tree, a bed of pretty, but neglected rose bushes and an excellent lawn, springy, damp and mossy, now spattered with fallen leaves from the apple tree. She bent down and touched it. It was soft in a way that pure grass never can be. She swivelled her neck to peer up to the skyline.

All around may be the factories, the city and industry but right here was something better. A green haven, a mossy place to return to. She turned back towards the house, pictured the long portico repainted and renovated, the glass cleaned of algae and moss, the windowframes restored or replaced, the sash windows thrown wide in the summer. She had sat on a hideous green plastic chair, getting colder by the minute and known for sure. This could be home.

Grant squatted beside her. 'So, Claire?'

She had nodded and hoped the estate agent didn't have an inkling of how enthusiastic these buyers were.

She rested her hand very lightly on Grant's shoulder. 'Let me do the talking.' She didn't trust him. His eyes gave too much away. He gave her a light, soft kiss on the mouth. It was a surprisingly erotic gesture.

Together they had stepped inside, the estate agent waiting for them, the question in his eyes.

Always begin with a negative.

'It wants a lot of doing up.'

The estate agent had his answer ready. 'Reflected in the price.'

'Shame about the fireplaces having been ripped out.'

'You can replace them from a reclamation yard.'

'At a price,' muttered Grant in her ear.

'Or put reproduction ones in.'

Claire did a mock shudder.

'We've already sold our property,' she said. 'We'll get a search done and then get back to you.'

'Other people are interested.'

Grant cleared his throat. Claire scowled at him.

When they were outside she'd scolded him lightly. 'We'll get it. It is lovely. But if he knows we're really keen . . .'

She took his face in her hands. 'Trust me,' she'd said, smiling. 'I'm a doctor. Remember?'

So this morning, at the very same time that Nancy Gold was slipping through the front gate of Greatbach 'In-Secure' Unit, Claire, wrapped in a huge, white bathsheet, was sitting on the end of the bed with a ticklist.

'You speak to the surveyor,' she was saying, 'and I'll talk to the mortage company. If we get our skates on maybe we can exchange by the end of the week.'

Grant threw the covers off in a fit of energy and she fished around in the wardrobe for something to wear.

So her mind was clean and happy, full of ideas for the new house, as she turned into the car park. She parked, picked her bag up from the back seat and turned around to meet a security guard.

'Morning,' he said, boxing her in as she locked the car.

'Morning.' Something must have struck her. 'Is anything

wrong?'

'One of the patients. Gone walkabout.'

'Which one?'

'Nancy Gold,' the guard said.

With an almost physical thump in her solar plexus she knew right then. Nancy was a vulnerable patient. She should have paid more attention to her. Had her mind not been full of Kristyna and Barclay and Heidi she would have spent more attention with the dangerous little doll.

Because her mind was concentrating now on Nancy she was at last facing the obvious.

Someone had made her pregnant. Had manipulated her into this position, taking what they had wanted, by pretending to give Nancy what she wanted.

That person had used Nancy's terrible yearning for a baby and had played with her, teasing her that if she played her cards right she could not only have her baby but keep it.

So first Nancy had had to escape.

To where?

To the same place, whispered the voice. To the place where glaze mixed with bone dust and chinaclay, fragments of pottery and slip. Slip, the mixture of clay and water, used both to decorate and bond. The same place where Kristyna had been kept prisoner by the same person who had learned his trade, cut his teeth, on Heidi Faro. Her feet moved fast towards the hospital main entrance and a telephone.

Siôna was waiting in the hallway. 'The night staff were busy,' he explained. 'She must have gone in the very early morning. We've got people looking all over for her.'

'Have you phoned the police?'

'No. Surely that's a bit premature? She might be . . .' The words faded into the grey air.

'Her baby is due next week,' Claire said fiercely. 'She's waited for this moment.'

A blue Honda pulled on to the car park. Rolf climbed

out, listened to what the security guard was telling him, approached with dragging footsteps, already looking drawn and tired and haggard around the eyes.

This monster was bigger than them. It would eventually swallow them all, staff and patients alike, and spit out their bones before belching and searching out more victims. It never could be satiated.

So what was the monster? Why – a disorder of the personality.

She knew it was an irrational fear and yet it clawed at Claire's heart, making it difficult for her to breathe. She gasped and both Siôna and Rolf looked across at her, concern etching lines across both their faces.

She dialled the police from the main desk telephone, using the 999 code. It seemed too urgent to locate the number for the local copshop.

The police make a great deal of noise. It's called 'showing a presence'. Quite suddenly, within seconds, all was activity. Tyres screamed across the car park towards each other as though threatening to collide, sirens blaring, blue lights blinking. And all Claire could think was what a great joke this was for Barclay. How he must be enjoying it. If he was watching.

Of course he was watching. Otherwise what was the point? If not for Barclay's entertainment. Sticks and top hats click-clacked across her mind. *'That's entertainment.'*

Paul Frank climbed stiffly out of one of the cars as though he too was dog tired. He stepped slowly towards her, his eyes hooded and defeated.

His first words were, 'Not -?'

'It's possible.'

What was she saying? Barclay's name had been on her lips since she had learned that Nancy was missing.

D.I. Frank looked even more exhausted, as though he

could have dropped to the floor, curled up and slept for ever.

Claire felt she must say something. 'It's all suspicion,' she said. 'We don't have evidence.'

Behind him she scanned the skyline. The tall towers of the blocks of flats stood against the sky, lights sparking against the greyness.

Somewhere, here in this city, she thought, he was waiting.

Nancy was cold. 'Stay here,' he'd said. 'Don't move. If you want your baby, Nancy, we must do it alone. They will take it from you the second it draws breath. They are your enemy, Nancy. Trust *me*, Nancy. Not *them*. Trust *me*.'

Chapter Seventeen

Most cities have their green areas, pretty places set aside for the urban dwellers to kid themselves the countryside is all around them, that they are cocooned in fields and trees and ozone. Stoke on Trent, being a loose collection of towns which ran in to one another, formed a long, thin city, bordered by ex opencast mining areas. ('Go for a walk in Bemersley,' the old-timers would say, 'and you can pick up lumps of coal from the path.')

Like the Cattle Market Pub in Leek, or the Boathorse canalside drinking houses, the names of the pubs give clues to the environment. The Lump Of Coal, The Winding Wheel, The Miners Arms, The Miners Rest, The Potters Wheel, The Jolly Potter.

And there is a trade-off to opencast mining. Part of the contract is to landscape the sites once the coal has been extracted, to improve the scenery and make it more environmentally friendly than before. Not as much altruism is involved as you might expect. The sites make poor building ground anyway, prone, as they are, to shifting and subsidence. Houses have to be built on rafts which makes them vastly too expensive. So instead these derelict opencast sites are transformed into Stoke on Trent's green areas, places where children might play, folk may take their dog for a walk or cyclists and runners get fit. They form nature reserves around ponds and seats are placed in arbours facing modern sculptures. But there is a downside too. These Arcadian fields are too near the city. Leafy glades can be places of concealment. They may form lovers' lanes but they are also hidey-holes where assaults could be committed or bags might be stolen, drugs can be shot into already scarred veins. Or it might be the place where you could take a car if you wanted to torch it.

One of these green areas is Bemersley, near the source of the River Trent. Bordering Bemersley is a picturesque country park containing two pools, Knypersley Pool and the Serpentine, both managed by Staffordshire County Council. Watching the pools and the car park beyond, stand two small semi-detached white-washed cotttages. Two up, two down.

Very early, on a frosty morning, in the house nearer the pool, Richard Dennis, a chartered accountant, lay in bed, silently staring at the window, alert only to the fact that something was not quite normal.

It is the light, flickering.

The phrase registered before the argument. It should not *be* light. A slight turn of the head confirmed the fact that by the L.E.D. radio alarm it was three am. Hours before dawn. As he watched, the radio alarm changed to 3:01.

That was when he heard the noise, a raging, crackling, angry sort of noise.

He sat up, threw his bedclothes off, glanced at the unconscious lump next to him which was his wife, padded to the bedroom window, drew aside the curtains and stared out.

A car full of petrol makes a fine blaze. Flames shoot ten feet high. It is a firework display with explosions of glass and sudden flares when the plastic melts and ignites. He watched the show and listened to the noise for a few seconds, the crackle, the air whoosh, the glass cracking like ice over a pond. Nothing more, he would say at the inquest. No screams.

The car must have burned, they estimated, for about an hour. The heat was so intense the fire-fighters could not get within thirty yards of it for twenty-five minutes. No one, sitting inside the car, could have survived for more than a few seconds. She must have been already dead before

Richard Dennis had woken up. At the inquest all these statistics would worm their way into Claire's brain, boring
trails so deep she would never forget them in either her
waking or sleeping moments.

But on that frosty morning as Richard Dennis stared
through the window and watched the car burn he knew
only a small part of the story. So he cursed, assuming it was
simply another stolen car dumped by joy-riders – not the
first to be torched here. He'd asked the Council to close the
car park at sunset but they had used the dual arguments of
night fishermen's access and straggling hikers who roamed
the country park and were late returning to their vehicle. So
Dennis always lost the argument. And this, he thought
angrily, knotting his dressing gown cord around his waist,
sliding his feet into slippers and stumping noisily down the
narrow stairs, was the result. He rang the emergency services before stepping outside to the crisp, wintry air, and the
still exploding car beneath a night sky speckled with a hundred million stars. When he was near enough to feel the
heat he stood and waited for the fire engine and the police.

Minutes later he was waving in a tanker with flashing blue
strobes.

There is something surprisingly bouncy about firemen
summoned to a blaze in the dead of night. If you ask them
how they can be so lively they will tell you that from the
moment they get the call adrenalin floods their blood
stream. Foam and hoses, noises and flashing blue lights.
Further sparks to ignite their love of the job. The chance of
heroism and bravery complete the adrenalin surge.

An hour later the car was a smoking, blackened wreck,
smothered in foam like suds of washing up liquid and the
firemen were staring at the unmistakable human form
which lay, face up, on the floor (the seats having melted),

fists bared, ready for a fight.

The well-documented, pugilistic attitude formed by the biological fact that muscle contraction is stronger in the flexor groups than the extensors. Knees, elbows and wrists are affected.

So the burning car had served as a funeral pyre. Not sandal-wood on the banks of the Ganges but rubber and plastic, fuelled by petrol on the edge of a Northern English city. There was no religious significance to the burning car – only expediency.

Immediately the crime scene switched gears. Not just a stolen car any more but a potential homicide enquiry.

In such a state of destruction it can be hard to identify a body and almost impossible to ever know for sure whether the victim was alive or dead when the car was set alight. Inexperienced pathologists might well mistake injuries for effects of the fire. Fractures, unexplained marks on the body, presence or absence of soot in the air passages, skin peeling. Strangely, other aspects of the crime scene can be easier to detect. Keys, still in the ignition, car doors open or closed, locked or unlocked, which gear the vehicle was in, handbrake engaged or not and the identity of the car itself with all the knowledge this brings in its wake. Stolen? Owner? Desire for discovery is implicit. A burning car is a beacon to draw the emergency services and the source of a fund of information via the police computer.

Richard Dennis would not go back to sleep that night. He had caught sight of a smoking ribcage, a corpse which he knew would populate a nightmare the instant he closed his eyes. Besides – the car park opposite his idyllic little cottage was now a bustling crime scene. A tent had been erected, more policemen arrived. And finally a yawning police sur-geon in jeans and a thick sweater, soon followed by a pathologist who carried a black Gladstone bag. So Richard Dennis made the coffee and followed events from the warmth of his kitchen. The only person he did not offer freshly-made coffee to was the journalist who arrived with notepad, sound engineer and a spare man balancing a camera on his right shoulder. Something of the accountant in him balked at being filmed relating the drama and seeing it subsequently on the evening news. It took until mid-morning for the body to be moved and the car-wreck shifted onto a low-loader. It took a whole day for the incident to filter through to Claire.

Like many she had heard the local radio station announce that a body had been found in a burning car near Knypersley Pool. But she did not connect the incident with Kristyna. The pool was at the other end of the city from Greatbach. So she'd simply heard the bulletin and driven on.

This was not what she'd expected.

Late in the day Paul Frank rang her and told her parts of it, that jewellery, dental records and *other sources* had identified the charred body as Kristyna's.

Bones, teeth, jewellery, the underwires of her bra.

The rest she filled in over the next few days from a variety of sources – newspapers, gossip and, worse, her own imagination. The charred and twisted corpse, the heat, the light, the suffering.

Once the car had been removed no mark was left in the gravelled car park but a rectangular, blackened patch in the centre which was soon smothered with bunches of flowers by a soft-hearted public and Kristyna's heartbroken partner, Roxy.

Paul Frank called in to see her a week later to relay the findings of the post mortem.

'As far as we can ascertain,' he said slowly, *'Kristyna was already dead before the car was set alight but the destruction of her body was . . .'* He stopped short, finding it hard to continue.

The missing word was *complete. The destruction of her body was (would have been) complete.*

Unlike the policeman Claire could not *reduce* Kristyna to the phrase *her body*. She could not equate that animated figure, always moving, jangling and talking, earrings flicking forwards and backwards, with the picture she held of a blackened corpse.

The one was life and movement, the other unmistakably stillness and death.

She simply gaped at him.

'There is one other troubling point,' he added, refusing to meet her eyes.

She listened, apprehensive and puzzled too.

'The car that Kristyna's body was found in.'

She waited, not too interested. It would surely be a car stolen in the last twenty-four hours from a nearby housing estate.

Her guess was wrong.

'It was *her* car. Her *own* car,' Paul Frank said with difficulty.

'How?' The word shot out like an accusation.

'You remember Kristyna was walking the day she vanished because her car was in for a service?'

She nodded impatiently. She knew that. *Everyone* knew that.

'We'd looked at it but only briefly. There was nothing there. We decided to leave it at the garage pending our enquiries.'

Claire felt her lip curl. Police incompetence was the phrase that rolled off her brain and over her lips. Even if she only mouthed them Paul Frank heard.

'Yes,' he said. 'I agree. Incompetence. But with hindsight . . .'

He shrugged. 'Anyway – it was on the garage forecourt

and was stolen some time last night.'

This too spoke of Barclay. Irony. Such subtle irony. All so fitting.

She almost smiled. It was so inevitable that she, intimately knowing the machinations of Barclay's mind, should have been able to predict this.

He *would* use Kristyna's car to incinerate her body in. After all. It was Kristyna's car. How apt. How appropriate.

She could picture him saying it, palms showing in the age-old gesture of honesty and inevitability, of something so absolutely fitting as to be obvious.

Paul Frank gave her a few more details, the fact that the body had been released for burial, that the cause of death had had to be listed as uncertain, but she hardly listened and he left soon after.

And now Claire's life entered a dangerous period. Like oil and water, her two existences slowly separated into two completely different entities – work and home. They could not emulsify and the complete segregation made her feel, at times, almost schizoid.

Home was happy, lively, optimistic, planning a future, swags of material, colour magazines, long discussions on the comfort of furniture, of the expediency of bathrooms, shower units over baths, of reds and greens and purples and gold. Olive-white, barley-white, sherbert-white and so on.

Work was worrying, depressing, anxiety-driven, frightening. Constant meetings were held reviewing security for both patients and staff. And all the time the Press haunted the place. The Medical Defence Union was mobilised, uttering their warning cry of protecting the general public from dangerous inmates while at the same time preserving patients' right to confidentiality; the illegality of imprisonment without a Section Order and restraint without due authorisation. The buzzwords were 'responsibilities' and 'reasonable care' and Claire felt she'd defaulted on both.

Most chillingly the Defence Union warned her against playing policeman. 'It is up to the police,' the senior barrister said in a condescending tone that made her feel an inadequate amateur, 'to investigate. Not you. You should neither hinder nor further their inquiries except where it is in furtherance of your professional responsibility which is to protect the general public. Keep your suspicions well wrapped up, Doctor. That,' he ended pompously, 'is my advice to you. Breach that and the Defence Union will document the fact that we gave you clear instruction but that you chose to ignore it.'

So at work she sat and worried at her fingernails while home-life became increasingly surreal in its giddy merry-go-round for a bright, beautiful home.

Sometimes she felt she would go mad with the dichotomy.

And all this time she was aware that Barclay was out there somewhere, watching for her, biding his time. He would come for her at some point as he had come for Kristyna and even possibly Nancy Gold because who knew where she had gone with her unborn child? It was inevitable that Barclay would return for her. She knew it, recognised as he sent her veiled warnings. Notes were moved, the computer altered. Once his name was inserted into a clinic, double-booking the two o'clock spot and she sat in her room beyond the appointment time, not seeing the flesh and blood patient who sat outside, stoically waiting, but paralysed, watching the door and waiting for Barclay to saunter in.

Afterwards she acknowledged to herself that if she had seen the 'A' for arrived opposite his name, followed by a knock on the door and then it starting to open she would, finally, have started to scream and maybe never ever stopped.

She was aware that Barclay was assuming folklore proportions, the massive size of the child's nightmare bogeyman. His shadow was everywhere, an embodiment of all the evil in the world. He was more frightening than anyone could possibly be because he was invisible, always hidden and possessed of the trio of supernatural powers of being everywhere, knowing everything, all powerful, the three attributes we normally give only to a deity.

Looking around the morning meetings she could see she was not the only one feeling the strain. They all looked years older than that short eleven months ago when she had first walked in to Heidi's room.

Gradually she retreated into herself, shutting herself off from Rolf and Siôna and the others, unable to confide in them because she knew, from bitter experience, that it is too easy to label your colleagues and watch them askance for signs of caving in, or mental disorder. Similarly they will watch you.

Psychiatrist, she thought, make yourself sane.

Chapter Eighteen

In 1986 Stoke on Trent had a Garden Festival. It was a conjuring trick. An ugly patch of waste ground was turned into a place of fun. For months the people of England – and further afield – stared at a waterfall made of Twyford's bathroom sinks and toilets, a Welsh garden with slates and model sheep, displays of china and a willow pattern bridge copied from Biddulph Grange. One of the clever aspects about the Garden Festival is that after it was closed the site did not revert to waste ground. The beneficial effects continued. Today it houses a retail park, Toys'R'Us, Comet, Morrisons and the others and a Festival park consisting of a multiplex cinema, a ski slope and Water World together with numerous restaurants, pubs and hotels.

Along the Western edge of the Garden Festival runs the Trent and Mersey Canal, once a thriving industry of transportation, now another place of leisure with a picturesque marina lined with narrow boats, a towpath walk and a canalside pub. Trips, complete with bar, are run for tourists, to see the sights of the Potteries from the water – Etruria's stumpy bottle kilns, Barlaston's Wedgwood and beyond – South towards Stone.

The Garden Festival of '86 fulfilled its remit. It turned an ailing city into a tourist centre.

The people of Stoke loved Festival Park. The queues on a Saturday and during school holidays testified to this, particularly when a new Disney film was showing, or some special promotion, a gala premiere performance, the seasonal sales, Dad Goes Free into Waterworld and so on.

But it had not succeeded everywhere. The area which immediately borders the canal, a stone's throw from Etruria – the fanciful birthplace of Wedgwood's classical Etruscan Ware – is where the car park is less busy. The police recognise these places as dark zones. Corners of the car park least used, farthest away from the cinema's lights, nearest to the black, oily canal, the area where people instinctively avoid leaving their cars, choosing instead to park them across the verge. The floodlights frequently get broken so it remains dark and unlit and dangerous.

Even prettied-up cities have their dark zones. The illusion of perfect England is only veneer thick. Beneath the surface, as in other cities, Stoke on Trent is in every way, a city of the post-millennium.

There is a dark zone in our minds too, areas we dare not visit because they frighten or intimidate us with their capabilities.

In this dark part of the canal the body of a young woman floats slowly down stream. As small as a child, face down, blonde hair floating like a sweet weed. She is tiny in the water except for her abdomen which is the swollen size of a full term pregnancy and dips down like the belly of a whale.

Nancy will have her wish. She will keep this baby with her for ever. They will never be parted now.

She floats through the dark zone, passed the underage kids experimenting with cheap cider and drugs, practising rolling joints. They glance across, see the woman and do nothing. They do not use their mobile phones to call the police. So Nancy's body bobs a little further down stream, towards the warehouses which once filled the narrow boats with their pottery but now are small businesses sponsored by the Prince's Trust. They make diverse objects, furry photograph frames, hand potted ashtrays, fridge magnets. It is here, opposite the A500, the so-called 'D' road which links the M6 Stoke South and Stoke North exits, that a young man is unloading his van, taking boxes of goods into the warehouse, ready for collection in the morning. Sensing without seeing that something is breaking up the surface of the water he glances over the top of his box and almost drops it. Over-carefully he sets the box down on the tarmac and tugs his mobile phone from his breast pocket. 'Police,' he says hoarsely.

Nancy has been found.

No more women are hidden.

Strangely enough Claire felt relieved when Paul Frank rang her and told her they had found Nancy. To know – whatever it is – is usually better than uncertainty. But the image of the child woman Nancy had been, with her sweet face and gold hair, humming lullabies, clutching on to an empty blanket, would haunt her for ever. Also she felt partly to blame. Nancy had been in *her* care. Her responsibility. She had looked the other way and Nancy had died.

She had let her patient down and she knew it.

'Drowned,' Paul Frank said. 'It's possible she simply found her way down there, lost her footing and ended up in the canal then couldn't swim. The banks were slippery. One of our officers almost lost his footing on the towpath. There's nothing to show it wasn't a simple accident.'

Claire flexed her toes in her shoes, wishing she could make a pretence of believing in this simple, neat explanation but alternative versions tugged away at her conscience. She wanted to believe Nancy's death was an accident but it stretched her powers of credulity too taut.

'They're doing some tests,' Paul Frank said, tucking the phone beneath his chin to leaf through his notebook, 'looking for things called . . .' He squinted at his writing. 'Diatoms?'

He obviously assumed it would mean something to her.

And it did. Claire felt a quickening. Diatoms were microscopic organisms found in water dispersed through the body by circulation. Diatoms are different in different waters – tap, river, pond, sea – a fingerprint, a means of identifying the water Nancy had drowned in as well as telling them whether she had been alive on entry or dead. If proof of the circumstances surrounding Nancy's death were possible, diatoms were it.

'When will the results of the tests be back?'

'A week or two,' Frank said cheerfully. 'And we're going to bank the DNA of the infant. It would be nice to know who the father was.'

'Yes.'

Claire put the phone down, not sure where this new discovery fitted into her ideas of events. One by one her theories needed to be tried and tested.

Kristyna and Heidi Faro had been killed by the same person.

Not Gulio – Barclay.

Nancy Gold had been sweetened, seduced and impregnated. But nothing in her had read Barclay as a Romeo in spite of Sadie Whittaker's view. And she found it hard to picture him as the father of Nancy's child. He simply didn't fit the profile. When would he have first met her? How and where had he seduced her? How had he kept her sweet throughout her pregnancy, refusing to leak his name? Finally how had he persuaded her to return to him?

Barclay's murders were brutal, in your face obvious, bloody, sadistic killings. Not a woman dropped into the canal, nine months pregnant.

Barclay liked his murders to look like murders – not accidents.

For the first time since she had met Barclay doubts crept in. He was a psychopath. He liked to play people, tease them, encourage them to fear him. He wasn't really about sex. Except violent sex and Nancy had not been intimidated by her lover. Rather she had been wooed by him. She had seen it in her eyes, those doll-like china-blues.

She tugged one of her textbooks from the shelf and flicked to the chapter on sexual behaviour in psychopaths. Promiscuity was there, short-lived relationships, sex so vio-

---

lent it bordered on rape. Manipulation of the partner. Her eyes roamed the room. Barclay had had a couple of ex-girl-friends whom he had strung along but there had been no pregnancy. Jerome Barclay was intelligent. He would know that a baby's father could be traced through DNA and blood grouping. Babies leave traces which can lead straight back to the father. Why would Barclay have taken the risk? He wouldn't want to have paid out for a baby for the next twenty-odd years. He liked his money too much for that – or rather – his mother's money. And it must have been obvious from the start that Nancy wasn't going to give up this baby.

Something about this latest happening disturbed Claire even more. She was used to feeling she understood Barclay's behaviour well enough to almost anticipate it. Certainly follow it through from conception to the act. But she had not anticipated this. Her instinct told her the motives were different. She frowned, sat, agitated at her desk, her fingers drumming out a gallop.

It was a difficult day, having to tell the others that Nancy had been found, knowing they were all forming the same picture, seeing the wide eyes, the tiny face, the blonde hair that formed a bright halo, Nancy crooning to the pillow, pretending it was her baby.

It was a long day. But it passed and more – and still there was no sign of him.

A week after Nancy Gold's body had been found in the canal Claire was summoned to appear in the coroner's court for the inquest on Kristyna.

She listened to Rolf talk about his last contact with her, watched Roxy deny that her partner had been preoccupied, say vehemently that she had no clue as to where she had gone, why and with whom.

Then it was her turn.

She was asked to describe Kristyna's state of mind on the

last occasion she had seen her.

It forced her to relive their last encounter, to conjure her up in front of her and she knew that whatever had happened to Kristyna had come out of the blue, unexpected, a tap on the shoulder, from an unconscious state through surprise straight to terror. And it had all happened quickly.

Only one fact emerged that she had not been aware of. The blood found on the coat was not human but rabbit's blood. The body found in the car had had both ears. Claire hugged this one small fact to her and found it of some comfort but again she wondered whether this had been yet another instance of Barclay's idea of a joke. He would have known the little touch about the ears would remind them of his past story.

At the same time another thought flashed through Claire's mind. There had been no independent verification of Barclay's stories. It could all have been made up.

Except Sadie Whittaker's tale. That had been no fable.

This was the trouble with Barclay – it was too hard to be sure what was fact and what was fiction.

The pathologist held back on the cause of death. He gave a sickening list of damage to the body, said flatly that it was not possible to say which had been done pre mortem and which post mortem because of the great heat and the tendency of bones to splinter and skin to split.

The only fact he could be sure of was that she had not been alive when the fire had started but had died sometime previously, probably more than a month before.

Claire rolled this fact around in her head. Dead – for around a month? Barclay had held on to her *corpse* for all that time.

Why wait? Only to set fire to it.

The answer banged back at her. Because he wanted to gain access to her car.

It was to be her funeral pyre.

Again – why? A formality?

She looked around her. Rolf was staring straight ahead and she knew he had switched all his emotion off. Siôna had his head in his hands, bent low, rubbing his temples as though he had a bad headache. Behind her, she knew, was the row of nurses, Kristyna's colleagues, sitting still as statues.

The coroner was a plump lady with straggly blonde hair and a dark brown cashmere sweater which strained across large, rounded breasts. She looked in her middle-fifties, and tired.

She finally adjourned the inquest pending police enquiries. And back at Greatbach they continued with their work mechanically, waiting for something else to happen as though it was inevitable and they had no influence over events but were being blown here and there. Puppets on loose strings.

The atmosphere settled slowly and uneasily. The morning meetings had resumed but they were different. Claire found it hard to concentrate. She would look at each staff member in turn and wonder what they were thinking. Once she found herself visualising a Daliesque image of a can opener cranking open their crania and herself peering into the matter, sifting through all that *they* knew, adding it to all that *she* knew or *thought* she knew.

But what was real and what simple paranoia or imagination?

Grant was no help. His mind was stapled to swags of material, colour charts, and the like. The moment she tried to discuss the situation with him his eyes would glaze and his face assume an abstracted look.

So time ticked forwards.

Then a week after the inquest Rolf stuck his head round her door with a friendly, 'Mind if I come in, Claire?'

She shook her head, knowing that the atmosphere in the hospital must be broken soon, like heavy, hot weather before an electric storm. The strain was too great. It was too hard not to confide in colleagues or trust them. So she looked with pleasure at Rolf's face, now almost gaunt. He looked ill and tired. She suddenly realised just how much they wanted this to be all over, like a painful course of treatment. For there to be an explanation, a conviction, safety. It brought it home to her how very tempting it must have been to acquiesce to Gulio's conviction. Had she been here then she would have terribly wanted it to be him and see him locked away in Broadmoor or somewhere else – for ever.

In law they call it settlement. It seemed a very complete word.

'Sit down,' she said, the warmth in her voice even surprising her. 'Come on in. How are you?'

He hesitated, surprised at her friendliness. They had all grown too used to keeping things back. 'Not good,' he admitted, sinking into the chair. 'I've been thinking about Heidi a lot lately.'

She was surprised. She had thought it would have been Kristyna he would have wanted to talk about. But she suppressed her surprise, put her head on one side and willed him to talk – and keep talking. She knew it would be an aimless meander which would probably get them nowhere. All it would achieve would be a release of the pressure inside his head.

'She was a powerful force here, you know, Claire. Her methods were innovative but they were clever too.' A pause during which his eyes flickered over her.

He was wondering whether he could trust her.

'We were working on a thesis – a way to treat psychopathy.'

'But it isn't amenable to treatment.' It was one of the basic laws of psychiatry.

'She believed it was.'

'How? Cognitive therapy?'

Rolf Fairweather hesitated. 'No,' he said bluntly.

'How then?'

He still didn't speak but flushed dull crimson. 'It was – unethical.'

She drew extra air into her lungs. 'What do you mean unethical? Where are her records? Her notes? What did you do?'

'We treated them as they treated us. We stopped being reliable.'

She thought, working this one out step by slow step. The psychiatrist letting down her patients, becoming inconstant. They who should have been the rocks of their existence. Letting their patients down would unleash only anger. Hatred and fury which had been the hallmarks of Heidi's murder. Finally she looked up. 'You're talking about a motive, aren't you?'

Fairweather nodded miserably.

'You let Gulio stew because. . .'

He put a hand out in a stop sign. 'The circumstantial evidence was overwhelming. The police didn't even look for anyone else. We all wanted to think . . . There was blood on his hands, Claire .'

'There's blood on a surgeon's hands, Rolf,' she said quietly. 'It doesn't make him a murderer.'

She didn't need to point out the implications – that had the right person been charged with Heidi's murder Kristyna would still be alive. And Nancy Gold. And Nancy's baby too – whatever his subsequent fate might have been. But looking at his face she knew he was already miserably aware of all this. It hung around his neck like the Ancient Mariner's dead bird.

'Where are your notes for this trial?'

He handed her a small buff folder he'd been nursing. 'We could never have published it, Claire,' he said. 'It was too unethical. We never could have got permission from the patients.'

Curiosity got the better of her. 'And did you think it worked?'

'Too soon to say but . . . ' He stood up, agitated now. 'It's better than letting them walk all over us,' he said angrily. 'They make such monkeys of us, Claire. They are always in the right. We in the wrong. They can default on appointments, then turn up when they don't have one, demand to see us anytime, refuse to take their medication, lie, cheat — ' He stopped dead just as she was about to soothe him with a, 'Hey. It's just a job. Cool it. Chill out,' sort of comment. But she stopped short and instead observed crisply. 'But we can set parameters, Rolf. If they don't stick to them . . .'

'Yes? What then? What really, Claire? If they don't stick to them and then commit a crime we're to blame. We can't win.'

She was silent. Unhappy.

She could not believe that Heidi, her heroine, would have been a party to this, to reverting to a reflection of her patients' animal behaviour. It was not so – surely?

The question hung in the air between them.

Rolf Fairweather stared back. The energy had drained out of him. He was pale, his breathing shallow, his chest wall heaving.

'Give me the file,' she said very quietly. 'I'll run through it and then discuss it with you after the weekend.'

He bowed his head and left, leaving the file on her desk.

Chapter Nineteen

What happens when you awaken the dragon?

You risk being burned by his breath.

As Claire leafed through the file Heidi's murder was falling into place.

Barclay would not have liked being crossed and yes, he was intelligent enough to understand what Heidi had been up to. So he would have smouldered. Planned his revenge with detail and malice. This, then, was his motive.

Claire read on.

There had been seven patients on the trial but Barclay had been by far the most dangerous with an impressive list of offences. Major cheque fraud, rape, assaults on his girl-friend, manipulation of his mother, physical violence, threats, a complete disregard for the law. The others had been less intelligent with fewer criminal convictions. Interestingly it would seem that Heidi's treatment had worked on six out of the seven. The others had stopped defaulting on their appointments within a couple of months. There was documentation of jobs begun and stuck at, even relationships lasting. Four out of the six had been discharged. Their behaviour had improved. Only Barclay's behaviour had not. He had remained resistant to Heidi's ideas.

His behaviour had remained unpredictable, his atten-dances at clinic erratic. Heidi had not achieved superiority over him. They had struggled until the end. Her end.

On \March the 14th 2003 Barclay had stormed out of her office, banging the door behind him hard enough to knock some plaster off the ceiling and into her cup of coffee. Impossible to stage-manage but unfortunate. It had finally provoked Heidi into threatening Jerome Barclay with a Section Order for antisocial behaviour.

Unwise.

Had he then festered over the weekend, planning her

punishment and sneaking back on the Monday evening?

Unseen?

She settled down and studied the document more carefully, word for word.

The first page was justification for what she was about to do:

'People who are diagnosed as having a severe personality disorder pose a very real problem to police and psychiatrists and can be a threat to the general public. There is no known treatment. It is not amenable to cognitive therapy – the patient simply agreees to the conditions, making promises which he (or more rarely she) has no intention of keeping. To deny them treatment is unethical from all points of view, ours, theirs and the public at large.'

Claire turned the page. *'We selected only patients diagnosed as having a personality disorder here, at Greatbach, using the criteria based on the World Health Organisation classification of mental and behavioural disorders, code F60 which describes "specific personality disorders not directly resulting from disease, damage or other insult to the brain, or other psychiatric disorder."'*

'Our proposed treatment is based on the premise that the only emotion you can rely on from this group of people is grudging respect for an equal or a superior – someone who plays the game equally well – or better than they – using their own (lack of) rules. Therefore Rolf Fairweather, Kristyna Gale and I have agreed to select our most severely affected patients and treat them disconnectedly for a given period of time – in this case three months. We shall then review them and assess whether there is any improvement in their behaviour using the following criteria: an acceptance of responsibility, expressions of remorse for previous adverse actions, acknowledgment of blame and an acquisition of reliability.'

Claire cupped her chin in her hand and stared into space. With this clinical proposal Heidi must have known she was signing her own death warrant. Or had she awakened the beast, without understanding just how dangerous that beast could be? Was this, then, the reason why Barclay had finally flipped and murdered her?

Barclay must have had a reason for committing such an action. Heidi's murder had not been committed on impulse. It must have been planned.

Claire read on.

'*To put it in the simplest layman's terms, we messed them around. Made appointments we were not here to keep, kept them waiting, denied them medication etc. Our rationale behind this treatment is the bootcamp of the United States. They prevent their villains from having the upper hand by dehumanising them, brutalising and robbing them of their preening identity and confusing them by breaking their own rules. The US now has lower crime figures per capita than the UK.*'

Claire nodded in agreement.

'*But in this country our police, government and left wing agitators have a loud and articulate voice. We tend to spend a great deal of time arguing our decisions from all angles. This prevents us from carrying out difficult or potentially unpopular courses of action – even when the benefits are unarguable. Were this treatment of even potentially dangerous future offenders to be made public outcry would follow. Our passionate desire is to anticipate crime and prevent it where possible. But our work has to remain subversive because we would be banned from testing our theories on the grounds of improbity with the result that science, yet again, would be robbed of an opportunity for advancement. Personality disorder would remain an untreatable condition. The only option open to us is to prove retrospectively that this treatment can work by monitoring the cohort of patients and proving that their anti-social behaviour is reduced.*

Thus also justifying the need for secrecy.'

Claire's eyes opened wide. This was danger-country for any psychiatrist both professionally and personally. Simply reading through the file she had a sense of doom. Heidi had not been authorised to treat any patients in this way. She tried to visualise Heidi, her heroine, as she had last seen her, lecturing from the stage in the Medical Institute, writing this and failed completely. Instead, leaning back in her seat, for some odd reason of association, a vision of Cynthia Barclay's pleading face swam into view, blue eyelids blinking rapidly like morse code, beseeching someone to sympathise with her son.

She heard that gravelly voice taking his side. 'They're not being fair on him.'

Claire had interpreted this as maternal indulgence, sticking up for her offspring against the cruel world. Now she was not so sure. She closed her eyes almost shut. Why had she thought of Cynthia Barclay at that very moment? Because, surprisingly, she did sympathise with her. They had not played fair with him. And this was an odd turn of events. The last thing she had expected was to find herself taking sides with Jerome Barclay against Heidi Faro, Rolf and Kristyna.

More – riding on the back of this was another, more uncomfortable idea. If Barclay had struck out at Heidi in frustration, because of the way his treatment was being handled, was it possible he had killed his mother through the same motivation? Even when the two crime scenes were so vastly different? Her next thought was blame. Did the responsibility for Cynthia Barclay's death lie ultimately at the door of this ill-judged clinical trial dreamed up by Heidi and her colleagues?

Had frustration at his situation driven Jerome Barclay to murder both his psychiatrist and his own mother and finally his psychiatric nurse? Was this the reason he had let her go?

Because he had no reason to kill her?

Barclay did not need a reason.

She screwed up her face, concentrating hard, and replaced Cynthia Barclay's pleadings with pictures of her own.

Heidi's murder had the hallmarks of a typical, helter-skelter psycho-killer whereas Cynthia's had been subtle with a controlled and orderly crime scene – if crime scene it was. It was still possible that Barclay's mother had taken her own life either accidentally or deliberately.

And Kristyna? Who knew? It was all so shrouded in mystery. She had vanished. No one really knew what had happened next. Act Two had been the planting of the coat which was so typical of the way Barclay would behave – the cruel tease, the blood dripped theatrically over the collar. And then the final act, the dramatic torching of the car.

Three deaths – each one different.

Was it possible that the difference in the crime scenes did little more than reflect Barclay's state of mind over the killings? Hatred and resentment towards his psychiatrist and his nurse but little more than weary disdain towards his mother.

She closed the file, stood up and shook herself as though to rid herself of the taint. It was up to the police now to pick Barclay up and question him. This was not within a psychiatrist's powers. She moved towards the windows, gripped the wooden sill.

She badly wanted him found.

She stared towards the door, visualising events as they must have happened, wondering now whether she should pass the known facts on to the police.

In her hand she held a clear motive for a brutal killing. She was sure now that Barclay had killed Heidi. Something held her back – the Medical Defence Union's warning, *Don't play at policeman.*

She decided not to and put the file in the bottom drawer of her desk.

So Kristyna and Nancy had both been found but Jerome Barclay remained invisible. Claire sensed he was near but cleverly concealed.

He would, at some unexpected time, reappear, popping up like a Jack in the Box, with the same silly grin on his face and stupid wobbling head.

In the meantime she had a breather, time to work with other patients. She had given Paul Frank a clue. He should work on it.

Kap Oseo had failed to make his second outpatient appointment. Claire filled the screen in, dictated a letter to Oseo's GP and kept her fingers crossed that all was well. When stable there had been a gentle side to the Jamaican that she had liked.

Two days later Detective Inspector Paul Frank arrived in her office unannounced and without an appointment.

'I have the result of the diatom tests,' he said, 'that we performed on Nancy. I thought you'd want to know the results as soon as possible.'

She watched his face, slightly plump, pale and sweating, already tending towards lines, an aging fifty-year-old. His hair was thinning but he had good, strong teeth. Frequently lately he'd worn an air of tiredness, bordering on exhaustion but today he looked better. Eyes bright with energy. Something must be going well.

'The results show that your patient drowned,' he said. 'But not in canal water.'

Her first reaction was one of disappointment. If Nancy Gold had merely slipped into the canal it would have been an answer of sorts. She waited for the policeman to elucidate. It had been a difficult enough case. Let him savour the moment.

He did, with a rueful smile in her direction. 'There are no or very few diatoms. The forensic lab is of the opinion she was probably drowned in a bath. Her heels are quite bruised as though she kicked against something hard. There is damage inside her mouth and nose which the pathologist is convinced was caused by someone pressing hard on her face as he or she held her under the water. Her body was then dumped in the canal.'

'As far as the pathologist could tell the baby was alive until the moment of Nancy's death. It was a little girl,' he added. 'Practically full term.'

Claire gritted her teeth. One word repeated constantly in her mind like the ratatat of a gun. Evil. Evil. Evil.

'Find him,' she begged. 'Get him in before he . . .' But her mind could supply nothing nightmarish enough for Barclay except, *finds me again*.

March arrived. The evenings were lightening, spring beckoned. Daffodils waved with joy, purple crocuses celebrated. There was a lightness in people's step. Everywhere people talked more quickly of optimistic subjects – holidays and families, Easter and the approaching summer. As she drove to work Claire saw signs of home decoration, scaffolding up, windows being knocked out, gardens being dug over. The celebration of the end of winter was almost primordial, probably because it had been so very dull and grey and wet.

But the change of season did not extend inside Greatbach. It was approaching the first anniversary of Heidi Faro's death and Claire had convinced herself that Barclay would want to mark the occasion. The feeling of inevitability persisted.

He would find her.

March the 17th this year fell on a Wednesday, a warm day with low lying cloud which returned Stoke to its native air of drabness. She was late finishing. It had been a busy clinic with two extra patients needing assessment urgently. So although she had planned to be safely at home by eight o'clock, eight fifteen found her crossing an empty car park alone and unlocking the door.

Familiarity. Actions we perform many times in a week, done unconsciously.

She climbed in, started the engine. And immediately sensed he was right behind her. There was an odd smell in the car, something clinical yet not quite clean. She saw his face in her rear view mirror and felt the taste of pure terror in her mouth as he pressed down the central locking device.

'Barclay,' she squeaked.

'I'm not the one,' he said urgently. 'I know what you're thinking but you're wrong. You've been wrong all along. It isn't me.' He laughed lazily. 'It never was. I didn't care what you thought while it didn't do me any harm but now it is and I want you to call off your dogs. The police want me. I've seen posters. It's been on the TV. It isn't me, I'm telling you.'

Two voices argued inside her head. *Evil evil evil* and the rational psychiatrist's sentences, *We should talk. Give yourself up. Confession is good – not for the soul – but for peace of mind.*

When will psychiatrists begin to realise they have no open access to the mind, no control over it? They are permitted to peer inside – that is all. The first voice screamed again in her ear. *Killer. Torturer. Murderer.* And she realised she had screamed out loud.

Barclay's voice, speaking quietly, rationally, in her ear. 'Don't turn around, Claire Roget. I want you to remember. If I really was the killer I could snuff you out now. Like this.' A snap of the fingers, a stroke of her neck.

She wanted to vomit. Dared not move. He might have a knife – a rope – a gun. Just his hands could be enough. She wanted to move but was stuck, rigid, to the seat.

This, then was how he had kidnapped Kristyna and persuaded Nancy Gold to walk out of Greatbach where she had at least been safe. This voice was so persuasive. So reasonable. So credible. It was easy to be lulled into trusting.

Her head snapped around.

'Killer,' she said. 'You don't fool me, Barclay. Give yourself up. Stop doing it.'

He was lolling back in the seat and she couldn't see any weapon. 'How can I stop what I never started, you stupid cow?'

The psychiatrist's half of her brain noted how well he was fitting into the mould. Plausible, convincing, a born liar, criminal, intelligent, failing to accept responsibilities for his own actions.

To try and distract herself she ticked them off on her fingers. Glib. Cunning, manipulative, shallow affect, callous, lack of remorse, empathy. She felt her jaw drop.

He had them all.

Slowly her brain froze. Sitting behind her, in her own car, was the man who had butchered Heidi, drained the blood out of her body. The same man who had killed Kristyna somehow, kept her for a month in some derelict potbank before incinerating her body in her own car. The same person who had drowned Nancy Gold and her unborn baby.

The terror was numbing. She heard a soft whimper and knew it came from her. It was a plea for her life. She was the bird caught in a cat's claws, the rabbit in a car's headlights, the mouse in the corner of the barn as the owl swoops down.

'I let you believe it,' he was saying, a smile curving his entire face, 'because I didn't care and it amused me. I'm not having fun any more, Claire. Call the dogs off. I'm telling you. Call them off.'

He unlocked the car door, opened it. And then he was gone.

She had heard it said that after a life-threatening event people take a while to phone the emergency services. Shock intervenes. Instead of summoning help immediately they wait, out of a fear that their attacker might return. Besides – she couldn't find her mobile phone in her bag. It seemed to have slipped away. When she did find it she couldn't locate the three nines. Her fingers missed the keys. She wanted to throw open the car door and get rid of the smell of him, the taste of him, the taste of her own fear. She wanted to be sick. But he might be outside – waiting for her. So she was unsure whether it was better to be inside the car or out. He was still here, inside, but outside might be worse. He could be lying in wait, ready to pounce. And outside was worse because the car was her only escape. After minutes or seconds – time had certainly stopped – blind instinct took over. She accelerated out of the car park, screeching through the security barrier the second it lifted and drove to the police station, parking right outside, leaving her lights on, her doors open, but having the presence of mind to pull the ignition key out of the lock.

The desk sergeant stared at her, as did the plain clothes guy carrying two mugs of coffee. 'Please,' she managed. 'Please.' Before sinking down on the seat. 'My car's outside.' She was going to babble, she knew it. She managed to say, 'Paul Frank. Detective Inspector. Please.'

'Just take it easy.' The plain-clothes guy set down the two cups of coffee. 'Now what's happened.' And suddenly she realised how much there was to tell. Too much.

'I'm a psychiatrist,' she began.

It was good starting ground. 'At Greatbach.' She heaved out a long, shuddering breath. 'We've had a lot of problems. Someone got into my car – this evening. Detective Inspectot Frank. He knows all about it. He's been managing the case.'

'OK.' The policeman looked suddenly decisive. 'Let's start with your name, shall we?'

'Claire Roget. Doctor – Claire – Roget.'

He scribbled it on a pad, went back behind the desk and picked up the phone, glanced across at her, closed the window.

Excluding her.

Claire wanted to burst into fits of hysterical giggles. *He thought she was a nutter. That she was the mad one. She drew*

back her lips to giggle and pressed them together.
Maybe she was. Maybe she was.
To laugh would be inappropriate behaviour.

The policeman must have spoken to Paul Frank. When he came back out again he'd lost the bothersome question from his eyes. And she thought how very ordinary he looked. Brown hair, average height, brown eyes, Chinos, an open-necked shirt. She would not remember him again.

'He'll be here in a minute. I won't start taking a statement from you. He'll get it himself. OK?'

She nodded.

'Cup of tea?'

She would have loved a gin. A stiff gin with plenty of ice and lemon, drowned in tonic water, but it wasn't on offer. She nodded. 'Tea would be nice.'

The tea was the wrong colour brown and it came in a styrofoam cup, well stewed. She drank it anyway.

Paul Frank arrived in a surprisingly short time, took one look at her and read her mind.

'You need a drink,' he said and pulled a ready-mixed G&T from his sports bag.

She could have hugged him.

Just the sniff was enough.

'Go fetch a glass,' he said to the brown-haired plain-clothes guy. 'With some ice in.'

'Now then. Let's talk.'

He led the way along a grey-lined anonymous-looking corridor to Interview Room I. Took the iced glass from the young policeman and closed the door behind her.

She spoke first. 'You do realise it's the anniversary of Heidi Faro's death, don't you?'

He bumped his forehead with the heel of his hand. 'I should have remembered. It only struck me as I was driving in. I heard the date on the evening news. I knew then.'

'Claire,' he said when she'd sat down at a pre-formed chair, across the table from him. 'Do you mind if I record this?'

'No.' The gin was restoring her.

'Now,' he prompted. 'From the beginning.'

But somehow it didn't come out as it had meant to. 'He says it isn't him,' she said steadily, swishing the G&T around in her mouth. 'He says you're suspecting the wrong man.'

'From the beginning,' he said again.

'He was in my car,' she said. 'Waiting for me.'

Frank sucked in a noisy breath.

Her mobile phone interrupted and looking at the display she knew it was Grant. They exchanged a few terse words and she flicked it off. Grant was too stunned to react.

'He was waiting for me in the car.' An involuntary shudder. 'I was so frightened. I thought, I believed I would die.'

Frank's face didn't move a muscle. He stared at her with a wooden expression.

'He said it wasn't him,' she repeated. 'He said that he'd had his fun but that now it wasn't funny any more and to call you off.'

She swigged at the gin, finding comfort from the cold of the glass.

Frank leaned in closer. 'You've seen him. You're a psychiatrist. What do you think?'

She stared back. Confusion reigned. 'He is,' she said slowly, 'a dangerous psychopath. Capable of violent, serious crime.'

Antagonised by his clinician which gives him a motive.

'What are you basing the assumption on?'

She hid behind the textbook stuff. 'Disregard of human life and suffering. He is capable, Frank. As a child he cut off a rabbit's ears, cooked a bird live in the oven, slowly warming it to prolong its suffering. He threatened his girlfriend. Terrorised his mother over a number of years. He shows a wanton disregard for law and rules and frightening cruelty.'

Paul Frank stared at her, hard for a minute. 'You saw the pictures of Heidi Faro,' he said.

She nodded, knowing he was doubting her word.

'And you heard the details at Kristyna's inquest.'

'Yes.'

'I agree that Barclay is all the things you say,' Frank said. 'But as for being capable of both these murders . . . I'm not convinced.'

She leaned towards him, almost as though she wanted to exclude the tape recorder from listening. 'But you don't think it was Stefan Gulio either, do you?'

Stefan's reedy voice came into her head. 'I hear screams. There is blood.'

She tried to convey this to Frank. 'He *hears* screams. He *sees* blood. He *picks up* the knife. He runs along the corridor. He makes no mention of the actual assault. Ever. Not in one of his statements. Imagine if he was summoned to see Heidi, is waiting outside the room. He would hear screams. Then he enters the room and sees mayhem. So he *runs*. And is *found* by Siôna Edwards.'

'But we've got no connection with Barclay. We don't even know that he was there that day.'

Time to produce her joker card. 'He had a motive,' she said.

Paul Frank looked dubious.

She explained as best she could the circumstances of Heidi's trial, including the fact that it had been unethical enough to be illegal.

And watched him remain sceptical. 'Claire, *Nothing* puts Jerome Barclay anywhere near the crime scene on the night of Heidi Faro's murder. No one saw him. CCTV didn't pick him up.'

She could almost feel the doubts crack the surface of her theory. She sat back in her chair, quiet now and listening to sounds in the rooms and corridors outside.

She took another drink of her gin. The ice cubes must be melting. It tasted watery.

'You see, Claire, I have a real problem with this.' Paul Frank was not meeting her eyes. 'If Jerome Barclay is all the terrible things you say why did he let you go tonight? Why didn't he kill you?'

She had no answer except possibly one.

Perhaps it had not been her time.

'It must be Barclay,' she said firmly. 'It must be. Because . . .' *If not Barclay and not Gulio – who?*

She held on to the end of the sentence and made an effort to speak to the policeman in his own language.

'He must know we're after him and seriously does want to speak to you.'

'I'm willing,' he said, 'I want to speak to him. But he must realise he is a suspect in a murder case.'

'Then make it public,' she said. 'I think he'll listen. Otherwise he is smart enough to know that he can never shake you off.'

She felt like a traitor towards Heidi, Nancy Gold and Kristyna.

Suddenly she felt helpless, almost in a state of collapse. 'So what next, Inspector? We wait for another murder?' She was struggling against rising hysteria. 'I can't do that, Paul. I can't. We've had three awful murders at Greatbach. Three people I knew.'

He jerked forward. 'But you didn't know Heidi Faro. You never met her.'

'I did.' It almost felt like an admission of guilt. 'I attended clinical meetings she was teaching at. I *learned* most of what I know from her. She was my mentor. My guru. A friend.'

'I see.' All of a sudden suspicion danced in his eyes. 'And then you took up her job, stepped into her shoes – as it were.'

She nodded very slowly, understanding he was heading somewhere she refused to follow and returned to her original line of thought.

'I can't just wait for something else to happen, Inspector. We're all at the end of our tether. And if I left no one would step into my shoes. The word would out that Greatbach is not safe. The place will close. Secrets will lie, the patients and staff disperse and you, Inspector, will have an unsolved mystery on your hands. Three murders. If you don't find some settlement, this is what will happen.'

She had not voiced this even to herself until now but having said it she knew it was the truth.

There had been criticism of the unit and their methods, a complaint that it was not as secure as it might be considering the inmates and their past. If on top of the events of the past years word got out about Heidi's so-called treatment of psychopathic patients they would be finished anyway and their work discredited. The treatment of personality disorder would slide back to the last century. She'd watched it happen to other forward-thinking psychiatric units. If they weren't achieving Government targets they would be closed. And in no Government paper were three murders considered a target.

Chapter Twenty

It took the police precisely eleven more hours to locate Jerome Barclay, and Paul Frank informed her briskly at nine o'clock that very night that her patient had requested she be present at his initial interview instead of a solicitor.

She'd been at home, watching a DVD with Grant, nicely relaxed in jeans and a T-shirt, but as soon as Paul Frank had spoken one sentence the adrenalin started to flow. Excited to be in at the kill she changed back into her work suit. At last, she told herself, they would learn the truth.

But driving in she still felt a mounting apprehension. Barclay was her patient. He would know of her involvement with the police investigation. What role would he choose for her?

She would soon learn.

Inspector Frank met her at the doorway of the police station and all around him was an excited buzz of static. All the police personnel were moving quickly. There was none of the sluggishness that had marked them before.

Murder has this effect on the police. Like a serious accident has on the medical profession. It is a challenge which stretches your skills.

'Let's talk,' Frank said, keeping his voice very steady. There was only the vaguest hint of a quaver that leaked his excitement. She followed him through a wide hallway, turning right into a short corridor and through a semi-glazed door with his name on.

No mention of Stefan Gulio now, mouldering in Broadmoor, she thought, with a hint of spite that surprised even her.

'So?' she said, glancing around the small, untidy office.

'We're not there yet,' he warned. 'There's a lot we don't know.'

'How can I help?' *Nail him to the cross?*

'I just need to know how to extract the right information from him, how to ask my questions, which questions to ask. I want to trip him up.' He looked as eager as a spaniel puppy.

'Then let him talk,' she said. 'Keep your questions, as far as possible, open-ended. Don't direct him unless he's veering way off subject. He's attention-seeking. He'll do anything to keep you listening. He loves the sound of his own voice. So let him enjoy himself. Just – let – him – talk. Give him a free reign. Ask him how he felt about Heidi, how well he knew Kristyna. Those sorts of things. But I'll give you a word of warning. Don't try and pretend you're his friend. He's too intelligent to fall for that one. He'll see right through it and lose respect for you. And then he'll clam up.

'One more thing, Paul. I'd leave his mother's death out of it for now. After all – you have two violent deaths, undoubted murders, to keep you occupied. The evidence to make him responsible for his mother's death is likely to be very circumstantial and he'll know it. He'll also know you won't be able to pin it on him and assume your case against him for the other two is equally weak.'

Something almost defeatist softened D.I. Frank's eyes so he looked vulnerable.

He was frightened. Not of Barclay but of failure, of having his quarry in custody and letting him go.

Aloud he said, 'The only trouble with giving him a free reign, Claire, is the time factor. The PACE clock ticks away. If he rambles on I'm going to have to release him without finding anything out. I can apply for a couple of extensions but I've got nothing on him. I can't charge him, Claire.'

She smiled, wanting to pat his arm. 'I know, but you will get there. I promise.'

'I hope so.' His face softened for an instant then he stood up, squared his shoulders, cleared his throat. 'He's refused to have a solicitor present. He wants only you.'

'Suits me,' she said bravely but as she walked along the

corridor she started to worry. What did he mean, he wanted only her. What game was he playing?

Frank pushed open the door of the interview room.

Barclay was sitting quite still, his hands stretched out in front of him, palms down, flat on the table. He looked up briefly as they entered, didn't smile. Didn't speak.

He was wearing a turtle-necked, grey cashmere sweater, sleeves pushed up to the elbows, exposing a gold watch on powerful-looking forearms.

Claire sat down opposite him, meeting his strange eyes without a smile and noting an answering lack of expression on his face. No curiosity, no interest, no fear. Nothing. Even though she had half anticipated this it still disconcerted her.

'Hello, Jerome,' she said – quite formally, aware that he would despise any greeting short of authentic.

He nodded back, swivelled his eyes around to watch D.I. Frank settling down in his chair.

Paul Frank switched the tape recorder on and announced their names into the microphone with the time and date. Then he addressed Barclay.

'You understand that we are questioning you in connection with the deaths of the psychiatrist Heidi Faro on March 17th 2003 and the death of Kristyna Gale on or around December 10th 2003?'

Barclay's eyebrows registered some surprise. Maybe that he wasn't being questioned about his mother's death too. Claire resisted the temptation to glance across at Inspector Paul Frank and see his face from Barclay's angle.

'Yes.' Barclay's answer was steady and clear. Ideal tape recorder material. Claire watched him closely. Still unsure what game he was playing.

'We'll start with the murder of Heidi Faro. She was *your* psychiatrist, I believe.'

'That's right, Inspector. And she helped plenty of other

people too.'

What a clever, consummate little actor he was. Convincing in his part of innocent, victimised patient. Playing co-operative. So far.

'Can you remember where you were on the day she died?'

'That's a long time ago, Inspector.'

'It is indeed, Mr Barclay, but it would be very helpful if you could tell us where you were.'

'It so happens I was at work.'

'You know we will be checking up on this.'

'As far as I remember,' he added.

Innocent eyes.

'What time do you finish work?'

'Round about six – the other side of town from here.'

He folded his arms. 'I remember the day particularly because that night it was on the news that there had been a murder at Greatbach Psychiatric Unit and I wondered who had been killed. If it was anyone I knew.' A faint smirk. 'And how.'

That was when she understood. Barclay wanted accolade, admiration, the slow handclap, fear for Heidi's mode of death. It had all been designed to provoke fear.

In spite of the presence of Inspector Frank it had its effect. Claire was chilled. She studied the performance with respect and fear. She had never before realised just how conscienceless these people were. And Barclay was giving it all he'd got. She was learning more about psychopaths than she could possibly have done from any existing textbook. She could almost feel Heidi Faro sitting on her shoulder, applauding.

Paul Frank gave her a swift glance before asking Barclay another question. 'How did you feel when you heard it was your own doctor who had died?'

Barclay had to think about that one. He had no appropriate response in his repertoire.

Frank was about to repeat the question when he

answered. 'Well – that's a difficult one. I thought . . .' His eyes rolled around the walls of the interview room. 'To be honest I wasn't that surprised. There are some dangerous people out there. And she – well – ' A swift smirk at Claire. 'She wasn't always fair on people, you know?'

Frank gave a startled look at Claire. 'What do you mean – she wasn't fair?'

Claire held her breath. She wasn't anxious for the police to even land on the fringe of Heidi's trial. Barclay fixed his eyes on Claire, knowing he had her on the run now. 'She let us down, you know. Used us. She didn't need to keep seeing me. She'd make appointments and then not turn up. She was unprofessional. She stopped some treatment which had been helping.'

This was news to Claire. 'What treatment?'

'I'd been having sessions with Rolf, the clinical psychologist. He'd been very pleased with my progress.'

Rolf had said nothing to Claire.

Paul Frank sucked on his lips. 'So – to recap – the evening Doctor Faro was murdered you were with your girlfriend, watching a film. All evening?'

'That's right, Inspector. Sorry to disappoint you.'

If the policeman had picked up on Barclay's little hints he had passed by on the opportunity.

'OK. Let's skip a few months forward to December the 10th.'

Barclay looked disappointed. 'Don't you want to ask me about my mother? She died too, you know.'

'Do you want us to?'

Claire tried to send D.I. Frank messages, not to get sidetracked. This was a delaying tactic. She was sure.

Barclay looked sulky. 'You did want to question me about her round about the time she died.'

Frank responded quickly. 'Well – ' Her advice must have got through. 'I think we'll concentrate on the two murders for now. If you want to add something about your mother later on we can talk about that.'

Barclay looked even more grumpy.

'Now then,' the D.I. prompted. 'Tell us about Kristyna. How well did you know her?'

Barclay pretended to think for half a minute or so. 'I suppose I really got to know her after Doctor Faro died,' he said. 'You see – she took over some of the clinics and spent quite a bit of time with me. I found her very pleasant. I liked her.'

*To Claire it was a bland statement yet sinister consider*ing her suspicions.

She felt she must speak. 'How did you feel about her?'

Surprise registered at the question.

'Like I said.' There was a taut warning in his face. 'I liked her. She was a pleasant person, quite helpful. Easy to talk to. Gave me a few pointers about how to behave if something annoyed me. How to make sure I stayed out of trouble. She wasn't like Doctor Faro. She was gentle – and more honest.'

'You didn't like Doctor Faro then?'

He was practised at an expressionless face.

'Not really.'

Still no emotion. Claire badly wanted to shock him into saying something.

'Do you remember making a comment about Kristyna's ears?'

Barclay looked at her as though she was odd. 'Her ears?'

It was turned into a joke which had the desired effect. Claire felt herself faltering.

'No. I don't remember saying anything about her – ears.' His smile reduced her to a fool.

But he didn't ask why she'd asked about ears particularly, she noted.

Frank must have sensed her discomfort. He butted in. 'And where were you on December the 10th last year, the day Kristyna disappeared?'

'In France,' Barclay said, with a bland smile. 'I sent you all a postcard, didn't I, Doctor Roget.'

She gave a reluctant nod.

'I returned on the 20th. Just in time to do my Christmas shopping like the rest of the population.'

'Not Kristyna,' Claire said through gritted teeth.

She was hating this levity when the very name, Kristyna, conjured up the terrible picture of that blackened corpse, fists up, ready for a fight. She felt a sudden rise of bile and desperately wanted to get out of the room, away from Jerome Barclay's mocking face.

'You can check my credit card statements if you want,' Barclay proffered.

She remembered the coat. 'And the night of February the 2nd?'

Some emotion crossed Barclay's face.

Triumph!

He hesitated before speaking. 'I think, Inspector,' he said, 'that you haven't done your homework thoroughly. I think you'll find that I wasn't in the country then either.'

Claire felt suddenly clammy and cold and recognised the symptom for what it signified.

Doubt.

And Barclay looked that little bit too confident.

Detective Inspector Frank must have picked up on it. 'OK', he said, 'we'll take a break now.'

Outside Paul Frank looked concerned. 'You know as well as I do that if he didn't put the coat in your car he almost certainly couldn't have done either of the other two murders.'

'There are ways round it,' she protested. 'He could have . . .'

But she knew already that if Barclay had persuaded someone else to plant the coat it would imply collusion. And there was no one he could trust. She felt her case erode like a sandcastle confronting the incoming tide. It was melting away in front of her very eyes.

'Go home,' Paul Frank said kindly. 'We'll keep him in the cells overnight, take a look at his passport and check with immigration. If we have any news I'll ring you.'

She dipped her head, exhausted now, by the effort, by the recent hype, by the sudden drop in her adrenalin level. She felt unbearably tired.

On the way home she chewed through every single possibility. Barclay had somehow slipped back from France, that any stamp found on his passport was a fake, that immigration would be mistaken. That someone else had masqueraded as him.

That . . . But none of it washed. He had looked just that bit too confident.

Grant was waiting up for her. At least she found him slumped across the sofa, barely moving as she let herself in.

'I thought you wouldn't be in for hours,' he mumbled.

She flopped down beside him. He sat up with a jerk. 'What's the matter?'

'I need a glass of wine first.'

He was soon back with a glass of rosé. 'Here,' he said. 'Drink this then tell me.'

She took two gulps before blurting out, 'It can't be

Barclay.'

'Why not?'

'Because he wasn't even in the country either when Kristyna was abducted or on the night the coat was planted.'

As concisely as possible she explained. Grant was frowning by the time she'd finished. He rapped out a couple of questions but ten minutes later the only question he was asking was the same one that had been burning holes into her mind. 'If not Barclay, then who?'

'Not Stefan Gulio,' she said. 'He was safely locked up when Kristyna was abducted.'

'He might still have killed Heidi though . . .'

'It's not impossible,' she admitted. 'People do commit crimes out of character sometimes. But . . .'

But underneath she was still doubtful. She had met Gulio, spent some time with him, made a brief assessment of his mental state and capacity. And she was as sure as she could be that Stefan Gulio had not strung his psychiatrist upside down before slitting her throat.

She looked helplessly at Grant. 'It wasn't Stefan,' she said. 'It just wasn't. He isn't capable of such practised evil. Barclay is. I sensed it clinging around him like London smog. But being capable of evil doesn't mean you committed the crime. He can't have killed Kristyna. It simply isn't possible.'

'Correction.' Grant interrupted. 'He could have *killed* Kristyna but he can't have put the coat in your car.'

'What good is that?' she asked. 'They are two halves of the same crime. The strange thing is that I can really imagine him planting that coat. It was just the sort of thing he would do.'

He yawned. 'Let Inspector Frank sort it out,' he said. 'It's time we went to bed.'

But in bed she couldn't sleep. Grant was tired and breathed heavily at her side but strangely enough, instead of finding it a disturbance, she liked it. It comforted her, soothed her, made her feel safe and secure.

There was another reason why she could relax that night. Barclay was in police custody.

She must have dozed and then awoken. It was lightening outside though still quite dark. She heard odd stirrings beyond the window, the sound of the next door neighbour's dog give his sharp bark once . . . twice.

In her mind she walked through the sequence of events slowly, trying to keep the pictures from being too graphic. Heidi. Cynthia. Kristyna. Nancy Gold. Their looks and sounds intertwined.

Blue eyelids, a pierced nose, an irritatingly flat voice with a slight Southern twang, Nancy's sweet, childish voice singing ever-so-softly, *Golden slumbers, Kiss your eyes.* Heidi, tossing her dyed hair self-consciously while expounding her theories on psychosis, Kristyna's silver-link bracelet jangling. Nancy rhythmically rocking – a pillow. Cynthia's wrinkled, pale hand, reaching for more pills, more gin. A cigarette. The deaths of four very different women.

She must have dozed off again or relaxed deep enough to allow the four women to creep from the shadows only to merge into one another. No longer four crimes but one.

Like the Chinese cube made of rectangles of wood it was a puzzle that seemed impossible to fit together to make one whole. But the law of medicine is to connect seemingly irrelevant symptoms into one logical sequence which is an illness then call it a syndrome. This happened so that happened which led to this and then to that and so on. Using this law of connection these were not random or disconnected murders but part of a wider, so far incomplete picture. Heidi *could* have been killed by Barclay or by Gulio or even by someone else. Cynthia *could* have committed suicide. It was possible that no one would ever know the truth about Kristyna – not even how or when exactly she had died unless the killer made a full confession. The only fact they all knew for certain was that someone had planted her coat stained with the blood of an animal in Claire's car and a few weeks later deliberately torched her body in her own car. *Why* was a matter for conjecture but destruction of forensic evidence was the most probable explanation.

Claire lay with her eyes wide open and willed her mind to meander along the dark crevices of the sulci of the brain and play the game of What If?

So she lay perfectly still, waiting for Grant to stir, welcoming the silence, the quiet and the almost dark, the lack of sensory stimulus. She stared into nothing and saw and heard nothing except the voices of the dead women and the people around them.

Whining. 'They're not being fair on my son.'

Victimised. 'I *hear* screams. I run along the corridor. I see blood on my hands. I pick up a knife.'

Jingling. 'If you want to meet a *real* psychopath — ' *Rolf's words.*

Confidently didactic. 'Patients diagnosed as having a personality disorder are notoriously difficult to treat. If you then explore those subdivisions of, say, schizoid, or dissocial, psychopathic, sociopathic, amoral and antisocial we then border on the criminal. Occasionally on the dangerous. It is this class of people that are troublesome to society.' Heidi's words.

Serenading a pillow with a crooning lullaby. Nancy.

And finally Barclay – threatening. 'Have you ever asked yourself what is the most indestructible part of a body? Teeth, bones, the underwires of a bra. Jewellery.'

'Keep thinking of the car, Barclay', she whispered. 'Think of the wires in the tyres, the numberplate, a body entangled. Think then of the two together. We will have you.'

The coat. She focused on the coat, recalling the scent of damp wool, Kristyna wearing it. Full and long, swishing as she walked. It had been an unusual coat for her to wear, rather conventional and old-fashioned compared to her usual style. The recall was so vivid that when Claire breathed in she inhaled not the musty bedroom air but Kristyna's perfume, an unconventional, kasbah scent. For some reason this brought vivid recall of her odd hair, spiky and red. And she asked herself a question she should have posed months ago. Why had Kristyna worn that conventional coat when a leather jacket would have been more her scene.

For forensics?

It was the nonsense answer. But leather doesn't hold on to cells and hair, like wool does.

It was a blind alley but with lighted windows staring down. She could make no possible connection between Kristyna's choice of clothes that day and her disappearance. It was something else to tuck away in an attic room, never to be used.

But the last vision was hers alone – a child, stealing towards a baby's cot, a thick blanket in her hand.

Most of us have intent. Only for a few does it translate into action.

We all have memories we must conceal to preserve our sanity. It was time she came to terms with this one. She had wished Adam harm but not acted on it. She had committed thought-crime. Was it then possible that in this Brave New World she was, in fact, a murderess?

No. She was not. So why was she accusing Barclay of murder?

The radio alarm started beeping very softly. In ten minutes it would grow louder. And then louder still. She slipped from between the sheets and padded downstairs to make coffee.

Grant mumbled something back as she placed the mug down on his bedside cabinet. Then he was suddenly sitting upright.

'Oh, hi,' he said gratefully. 'Thanks.'

It took seconds for the caffeine to find its way into his bloodstream. 'So,' he said, yawning. 'Where are you up to?'

She set her mug down deliberately on the bedside cabinet. 'I don't know where I am,' she said. 'I know where I should be. I'm a psychiatrist. My office is the bloody murder scene. I know all the protagonists in this. If I *really* understand anything about psychopathy I should have arrived at the solution before the police and the evidence should be supporting me.'

She flung off the bedclothes, suddenly energised. 'I should be there.'

'Hey,' he said, protesting, laughing and tugging the duvet back over him. 'Hey. You're not a copper.'

'I'm better,' she said, vanishing into the shower. 'I'm a psychiatrist.'

Twenty minutes later she was dressed in a short, pleated skirt and cropped sweater with high-heeled cowboy boots. Grant took one look. 'I see you're not about to act the shrinking wallflower.'

'I've got a reason,' she said earnestly, 'for this. I've got plans for today.'

The telephone blasted out and she knew before she answered that it would be Inspector Frank, that he would have confirmed that Barclay had been out of the country when the coat had been planted in her car and that he would have let him go free.

She just knew it.

And she was right.

'Have you an address for him?' she asked, her voice tight with irritation.

'All taken care of. ' He was soothing but she still fizzed. 'So that's that?'

'Not exactly,' he said warily. 'We've still got unsolved crimes here.'

'Right,' she said. Her interest was waning. If Barclay was not a killer they were all wrong. Heidi, Kristyna, Siôna,

Rolf.

Rolf. She brushed her teeth hard and fast, spat the tooth-paste into the sink.

Rolf.

She had a question for him.

He was in the staff room, eating a biscuit and drinking a mug of tea, looking surprisingly relaxed in a red open-necked shirt and black jeans. 'Hi,' he said. 'Good morning. How are . . .'

'The police pulled Barclay in yesterday,' she said.

The news seemed to add to his good humour. 'Wonderful. Good.'

She regarded him very steadily. 'Why do you say good?'

Rolf grinned at her. 'Now why do you think? Coffee?'

'Mmm.' This was turning into an interesting conversation.

'What do you think he has got up to?'

Rolf was too intelligent to do anything but consider the question carefully.

'Well now,' he said. 'We have a number of interesting crimes. Four women. Three certain murders. And we've all mooted the point that there could be a Barclay connection.'

'We have,' she agreed, sitting right back in the chair and crossing her legs.

'So?' He was puzzled.

'Let's get at the truth, Rolf,' she said softly.

'What do you mean?'

For the first time since she had entered the room Fairweather's confidence wavered.

She took her advantage. 'Do you mind if I ask *you* a question?'

'Not at all.' The long, thin fingers wafted elegantly.

'The sessions that you had with Barclay,' she said. 'He told me that they had helped him. What did you do?'

'Mainly agreed with him when he expressed negative thoughts.'

'I don't understand.'

'Instead of making it an issue when he didn't like something I'd agree with him – about people, about situations.'

'Which people?'

Rolf sucked in a deep breath. 'Heidi mainly.'

'It was about this trial, wasn't it?'

Rolf licked his lips. 'Mainly that.'

'You sided with him against Heidi, encouraged his aggression against her.'

Rolf was too smart to fall for this. 'No,' he said steadily. 'Not that. I merely . . .'

'You merely let him think you were in agreement with him.'

Rolf said nothing.

'And what did you really think?'

'I was fed up,' he said. 'You have to understand. I'd worked with psychopaths for years. We'd got nowhere – ever. Made no difference. Then along comes Heidi. Full of the most wonderful ideas. Completely controversial.' He took a sideways look at Claire. 'I don't know if any of you ever realised just how controversial she was. She was up to all sorts. But she got results. That was the wonderful thing about her.'

'You really liked her?'

Rolf nodded. 'Oh I did. I applauded her when she went in for this study. I thought it was wonderful. But it was unethical. It was never going to be used as a treatment programme. It couldn't have been so it was no use. I tried to get her to switch to another treatment programme – one which *might* have passed the ethics committee – but she refused. She'd lost her judgement completely. Once Barclay realised that she lost her authority with him.'

'But you let Stefan . . .'

'You don't understand. None of us here knew anything for sure. The police came barging in. The crime scene was – well – horrific. Stefan was whimpering in the corridor. No one could get any sense out of him. The police just fingered his collar and that was that. None of us knew for sure what had happened.'

'Was Barclay even around that day?'

'We *think* so.'

'And did you mention that fact to the police?'

'What would have been the point? We didn't know Barclay had been around. We didn't know whether he'd challenged Heidi and we didn't know for sure whether Gulio had suddenly taken it into his head to go for his psychiatrist. Besides . . .'

It came to her then. 'You were worried that the details of the clinical trial would be made public.'

Rolf nodded. 'Heidi was dead. The police believed they had the right person. We didn't know anything for sure.'

'Who was in on this?'

'Only Kristyna and Siôna. We didn't really talk about it. We just knew. It was a tacit understanding. All we did was allow the police to get on with their investigation, Claire. All we had were ideas.'

'Which you didn't pass on to the police.'

'I don't feel guilty about that.'

'Even though Kristyna's dead.'

'But that can't have been anything to do with Barclay.'

So who was it to do with?

Chapter Twenty-Two

She found Siôna on the ward, pouring out cups of tea from a huge, aluminium teapot.

'I think we should have a private word,' she said. 'Alone.'

He sensed immediately that she was disturbed, ushered the two care assistants out and closed the door very carefully behind them. There was real deliberation in the act.

'Rolf's told me about the clinical trial,' she began.

He nodded uncomfortably. 'I thought it was best you knew.'

'I'm not sure where it leaves us.'

He didn't look at her. 'It never was a good idea. Personally I thought she was mad to even consider doing it. If she'd been found out she'd have been in Shit Street.'

'Did you try to dissuade her?'

Siôna smirked. 'You knew Heidi. She wasn't one to listen to criticism. She was always sure she was right. And she wasn't going to change her mind.'

There was real dislike in his voice and in his expression.

Claire went suddenly very slightly dizzy. She had felt like this when she had been on a fairground ride once, when the world had spun around her, leaving her sick and weak, unsure which was sky and which the earth. She was seeing Heidi Faro from a new angle.

How little we know people. Suddenly her mentor seemed a flawed person, so anxious for accolades, to break new ground, that she was not above behaving like one of her patients, disregarding law, ethics, human consideration even.

That was when events started hurtling around her mind like loose objects in a poltergeist's room.

Such behaviour bordered on the psychopathic.

She decided then that whatever the consequences the police must be put in the picture. She rang Inspector Frank from her mobile phone while sitting in her car. He listened without comment and she pictured his forehead creased with frown lines.

It was an unwanted complication.

'Do you seriously believe this has bearing on her murder?'

'It wouldn't be the first time a psychiatrist abused the position of trust,' she said flatly. 'It's happened before. And our patients are an unforgiving lot.'

His silence spoke volumes. 'OK then,' he said. 'If you think it's justified we'll come in tomorrow and talk to some of your colleagues.' He paused before asking, 'And was Kristyna in on this?'

'Oh yes,' she said.

She returned to her office and closed the door behind her. She needed to be in there, alone.

And so she had turned full circle. She was back at the very beginning, in the cream-painted room, standing in the exact same point – in the centre of the floor – breathing in a recalled smell of paint. But things had changed. More than a year had gone by since Heidi had been murdered; months since she had started her new job. Three more women had died and if anything the situation was worse. It had spun wider out of control. She didn't believe anyone had been charged appropriately with any of the crimes.

What she craved was this:

Order out of disorder. Logic out of chaos. Form out of entropy. Some sense out of it all.

The words marched through her brain like an invading army. Claire sat down at her desk. From the top right hand drawer she drew out a blank sheet of paper. From the centre drawer she found a pen. And then she started to doodle.

Most people when they doodle draw the same shape. Hers was always a ballet shoe, a toed ballet shoe, en pointe, ribbons neatly criss-crossed. Always at the same angle. Never two feet. Always just the one, shaded and pointed, the leg sketched in through the swell of the calf to the point just below the knee. It reminded her of a trip to the theatre when she had been six years old to see the ballet, Sleeping Beauty. It had comforted her then through a poorly understood spate of parental quarrels. It had had the same soothing effect through the years and worked again, today. Trips to the ballet and other such treats had stopped completely when Adam had been born.

Maybe because the form was so obviously feminine her thoughts flew away from Barclay and towards Nancy Gold and the child she had been expecting.

Or more precisely the *father* of the child she had been expecting.

She ringed the word *father* and shaded in the area around it to denote mystery. No one but dead Nancy knew who that father was.

But they could find out.

Something about her liked the vagueness of the generic term so she continued in the same vein.

Mother.

Cynthia Barclay. Three questions sprang to mind. What sort of a person had she been? How much had she known about her son? And how had she really died? Again a dead person knew the answer although it was possible that Cynthia had died in a confused, alcoholic haze without ever knowing the precise circumstances.

Next the *doctor.*

Doctor Heidi Faro, as she had appeared the last time she had seen her, flicking her dyed auburn hair from around her face, stamping heavily around the platform in the clumpy brown shoes.

Not like the ballerina's footwear which she was softly shading in.

Using the words in the abstract helped her to lose her intensity and blur the focus.

But she had no generic term for Kristyna. Except, maybe, nurse.

So how had she fitted into all this? What exactly had been her connection with these disjointed, dysfunctional crimes? How exactly had she been spirited away? Why?

And all of a sudden Barclay seemed a less plausible concept. He was fading as a chief suspect.

She sat with her middle fingers centred on her temples as though she was a clairvoyant.

Focus on the child.

Focus on the father of the child.

Focus on the doctor.

Focus on the mother.

Then separate them out. Spin them apart like a salad spinner.

Then start again with Heidi Faro. The first to die.

Why had she died?

Had it been Gulio after all?

Claire sat right back in her chair. The police had never needed a reason to put him in prison for the crime. He had been mad. Locked up. Put away. That was enough for them. In their book anyone who was not the norm was capable of any dastardly deed.

So slowly Claire drew all the facts into focus. Her assumption had been all along that it had been Barclay who had killed his psychiatrist because he was capable of doing it. Barclay didn't need much of a reason.

But what if it hadn't been Barclay?

She put her head in her hands and peered through her fingers, side to side.

Then who else?

Separate the crimes, Claire. The order came from nowhere.

At the same time she pressed her fingers hard against her temples, irritated with herself. She needed clues. Not guesswork. Not witchcraft or clairvoyancy.

She needed reasons. Logic.

Nancy's voice sang to her.

Golden Slumbers Kiss your eyes.
Smiles awake you when you rise
Sleep pretty darling do not cry
For I will sing a lullaby.
Her voice sounded clear.
With a message sewn in.
Claire started to draw a second shoe, foot pointed.
Unconnected with the first leg.
The two feet danced independently of each other. Not right and left but two one-legged dancers.
What did she know about the people who had died?
Very little.
Heidi first.
She dropped the doodles on the floor and drew out another sheet of clean paper.
Heidi Faro, she wrote.
Brilliant psychiatrist, ground-breaker on personality disorder, desperate for recognition. Carrying out a successful but unethical clinical trial on a selected group of her patients.
That would have seriously pissed Jerome Barclay off. Enough to have made him take the ultimate risk. That was her assessment as a psychiatrist. She drew a thick black line underneath this.

Next name:
Cynthia Barclay
Barclay's mother, benevolent, a bit stupid, taken advantage of.
She could see no real reason for him to have murdered his mother. But suicide? Would she have done it?
Claire thought very carefully about the circumstances surrounding Cynthia Barclay's death. What had happened immediately before Cynthia had swallowed the fatal pills?
Tablets and alcohol. Not a terribly reliable way to kill yourself – or another.

Nancy.

Unhinged. Murdered her child, yet desperate for another one, a woman who acted before thinking. The baby was a nuisance, preventing her from having the partner she wanted, ergo she removes it.

Only afterwards does she regret the action.

Claire looked at what she had written.

It was the word *desperate* which sprung off the page at her. Two people desperate for different things.

Next Kristyna.

Here was the puzzle. There was no desperation here. Kristyna had been happy, well-adjusted, in a stable relationship. And a psychiatric nurse here at Greatbach.

So. How were they all knotted together?

And then the phrase entered her brain again. Not boring this time but wafting, like a wispy, insubstantial cloud. Nancy's desperation for a child. Perhaps that had been the start of it all.

She picked up the phone.

Oh yes, personality disorder lay right at the heart of the events here, at Greatbach. But there are various types of personality disorder, subdivisions characterised by various other characteristics.

Like: Preening conceit.

Narcissism.

Lust.

Dominance.

Psychopathy.

Many people display various characteristics of personality disorder to various degrees. Some are able to suppress it so well they never come to the attention of the police or the psychiatrist.

Some may even work in the profession themselves. Nurses are not immune from pathology.

What if Kristyna had not been all she had appeared?

Another idol with feet of clay.

The knock on the door startled her. Rolf stuck his head round. 'Couple of us are going for a drink,' he said. 'Care to join us?'

But she knew now she must distance herself from them. 'Not tonight, Rolf,' she said. 'Maybe some other time.'

What a useful phrase it is, 'Maybe some other time.'

We all know the time may never arrive.

Already feeling a traitor she spoke to Inspector Frank for less than a minute. He didn't ask why or look for justification. Serious crime is justification in itself.

Afterwards she would be humbled by the faith he had in her. Embarrassed, humiliated. But on that night she felt only the triumph of being listened to.

Chapter Twenty-Three

How the tables turn. What is up is soon down – and vice versa. A position of superiority reversed into one of vulnerability. On the following day Jerome Barclay rang her up and asked, quite politely, for an appointment.

She acceded and arranged to spend half an hour with him on the following day.

That night she hardly slept. It was walking into the lion's jaws. She was frightened, yet excited. She could not reconcile herself to rethinking. To her Barclay was evil, someone whose only remit was to cause harm.

So why did he want to see her?

She tossed and turned all night, trying to enter his mind and work out what it was he wanted from her.

She arrived at work half an hour early and spent the time looking out of the window, watching the front door.

He turned up at the agreed time, ten o'clock on the dot, and deliberately, to lay ghosts to rest, she saw him in her room.

Heidi's room.

He lolled in front of her, sitting low in the chair, almost challenging her to use the phrase, wasting my time, and came straight to the point.

'I think you have suspicions of me,' he said.

She could not deny it.

'I haven't been in any trouble for a long time now. Nothing serious has ever been proved against me. It's not as if *you're* carrying out an undercover illegal clinical trial. I'm no good to you. I'm not a danger to society and never have been. Let me go, Doctor Roget.'

'But it's *you* who have come in to see *me*.' she reminded him delicately.

He blinked.

Then leaned forward. 'I'll make a deal with you. If I reoffend I'll come back. You can study me like an ant in a Bug-Box. But for now I just want to get on with my life.'

She eyeballed him. 'When will you start telling the truth, Jerome? What happened to your father.'

Barclay looked surprised. 'My *father*?'

She nodded.

'But that was years ago. I was just a kid.'

'I need the truth, Jerome. It's a good place to start.'

He thought about that and then sneered, his top lip retracting like a horse's to show his teeth – and his disdain. Slowly he shook his head. 'Wouldn't be wise, Doctor Roget.' His eyes worked their way around the room, his brain obviously flashing through possibilities before he added, 'I might have tinkered with some of my father's stuff. He was a diabetic, you know.'

'Your mother told me.'

A sudden flash of anger. 'I thought she would.' Followed by a gleam of appreciation. 'You are thorough, Doctor Roget. I will give you that. You're a worthy match for me.'

She dipped her head. 'And your mother?'

Barclay looked bored. 'My mother was a miserable old soak,' he said coldly. 'The best thing she ever did was to swallow enough booze and drugs to make sure she didn't wake up. She died happy.'

His eyes challenged her so hard she knew he had killed her. She also knew she would never be able to prove it. He would get away with it again.

Fear a clever killer.

She leaned across the desk. 'I *know* you're guilty, Barclay,' she said, feeling flames light her eyes. 'I think you possibly killed your brother and your father. I also know the only reason you've never been inside for a good long stretch is because you threatened both your mother and Sadie Whittaker. One day you'll pay for your crimes. It'll all catch up with you.'

'A moralist,' he said, mocking. 'How refreshing. Maybe

one day it will catch up with me. In the meantime you don't have a stick to beat me with. It's time to say goodbye. I want you to sign a statement releasing me and stating that I am no longer a danger to society.'

She experienced what she knew Heidi had then, real hatred for a patient, for the blatant way he was mocking the system, destroying it and cocking a snook from the sidelines.

But for now she could do nothing but let him go. He was right. She had nothing against him.

'OK then,' she said finally, 'but I warn you now. If you come before the courts again I will give evidence, Jerome. I will say that in my opinion you are a dangerous criminal capable of acts of unprovoked violence.'

Barclay treated her to a penetrating stare. 'You're threatening me?'

'I'm simply stating a fact.'

'I don't care about you,' he said in a measured voice. 'But I will tell you one thing. I didn't kill Heidi Faro. I didn't string her up. I didn't cut her throat. I didn't butcher her. Take my advice. Look a bit closer to home.'

He stood up. 'And now, goodbye.'

Paul Frank arrived at one o'clock, with a team of officers. They commandeered a room in the main building, along the corridor from her office. For more than an hour she heard the sounds of people's footsteps walking there and back, past her room. She knew what they were doing. The detective did not call on her.

He was concentrating on the men.

At four came the knock on her door that she had been half expecting. Rolf's face appeared round the edge. 'Care for . . .?'

'I'd love to,' she said. 'Really love to.'

He waited until they were outside before suggesting, 'I'll give you a lift.'

She shook her head.
She would not go the way of Kristyna.

All was still muddled in her brain except that in the distance she could see the blurred halo of the truth. It was out there, simply needing to be discovered and recognised.

She knew bits.

They wandered across the road to the pub.

It was quiet, few people at the bar. They were served straightaway.

'White wine spritzer,' she said, 'with Slimline tonic.'

Rolf bought himself a pint and they sat and faced each other.

That was when she realised she did not know where to begin.

'I don't know much about you,' she said. 'Not really.'

Something in the dark eyes recognised the fact that she was fishing for anything that would nibble.

'What do you feel you want to know?'

'Let's start with your family, Rolf.'

'Why do you want to know, Claire?'

An innocent enough sounding question but his response was not innocent. He was a man who had something to hide.

'I already told you,' he said carefully. 'I have had the same partner for a number of years. She works at the university.'

It told her nothing. None of the members of staff had ever met Rolf's partner. He came to all the events – dinners out, Christmas party – alone. It sounded reassuringly normal. But who could know? Only two people had had open access to Nancy Gold. And if her theory was correct one of them had begun the chain of events which had led to three murders.

So she played the game, gazed innocently back at Rolf Fairweather and asked him whether he would have liked children.

'My partner already has a child,' he said.

'How old? A son or a daughter?'

Something bold beamed back. 'Why do you want to know?'

It was no use pretending. He knew this was not a social question.

So she said nothing.

He took a deep draught from his pint and set it down on the table hard enough for a little to slosh out and form a puddle. In it she watched the reflection of the one-armed bandits flashing out their garish colours, red, blue, yellow.

'My partner is thirty-nine,' he said, watching her face for any response. 'She was a psychologist too. We met in university. Her son is ten years old and has severe autism. He is a full time job. She switched departments so she could look after him.'

'I'm sorry,' she said, knowing that the 'full-time job' would get no easier and would never end except with death.

'Our lives have been completely changed,' he said, with another sharp swig at the beer and a twisted smile, 'by Martin's illness. We thought – oh never mind what we thought. When we met we certainly didn't imagine our lives following this particular path. Still.' He finished the beer while she searched his face for bitterness of resentment. She did not see it. Either it was not there or he was very good at concealing his innermost emotions. She didn't know which was true.

Suddenly his focus turned away from himself. 'And what about you, Claire? Life has changed for you in the last year, hasn't it?'

She couldn't deny it. 'It certainly has. Another beer?'

'Half,' he said. She bought it and herself a Diet Coke and returned to the table.

'Why did you take the job in the first place?' he asked curiously. 'Most psychiatrists would have gone anywhere but Greatbach. Why did you walk into a dead woman's room, a murder scene?'

'Because . . .' She thought for a moment. 'Because I

admired Heidi. I wanted to continue the work she had started. I'm interested in personality disorder. It fascinates me.'

Fairweather sneered. 'This isn't an interview,' he said. 'This is for real.'

What it is to see the skull beneath the skin.

Fairweather's face had altered. There was something greedy in it.

She wanted to get out of the pub. But – she looked around her. In here were half a dozen people – maybe a dozen. The beer-bellied landlord. Phones, barmaids, civilization. Out there . . .

She shivered. Out there was an empty car park.

Images of the scene of crime pictures of Heidi's murder scene flashed back into her mind.

Gulio, cowering in the corner, knees hunched up to his chin.

She stared helplessly at Fairweather.

'Was it you,' he asked.

'Sorry?' Her voice sounded strangled.

'Who suggested they DNA test us?'

She nodded.

'Why?'

'To find out who was the father of Nancy Gold's baby.'

'You suspect a member of staff?'

He sounded genuinely horrified.

She nodded. 'But . . .

She grabbed her bag. 'Don't you think we should talk about this somewhere more appropriate?'

'Fine by me,' he said carelessly. 'I'll call in tomorrow.'

So this, then, was how it had been done. She was beginning to understand that the deaths at Greatbach had followed a pattern. Except that it had not been one pattern but two. Barclay's pathological character had been intertwined with a deeper character, one who had been capable of so much worse. Not only the teasing, cowardly hints and provocations but murder.

The double helix of evil.

But ideas were not enough. If the case of both Barclay's parents had served anything it had proved that you needed evidence. Hard evidence. Suspicion alone was not enough. Whether he was innocent or guilty of murdering his parents or not she would never really know. Except that he would never be successfully convicted of either crime. She needed this burden of proof. And for the first time in her life she understood the true weight of the word. It was a burden.

She sat in her office the next day, restless and distracted, finding it hard to concentrate until she gave up and walked across to the ward. Siôna was in one of the side rooms, talking to a patient. A new, young patient named Julie-Anne who had suffocated her baby brother in a fit of jealousy.

Claire had read the notes and met the girl briefly, feeling a shudder of recognition as the girl had told her the stories which proved how much more her parents had loved the child than her.

She had lifted a tear-stained face up to Claire's. 'And now they'll always hate me.'

Claire had felt physically sick.

It could have been her.

Siôna had lost weight; his beer paunch had vanished with the worry and his face seemed lined and set in a permanent scowl which he failed to eradicate as Claire walked in. She knew he simply wasn't enjoying his work any more. She had heard rumours that he was considering emigrating to Australia.

And she suddenly didn't know what to say.

She felt embarrassed and responsible because Siôna had only altered since she had been here and events had spiralled right out of control. She felt she should have done something. But what could she have done? She was as much a victim of events as he was.

She sat down in the chair next to Julie-Anne and motioned to Siôna to continue with his 'chat'. He was good, there was no doubt about this, teasing out the most relevant facts – how much planning had gone into the assault, what she had done when she had realised the child was dead, how her feelings were now.

The three main ingredients of murder – forethought, the deed itself, remorse.

All documented neatly, pigeon-holed, as eventually all crimes must be. They all follow their own predictably straight lines. However dreadful a crime is committed they've all been done before and will happen again. And again. They are lined up in all our futures, waiting for the necessary elements: an evil mind, an evil act, a victim. An opportunity.

Claire interjected with a couple of questions of her own and the three of them talked for an hour – an hour and a half – while really she wanted to ask Siôna two questions:

Who? And why?

With his perceptive skills how much did he understand?

But the opportunity did not present and she wandered, still fidgety and dissatisfied, back to her room, frustrated again that the window would open only a regulation four inches.

She stood and stared out at the concrete square, the four benches, the pots of flowers. She smiled. As usual patients and staff were mingling. Sometimes difficult to tell them apart.

The thought struck her then. This had been Heidi's window too. Maybe she had seen something from it. The next question, inevitably, was what? What could she have seen?

When the magician whips his black cloth off the audience gasp with shock. Because what they see is not what they expected to see. They have been deceived. But it is only a trick of the eye, a diversion of the concentration.

Claire gasped.

Seeing all. Seeing what Heidi Faro had seen and challenged. Then died for that knowledge because it is what we protect, our secret self, the part we try to hide from public view. That inner, shameful self.

Claire stared, weakened, stared again and felt frightened. Because she knew now it had been the view from this window which had led to Heidi's death. And seeing it she too was in that same danger. So real she could taste it. Rancid and sweet. Foul and sickly, as deadly as sugar had been to Barclay's father.

Rolf stood with his arm casually draped around a young, female, inmate. No more than eighteen years old, the girl was small for her age and immature in character too. She had been sentenced to Greatbach for an indefinite period after setting fire to her parents' house following a family quarrel. The immature do this, an inappropriate response to a crisis. Except that her mother, her step-father and her younger brother had all died in the fire while she had watched and exulted. Even observed by bystanders to be fanning the flames with a teenage magazine.

Inappropriate behaviour

At any other time, without this heightened sensitivity the atmosphere at Greatbach had created, she might have taken Rolf's casual gesture for nothing more than a close chat. But as she stared and studied, she read anguish and discomfort in the girl's face, perceived that the girl was try- ing to pull away and that Rolf's grip on her shoulder was tight and making her wince.

He was taking risks. Who knew who might be watching?

She was.

Heidi had.

There was a quick movement in a window opposite. Little more than a flutter of the wind, something dark, altering the light and shade behind the glass.

Claire jerked away from the window. She did not care to be observed taking the part of a voyeur.

Her eyes roamed along the windows and she reflected what a sinister place Greatbach really was, full of watching eyes and people who had done terrible things to other peo- ple, family, friends, strangers. All in the name of an imbal- ance of the mind. According to some psychiatrists no more than a microscopic amount too little or too much of alu- minium or magnesium or some other element in the brain.

Suddenly mental illness seemed to her the most terrify- ing of all diseases. Invisible. Unpredictable. And worse – hijacked by evil people as an explanation for their cruelty.

She moved back to the window, mesmerised, drawn to it as though it was a sticky surface and she a fly. Watching as Harry Sowerby, suicidal after a recent high, shuffled towards the pair, Rolf and the girl. Rolf's eyes flicked upwards, towards the windows or the sky. There was another movement behind the window opposite. When she looked back down she looked right into Rolf's eyes. He knew he was being observed.

She jerked backwards again, out of sight, knowing he was grooming the girl.

As he had seduced Nancy Gold. And made her pregnant.

The DNA would prove it.

But the result would take a week.

He had until then.

Claire put her hand to her mouth and tasted the danger

in this place.

People were vulnerable. Patients and staff alike because here there was an opportunity to dominate and humiliate.

The mad are especially vulnerable when they are mixed in with the bad, the sheep with the goats.

She should know because she understood pathological character and where it could lead people – perpetrator and victim alike. What her patients were ultimately capable of. And the staff.

The staff. You could not discount them merely because they were health workers. They are not immune from disorders of character. They can dominate, humiliate, lust after, lie, cheat. They are capable of all the usual vices. Plus a few more.

It was a fine spring evening when she left the hospital that night. The birds were singing their spring mating message, the sky was blue. So she was deluded into feeling safe. This was not a dark, cold night in December.

But the minute her car failed to start, the engine turning impotently over and over, failing to fire, she felt uneasy.

She looked right across the almost empty car park, along white-outlined bays with the warmth shimmering above. No one was here. It is strange how there are sudden pools of emptiness in the most normal of days, unexpected silences, an abrupt lack of people as though time holds its breath.

In a minute – two minutes – the car park would fill again.

But it didn't.

She knew then.

Kristyna had had trouble with her car.

Before she had vanished. Before she had turned up in the funeral pyre. She too had fallen through one of these holes in time. We are too dependent on the internal combustion engine. Sometimes it forms the barrier between life and death.

She lifted the bonnet, hoping for something easy – a

stray wire, a loose spark plug.

There was nothing.

She locked herself into her car, tugged her mobile phone from her bag and cursed the fact that Grant had no car. He could have picked her up, returned her to normality,

As it was she could submit to her hysteria and call the emergency services for nothing more than a non-starting car or she could rationalise and ring for a taxi.

But she had no number.

Panicking now she sat back in the car, stupidly turned the engine over one last time and wondered which number to ring.

Only to say she was vulnerable and frightened?

She would feel foolish.

So should she walk?

Eventually she rang the number the insurance company had given her for emergency breakdown – and was put in a queue.

She heard his approach, softly, steadily, measured, quiet steps. Then the car door was pulled open, the phone taken from her hand, the end call button pressed.

Chapter Twenty-Five

'Get out,' he said. Not aggressively or roughly but matter-of-factly. In his normal voice.

She shook her head.

'It'll be easier for you if you do,' he said.

Still she shook her head, tried to pull the door closed. It was futile. He was in the way.

'Come on,' he said, still in the same tone. 'Don't be silly, Claire.'

But fright can sharpen the senses so she was not paralysed but pumped full of adrenalin. He might have killed Heidi, watched Gulio take the rap, murdered Kristyna, witnessed – even encouraged – her suspicion of Barclay but he had met his match here. She would not submit.

Foolish woman, do you think Kristyna or Heidi submitted? Do you think Nancy Gold submitted? They all thought they could fight, ultimately win.

They all lost.

It was the ordinary voice which made her most frightened. It made her sick, unable to move, unable to think rationally. It fed her terror.

'Please,' she said and watch his lip curl.

'What are you begging for?'

'You're not going to get away with it.'

'I suspect not,' was his answer. 'Ultimately. Now get in my car.'

He must have suspected she would try to run because he looped some nylon sailing rope around her hands and pulled her out of her own car. Struggling chafed her wrists and his grip was iron fed. The long, thin fingers were too strong and supple. Without any warning he pressed on points either side of her neck and she went faint. Felt sick and dizzy and knew he could kill her here if he wanted to. No one was around to see or care.

She noticed he took her keys out of the ignition,

removed her handbag, locked her car door behind her, made it look like a simple breakdown, less suspicious.

She was on the back seat of his car, fumbling with the door handle.

He half-turned. 'It's a childproof lock,' he said disdainfully and concentrated on his driving.

She knew where he would take her. To the place where bone and china clay lay discarded on the floor. Where shards of porcelain and pottery were broken and sharp. She knew she would see the place where Kristyna had died and that she would share the same fate. Ultimately.

He manoeuvred through light traffic, swung in the opposite direction to the town centre and drove silently.

She had known it would be Longton. She could see the tops of bottle kilns, the tall potbank buildings, neglected, dirty, Victorian bricks. She heard traffic splutter and accelerate.

When they arrived she would have another chance.

It was a shock when he turned, rattling, into an alleyway, buildings all around and through a steel door topped with razor-wire. He left the car to padlock them shut behind him. More than ten feet high. She knew then she was trapped, seeing the same view that Kristyna had before she died.

'I want you up the steps,' he ordered, his voice strengthening, becoming more sure of himself. 'Don't try anything. It'll be harder for you if you do. And there's no point anyway.'

Her bag was on the front seat. She looked away from it but caught the dark blue of the leather on the bottom corner of her vision. She had a brief flare of hope. Mobile phone. Access so easy to summon help. A swift vision of a police helicopter, hovering in that blue, blue sky.

But he read her mind, snatched the strap, threw it on the floor. Then he met her eyes with happiness and triumph.

She looked away from it.

The steps were little more than wooden planks forming a staircase to the third floor. They looked unsafe and wobbled as she climbed. The bricks were a mixture of red and yellow, stained with years of grime. The windows were dirty too. It had the air of a derelict site. In the centre stood a fat-bellied bottle kiln.

Still dizzy from the assault on her vagus nerve she stumbled upwards, he dragging her behind him by the sailing twine. He threw open a door with flaking red paint and threw her in to a large, dingy room. 'And if you have any ideas of escaping,' he said, 'just look at the window.'

There was only one. Tiny, covered with chicken wire. As instinctively as a newly wed viewing a house she crossed over to it and peered through. On to people, small as Playpersons, far below, going about their business in a supermarket car park. The one place where people are guaranteed not to look around them. Certainly not up at an ugly, derelict building. Too much is going on at floor level. The daily trial of life of everyday shopping. The search for a parking lot, acquiring a trolley, making sure car doors don't bump, controlling the kids, locating the elusive shopping list. And that is before you have run the gauntlet of double-glazing saleswomen and charity collectors to arrive at the shop itself. And after you have spent twice as much as you intended the whole rigmarole starts all over again, loading up the car and dumping the trolley somewhere where it won't cause damage. Then there is the trip home.

No – no one has time to stand and stare. They are all far too busy.

Claire put her hands up against the window and saw where other hands had prayed too. This peek at normal life was tantalising and awful. Extra torture.

Fairweather slammed the door behind him and walked towards her.

'You just had to meddle, didn't you, Claire? Spy on me from the window. Play the clever doctor. I did try to warn you, didn't I?'

She could still play at being in control.

'No,' she said. 'You were the one to suggest Barclay to me. You did nothing to allay my suspicions about Gulio being responsible for Heidi's death. You wanted me here, Rolf.'

His eyes were expressionless.

He didn't care. Whatever she felt, however frightened she was was immaterial.

He simply didn't care.

He walked towards the door, passed through.

Then she was alone.

She heard him shoot a bolt, the rattle of a padlock and chain, footsteps receding down the steps.

When he came back she knew he would kill her.

Even so, she didn't feel frightened now but very very angry.

Chapter Twenty-Six

She knew it all now – too late.

Rolf had been in a position of authority, deceiving all who came into contact with him. He had that most dangerous attribute of the psychopath – plausibility.

Nancy Gold with her desperation for a child must have been an easy target. She would have suited him well, childlike, easy to influence, available.

But one thing she couldn't work out. Fairweather must have realised the child Nancy bore would ultimately be tracked back to him. Surely he wouldn't have taken such a risk? It would have meant at the very least losing his job, at the absolute worst a prison sentence.

He couldn't have afforded to take such a risk.

But he had.

Heidi, with her understanding of personality disorder, must have suspected something about her colleague was not quite right. Maybe she had had her suspicions about Fairweather and the female patients or maybe he had said or done something that made her doubt his integrity.

Possibly one of the patients had said something. Possibly even she had had even more concrete evidence.

Something beyond mere suspicion.

Like watching him through a window.

She must have rumbled him somehow, realised exactly what he was doing, challenged him. And the drama had begun.

It must have suited Rolf to watch Gulio being bundled into the police car. In fact she wondered whether he had been the one to summon Gulio to Heidi's office. It had always puzzled her what he had been doing there at that time of day, long after she would have normally stopped seeing patients.

Through the gloom she looked at her watch. Seven o'clock. It would be dark soon. Panic burst through her reason. She must get out of here. He would return, find her, kill her. The door. She ran to it, flung herself at it, pulling and pushing on the handle. But it didn't budge an inch. The window. But it was covered.

She pulled her shoe off, tried to break the glass. Then saw the scratches on the window frame and knew it would be reinforced. Panic burst through again like a drowning man breaking the water-surface. *Kristyna tried this. And Kristyna had died.*

'Not you too, Claire,' she whispered.

Next she walked the perimeter of the room. It was large, rectangular, darkening and cold but not damp.

It smelt clean and dusty. Dry, old dust. Crushed bones.

In the corner someone had swept a small pile of pottery dust, china clay and ground bone, tiny, glassy flakes of glaze. Her footsteps sounded muffled and hollow as they paced the room. She tried to distract herself by humming and walking the length and then the width.

There was no escape.

And he will return.

There are always questions you can whisper to yourself when you think you might die. Have I led the life I wanted to live? What more did I want from it? In some crystal ball is there only blackness and oblivion for me? Do I have a future?

Then the practical issues. Who will miss me? Who is missing me right now? Grant. What is he thinking, right now? That I am working late, that I have forgotten to tell him about a medical meeting or a social engagement? He will be trying my phone, puzzled – and a little hurt, possibily irritated, in view of this new détente we have achieved between us.

I wish I could tell him that I loved him, that I did care, that I did value the person he is.

There was paper and a pen in her pocket. An old, necessary habit, for a forgetful mind.

She began to write.

Gradually the light leaked away through the window and she was alone with her thoughts. Cold and numbed, hardly able to think, she made an ill-formed plan.

She would escape. She would not be another victim for Fairweather.

She did not sleep but dozed like the condemned woman in her cell, trying not to think about death but life.

At some time in the night she heard some scratching and knew there were mice here. Little friends.

She began to dream, still awake.

If this were Disney I would tie a note to the mouse's neck, having coaxed him towards me with chocolate crumbs I found in my pocket. He would scamper to the Tesco's car park and alert some of the late night shoppers. They, in turn, would look upwards to the window and see my frantic wavings before storming the building with their lists and their trolleys.

It made a nice, comforting dream.

She sat, propped up against the wall, half in and half out of the dream, fumbled in the inside pocket of her coat and found her one chance at salvation.

A steel nailfile.

It was not exactly an automatic machine gun but it was a chance. Her only chance.

She must go for the neck or the eyes. Somewhere easily vulnerable.

Dawn stole in through the window watching her practise how to hold this feeble weapon, how to thrust, how to make contact. Maim, disable, take out. The euphemisms we associate with war and killing.

It was still early when she heard footsteps steal up the stairs, the subdued rattle of chains, the click of an oiled lock being slipped back. She scrambled to her feet. Upright she would have a better chance of survival.

The door yawned open.

In battle they yell to frighten their opponent, confuse him, startle him, intimidate him.

Instinctively she did just that. Yelled and screamed like a mad Mohican, belted towards him and thrust the nailfile deep into his neck where she hoped his carotid artery was.

He gurgled and, stronger than she, pulled her hand away, put his finger over the tiny wound. She thrust again. Surprise was on her side. That and desperation gave her strength.

This time she did catch the carotid artery in the angle of his jaw. Just where you might feel for a pulse. There was a satisfying spurt. His eyes rolled. He knew he was in trouble.

She thrust again, found the jugular vein this time.

Heard screaming, 'I will kill you. I will kill you.'

Caught the shock in his face and knew the voice was hers.

Then she ran.

Out of the door, stumbled down a few steps, grabbed the hand rail and looked up. Above her Rolf Fairweather was staggering out of the door, his hand held to his neck, blood seeping through his fingers and she knew she had not disabled him sufficiently yet.

She heard his strangled cry of hatred, saw the rope looped in his hands and knew how Kristyna had met her death.

Mumbled a prayer for the dead and prayed that she would not join them.

Ran down to the ground floor. Two steps at a time and felt as trapped as a rat in a cage.

There was no escape.

He was three flights up, his hand held to his throat, blood not seeping now but spurting through his fingers.

She read the coldness in his eyes.

His car had been reversed into the yard, behind the gates ten feet high, padlocked and impenetrable.

Still she ran towards it. Rattled it impotently, turned to the car.

It was locked. And Fairweather would have both the keys to the car and to the tall, steel doors she could not possibly climb.

'Shit,' she muttered to herself. 'Shit. Shit. Shit.'

She heard the clatter of footsteps on the stairs and knew *he* still had a chance while maybe *she* did not.

How quickly the tables turn in this terrible game of life and death.

His finger was pressing hard to his neck wound.

He had reached the ground floor. Without surprise now to give her strength and opportunity she could not overpower him. He was in the yard. They skirted each warily, like a pair of sumo wrestlers in a too-small ring.

She read murder in his face and knew if she did not think of something she would soon die.

Chapter Twenty-Seven

Crazily she could hear everyday sounds outside the steel doors. Police sirens, traffic jams, car radios, people. Normal people. Leading normal lives.

A possibility of salvation?

Slowly she took off her coat and threw it as high as she could over the door. But it stuck on the razor wire, a beacon – if anyone cared to look.

Fairweather's eyes flickered from her to the coat. Blood still dripped through his fingers but it was not spurting. It must have started to coagulate. The wound had been too small – too shallow.

You can lose pints of blood this slowly before the body registers shock.

She ran to the gates, began kicking them. Found a sliver of the world in the crack between the two doors. One centimetre wide.

This was how desperate she was to re-enter that real world. One centimetre.

An eye peered back at her. Unblinking.

Then she felt herself grabbed from behind, felt the warm stickiness of his blood on her neck – the rope loop around her neck. He tried to jerk the life out of her. She put her hands inside the rope and sunk to her knees.

He'd been ready for this – a penalty of both being trained by the same *Protect yourself in the Health Service* practical session.

He took a step back so he was dragging her along the floor.

Her last conscious picture was of the eye, unblinking, in that precious centimetre of the safe world outside.

Her last conscious thought was that the eye was that of a child.

Chapter Twenty-Eight

She found it all out afterwards, that she owed her life to a six-year-old child and his mother who believed the mad story he told.

'There is a man in there all covered in blood strangling a lady and she wants me to help her.'

Bless all those American movies, E.T., Sleepless in Seattle, where a small child is the hero or heroine. Where children are trusted and believed by adults. Whatever stories they tell.

What did the mother do?

She put her eye to the one centimetre which looked into some movie hell where all that her son had told her was true.

What did she do next?

She fished her Pay As You Go phone from her bag and rang the police.

All this happened while Rolf Fairweather tried to finish her life.

It is all a dream. A yellow helicopter hovers in the grey-blue sky. A police marksman sits in the open doorway, his gun trained on Fairweather. Fairweather staggers towards the steel doors. The doors are sprung. Hundreds, thousands of police pour in like the United States Cavalry in an old Western film. Huge, dark-blue-uniformed Saviours. An ambulance winks its bright blue eye at her. 'Don't you worry, duck. You're going to be fine. We'll 'ave you right as rain and in the 'ospital in two shakes of a lamb's tail. Just you 'ang on in there.'

In books the heroine would lose consciousness.

Claire did not. Dazed, she mumbled nonsense and felt herself bumped on to a stretcher, straps fixed around her chest and lifted into the ambulance where she stared up at the cream-coloured ceiling and the brown eyes of a junior, uniformed officer. She heard the siren slice through the streets of Stoke, felt the bumping and swerving of over-excited ambulance men who cornered too fast while she felt sick, weak and dizzy and mumbled that she wanted Grant.

To feel his arms wrapping around her and *his* voice telling her that she would be all right, that she would live, that Rolf Fairweather would kill no one ever in his life again, that he would be in police custody and incarcerated.

At the hospital the senior trauma consultant examined her from head to toe and pronounced her fit. She had no injuries except shock and fright and a scar inside her brain.

Scars never really heal. They cease to hurt every day. They don't bleed or cause problems. But they stay with you for ever. The best you can hope for is numbness.

Chapter Twenty-Nine

It all came out in court.

Cynically Rolf Fairweather chose the plea of insanity to explain his actions. As she had known he would. And as she knew he wasn't.

Insanity is a condition – not an excuse.

Claire herself was too involved in the case to assess his mental condition and she wanted to speak to the psychiatrist herself. But she was not allowed to. She worried he might fool the doctor as he had fooled her and Heidi and Kristyna and Nancy Gold and everyone else at Greatbach Secure Psychiatric Unit.

He was not insane. He was not even disturbed but the prime manipulator in life's grim game, in the charade that was, to him, simply fun.

Claire faced statements and counter-statements, court appearances and endless interviews. And Fairweather himself across a courtroom crowded with familiar yet unfamiliar faces. No one was quite the person they had initially appeared.

Siôna appeared shifty, Grant a support. And Barclay . . .?

As the facts came out she still suspected Barclay of having murdered his mother – or as he would have put it, *put her out of her misery.*

Much of what she had surmised turned out to be true.

Gulio was summoned back to court, blinking in the bright lights and unable to conceive that what everyone had been so sure about was now in doubt.

He had not killed Doctor Heidi Faro.

Somehow a patient psychologist delved into the deepest darkest corners of his memory and found hidden behind all the statements that had been planted there, like a thick hedge, to grow and conceal the truth, a memory that Rolf Fairweather had told him Doctor Faro had wanted to see him that afternoon.

His memories were revised, the sequence at last making

sense.

He had heard a scream, run along the corridor, opened the door, seen Heidi and the blood, picked up the knife and run away, the door jamming behind him – only to be found and accused of the crime he had not had the wit to deny.

The DNA test on Nancy's dead child proved that Rolf Fairweather was the father.

And Kristyna?

Rolf stood in the dock and smiled each time her name was mentioned. His glance across the crowded courtroom at Claire spoke volumes. Allow me to keep some secrets, it whispered.

But she knew that at some point when she had started questioning Heidi's death it had sparked something off in the psychiatric nurse's mind so her suspicion had turned. Maybe even Nancy Gold had let something slip.

We never know everything.

The plea of insanity was given due consideration.

Chapter Thirty

And rejected.

In the end Rolf Fairweather was deemed responsible for his actions, found guilty of the murders of Heidi Faro and Kristyna Gale and sentenced to life imprisonment with a recommendation that he serve not less than thirty years.

It was a more satisfactory end.

Stefan Gulio was given an unconditional discharge and compensation paid to the tune of a few hundred thousand. He was reunited with his mother and, briefly, became the target for young, female fortune hunters.

He dealt with them with equanimity and a certain amount of puzzlement.

Months later. And it had all come out. The whole story. Long after the newspapers had finished gorging on the stories of psychologists who lacked principle, psychiatrists who took advantage of their patients' minds and psychologists who took sexual favours from their patients' bodies.

Because it all came out in court. Oh yes. Fairweather had pulled out all the organ stops. Pointed the finger at everyone. Typical behaviour this, to fail to take responsibility for his own sins, shifting the blame onto others. And with such rich feedings it is not surprising that it takes the tabloids a long time to abandon the trough of salacious headlines.

Claire had become a mini-celebrity, being challenged once or twice in the street by people demanding why she was ill-treating people with mental disorders, or what she could do for a son with a temper, a daughter with learning difficulties. She had even had an offer from the local TV channel to host a chat show and discuss various current issues concerning mental health.

The fame had become part of her life. She continued working at Greatbach, while moving round the lecture circuit. At the point when she had been closest to death she had known that if she lived her life never would be the same again. Like a scar after an operation the site still sometimes ached. She still had flashbacks. Rolf stroking Kristyna's arm, that morning in the meeting, Heidi, strutting from one side of the stage to another, pushing back the shining hair while her heels clumped loudly on the boards, Nancy Gold, singing to a wrapped pillow case.

To preserve her sanity and sense of proportion she and Grant distracted themselves by working their way steadily through the house, making it good, forming a small planet from which they could remain untouched by the outside world. She often sat underneath the gnarled apple tree and thought how easily it could all have been so different.

She could have been a celebrity by being another murder victim.

But it was another incident which brought about completion.

It was a Saturday morning, a free weekend for both of them and they were looking at sofas in the Potteries shopping centre, on the top floor of Lewis's department store. She favoured ivory leather, Grant red, ethnic wool.

A man was standing in the centre of a crowd, shouting that the beers were all on him, that *everyone* was invited to his house for a party tonight. The man was not young. He was dressed in a scarlet Santa suit which looks odd in late springtime.

He must have hired it.

As she watched two police arrived and good naturedly they hustled the man away.

Harry Sowerby, ready for yet another Section.

Then she noticed someone else.

Standing in front of her, watching the small act being played out in front of them was a black man, standing with his wife and a tall, skinny son. Now the drama had finished he too was looking at the sofas and like Grant his taste was for the ethnic red wool, set out with two armchairs. He looked familiar. As they drew nearer the black man gave her a broad, knowing wink. 'Why Doctor,' he said.

It was the voice that told her. She stared at the man, at his smiling wife, at his tall, skinny son.

'Kap,' she said softly. 'Kap. It is you, isn't it?'

'That's right, Doctor. Quite famous lady now.'

'Still just a doctor.'

Doctors often ask their patients how they are when they meet them, accidentally, in the street. It is only polite. But there was no need to ask Kap anything. His wide smile, the casual way he was linking arms with his wife, the glance of pure affection and admiration his son gave him. Even the acceptance that she was a doctor he had once needed but was now able to discard.

It was a story with a happy end.

Mostimes psychiatrists get it wrong. Just occasionally, once in a while they get it right.

She knew now why Kap had failed to keep his appointments. Praise be. He had no more need for a psychiatrist. He was better.

She shook his hand, that of his wife and of his tall son, resisted the temptation to pat just one of his thick, Rastafarian dreadlocks.

'It is so good to see you,' she said warmly and genuinely.

So they passed by each other, to buy furniture for their homes. She put her hand in her pocket.

Her fingers closed around a scrap of paper. Nothing much, just the top sheet of a stickup pad. She knew instantly what it was.

She linked her arm through Grant's.

'When I thought I was going to die,' she said, 'I wrote you a note. Telling you things I probably wouldn't have said.'

He grinned.

'Do you want to see it?'

In a sudden, husky show of affection, he pulled her head onto his shoulder, his lips brushing her hair, as he drew in a deep suck of air. 'I don't need to see it, Claire,' he said. 'The fact that you wrote to me. I think I can guess what it says.'

She nodded.

'No need for words,' he said, 'except to say that life will be different because of this experience. We'll be different. Our relationship will be different. Every time you or I stop valuing life itself we'll remember.'

'We'll remember,' she echoed. They linked arms and continued walking.

And Jerome Barclay?

He is out there – somewhere, free to continue. With what? We shall have to wait and see.